NEW YORK REVIEW BOOKS
C L A S S I C S

S0-BBW-496

BACK

HENRY GREEN (1905–1973) was the pen name of Henry Vincent Yorke. Born near Tewkesbury in Gloucestershire, England, he was educated at Eton and Oxford and went on to become the managing director of his family's engineering business, writing novels in his spare time. His first novel, *Blindness* (1926), was written while he was at Oxford. He married in 1929 and had one son, and during the Second World War served in the Auxiliary Fire Service. Between 1926 and 1952 he wrote nine novels, *Blindness*, *Living*, *Party Going*, *Caught*, *Loving*, *Back*, *Concluding*, *Nothing*, and *Doting*, and a memoir, *Pack My Bag*.

DEBORAH EISENBERG is the author of four collections of short stories and a play, *Pastorale*. She is the winner of the 2000 Rea Award for the Short Story, a Whiting Writers' Award, a Lannan Foundation Fellowship, and five O. Henry Awards. *The Collected Stories of Deborah Eisenberg* won the 2011 PEN/Faulkner Award and in 2015 she was awarded the PEN/Malamud Award for Excellence in the Short Story. She lives in New York City.

OTHER BOOKS BY HENRY GREEN
PUBLISHED BY NYRB CLASSICS

*Blindness**
Introduction by Daniel Mendelsohn

Caught
Introduction by James Wood

*Doting**
Introduction by Michael Gorra

*Living**
Introduction by Adam Thirlwell

Loving
Introduction by Roxana Robinson

*Nothing**
Introduction by Francine Prose

*Party Going**
Introduction by Amit Chaudhuri

*Forthcoming in 2017

BACK

HENRY GREEN

Introduction by
DEBORAH EISENBERG

NEW YORK REVIEW BOOKS

New York

THIS IS A NEW YORK REVIEW BOOK
PUBLISHED BY THE NEW YORK REVIEW OF BOOKS
435 Hudson Street, New York, NY 10014
www.nyrb.com

First published by Chatto & Windus. Chatto & Windus is part of the Penguin
Random House group of companies.

Library of Congress Cataloging-in-Publication Data
Names: Green, Henry, 1905–1973, author.
Title: Back / by Henry Green ; introduction by Deborah Eisenberg.
Description: New York : New York Review Books, [2016]
Identifiers: LCCN 2016019421| ISBN 9781681370101 (paperback) | ISBN
  9781681370118 (ebook)
Subjects: LCSH: World War, 1914–1918—Veterans—Great Britain—Fiction. |
  London (England)—Fiction. | BISAC: FICTION / Psychological. |
  FICTION / War & Military. | FICTION / Literary. | GSAFD: Historical
  fiction. | Love stories.
Classification: LCC PR6013.R416 B3 2016 | DDC 823/.914—dc23
LC record available at https://lccn.loc.gov/2016019421

ISBN 978-1-68137-010-1
Available as an electronic book; ISBN 978-1-68137-011-8

Printed in the United States of America on acid-free paper.
10 9 8 7 6 5 4 3 2 1

INTRODUCTION

IT'S NOT that little is known about the author—actually we have a relative wealth of information about him. In addition to his nine novels, of which *Back* is the sixth, he wrote a memoir, *Pack My Bag*, in 1940 when he was thirty-five. There is also *Surviving*, a collection edited by his grandson Matthew Yorke, which contains a number of stories, early works, essays, and reviews, as well as an interview of him for *The Paris Review*'s Art of Fiction series, and *Romancing*, a lively and insightful biography by Jeremy Treglown. He was admired and written about by some of the most admired and written-about writers of his generation and subsequent ones. He was socially visible, and various sets to which he belonged included people who exchanged amusing, polished letters with and about one another. But his character and life are such a tumult of contradictions and incongruities, and his fiction is so various, that almost anything one initially thinks to say about him produces in one's mind an equal and opposite reaction.

But at least we can start with a name, as introductions generally do: His name was not Henry Green. In his personal life he remained Henry Yorke as he was born, and about his choice of Green as a nom de plume, his old school friend Harold Acton said, "There are Greens of so many shades writing novels that one wishes he had selected another colour." But, as he could have selected *any* name, however colorful, august, or striking, perhaps that was the point—that Green could be the name in England at that time of any writer, of anyone at all.*

In *Pack My Bag*, which for a memoir is conspicuously light on names, Green says, simply, "Names distract." But in any case, whatever the reason for it, his choice of "Green" was characteristically complex—both declarative and evasive, on the one hand defiantly lacking distinctiveness and self-importance, and on the other conveying a faint, defiantly arrogant suggestion (or, if you prefer, a touching writerly hope) that a puffy pseudonym would be entirely beneath the dignity of his work, a demeaning appeal for popular recognition, as if Albert Einstein were to have worn little pink ribbons in his messy white genius hair. And perhaps—although Green made only the most halfhearted and short-lived effort to remain anonymous—his choice was partly designed to blur the rigid grandeur of his background: His parents, Maud and Vincent Yorke, were both from dauntingly "important" families.

Green published his first novel, *Blindness*, when he was twenty-one and immediately afterward dropped out of Oxford to work for a time in the Birmingham factory of his father's manufacturing firm, Pontifex. And for two years—which seem to have been among the happiest of his life—he spent his days laboring in the foundry, and wrote in his lunch hour and after dinner.

Within a few more years, he was leading several somewhat incompatible lives—that of an upper-class county gentleman with an impeccably upper-class wife, that of a London socialite, that of a hardworking northern industrialist, and, although he avoided most publicity, that of a famous literary figure with increasingly bohemian friends.

In 1939 he added another, volunteering for the Auxiliary Fire Service in London, an occupation that provided the setting for his novel *Caught*, published in 1943. He did so partly to avoid conscrip-

---

*If anybody knows what determined his choice, I'm not aware of it. A friend, the writer András Nagy, wonders if it might have been a reference to Gottfried Keller's *Grüner Heinrich*, which doesn't seem impossible.

tion, though during the Blitz, which began in 1940, it might well have been as dangerous as fighting. Still, it spared him the horror of killing anyone and it also enabled him to get to the London office of Pontifex, where he was now a manager, with relative ease.

The bombardment of London, the tumbling, flaming city, the terror of Nazi domination, and the prospect of imminent death generated a fever pitch of high life among Green's acquaintances. Green was handsome, tremendously charming, and entertaining; he loved to have fun, to talk, to laugh, and when he turned his attention on someone its light must have been like the sun. He loved his wife, Dig—who seems never to have acknowledged his affairs—and her sister, and a startling number of other women.

The implicit charter of his marriage to Dig was, apparently, that he would never leave her. And while she and their young son, Sebastian, were safely installed in the country, Green—having provided himself by means of an unassailable marriage with both a license to frolic and a safe arena in which to do it—was often out dancing into the morning with one young woman or another.

How the rather languid Henry Green managed his multiple romances, his family life, his business responsibilities, his fireman's duty, and all the writing, in addition to an amazing amount of drinking, is an absolute marvel. In contrast to his father and brothers he had always been rather passive, and it seems likely that a fundamental passivity may have enabled him not only to mop up the essence of people with which he created fictional characters, but also to assume various identities with facility himself and to slide between roles with a minimum of energy-depleting friction.

All Green's books are relatively short and unobtrusively but highly condensed. And anyone who has read several of them will almost certainly have observed not only how different they are from one another, and in how many ways, but also that one of their shared features is how stunningly different they are from anybody else's.

Although Green had read a lot when he was a student at Eton

and Oxford, and in the later part of his life claimed to read a novel a day, it's as if he was the first writer on the planet and had never learned what a novel is supposed to be like.

Nothing in his novels—including almost any sentence—proceeds as one might expect, and although nothing seems arbitrary, the books are surprise after surprise. Green seems to have been free, or to have made himself free, not only from literary conventions but also from conventions of thought, such as our unexamined assumptions of what a narrative is—what merits attention, how something comes to occur, and the language and constructions in which the elaborate workings of human behavior can be expressed.

The experience of reading Green, or so I find, is far more animating than the ordinary reading experience and extends far beyond the usual confines: It can be almost physical, as if the thought or sensation expressed on the page were being generated by one's own, not the author's, mind.

The freshness and force of the work is somewhat uncanny. Besides an extraordinary radiance, an accuracy of insight, an oblique approach to the material, an exquisite precision, a sheer unexpectedness of content, and a gleeful humor, the reader is likely to come across exposition so blunt as to be nearly perfunctory, bizarrely awkward transitions or passages, and syntax so convoluted and so personal that he or she is sometimes obliged to go thrashing through sheaves of clauses, only to be stranded when they simply combust rather than resolve grammatically, possibly owing to the large amount of alcohol Green was regularly pouring into himself.

Yet one is mesmerized, thrilled, transported, often by the very recklessness entailed by an underlying and urgent purity of vision. One feels that Green is simply pressing into service whatever means he can find or devise to accomplish what he needs to—to represent what it's like to be alive at a given moment, in all its reverberant and perplexing depth.

He writes incomparably in the fine print of experience. No fiction writer whose work I've encountered is more adventurous or better able to squeeze into the fissures of consciousness. He renders on the page the intractable, ambiguous, and mutable plasma of reality, and he depicts the manifold oddness and confusions of human encounters with a very light and very sure hand. Other people write books, Green fits the entire, multidimensional universe onto flat surfaces.

From the outset Green was a wizard of talk—putting onto a page what talk really sounds and feels like. His second novel, *Living*, published in 1929 when he was twenty-four, is set largely in industrial Birmingham, a milieu he knew well from his father's factory.

The speech of the men he worked with was an idiom and sound utterly alien to him, and he was enchanted by its vitality and expressiveness. The ringing language of these large, eloquent personalities, the metal and fire of the foundry, and the precariousness of the workers' physical and financial security provide a sort of bass line to the book. In counterpoint that is pure joy to read is the noodling treble of its few characters from Green's own class—wildly satirical gargoyles, primarily the rich factory owner's light-minded wife and clueless son, who, like the author, is soon to assume complete power over the lives of his workers.

In addition to the voices of proletarians, plutocrats, and patricians, Green was fully conversant with the voices of servants. When he was not quite seven he was sent off to school, but until then he spent more time with his family's servants than with his parents or two brothers, who were, themselves, away at school. And his novel *Loving*, published in 1945, is set during World War II in an extremely grand Anglo-Irish house peopled not by its owners, the Tennants, but almost entirely by its staff of English housemaids, scullery maids, cook, butler, butler's assistant, and governess, as well as the Irish caretaker of the estate's peacocks, who is seen by the others as a sort of grunting, hairy beast.

Green sent *Back* off to his editor in August 1945, a week before Hiroshima was bombed. It contains no aristocrats, no servants, no rich bosses, no working class. The characters are entirely middle class, a demographic with which Green was considerably less familiar, though he had sufficient acquaintance with it to reproduce its many voices to apparent perfection in the book.

During World War I his parents had opened up their large country house, for as long as they could stand it, as a convalescent home for officers.

As these officers were badly needed back in France they did not stay for long. Each holiday from school there was a new outfit and better still we got the most marvellous food because we were feeding them up to go back to be killed....

In the war people in our walk of life entertained all sorts and conditions of men with a view to self-preservation, to keep the privileges we set such store by, and which are illusory, after those to whom we were kind had won the war for us. That is not to say the privileged did not fight, we did, but there were too few of us to win. The effect of this on a child of my class was to open before his feet those narrow, deep and echoing gulfs which must be bridged, narrow because after all they were officers, deep because in most cases they had as civilians to come over that rope bridge over that gorge across which intercourse is had on the one side by saying "sir" and on the other "my good man." That is to say I began to learn the half-tones of class, or, if not to learn because I was too young, to see enough to recognize the echoes later when I came to hear them.

The fact that Green was somewhat hard of hearing might have contributed to the acuity of his listening, and in any case, by the early 1940s, when he was writing *Back*, those echoes were resounding. Urgency, terror, shortages, and privations were dissolving Britain's steely class demarcations, and the Labour Party victory, which was to inaugurate vast, equalizing reforms, was not far off.

Back, which reflects the fractured world in which Green wrote it, concerns what happens to a mind dislocated by violence—a subject that, frankly, ought to be of intense concern to us right now. The book opens as its protagonist, Charley Summers, having lost one leg to a German mine, returns from a POW camp in France to visit the grave of his beloved, Rose, who died at just the time he was interned.

No more than that is needed to activate the title. *Back*? Back to *what*? Blocked passage, annihilation, irretrievable loss—there can be no return to Rose of the spectacular red hair, no return to home, no restoration to a sound body; a wooden leg will have to do for all of it.

Charley is damaged mentally and emotionally as well as physically, but if health requires a grasp of reality, what happens when reality has become unrecognizable?

As Charley disembarks from the bus that has brought him to the graveyard, the scene appears to us as it does to him, saturated with familiar threat: Rain clouds are amassed, the church tower is built on high ground, and there are "slits, built for defence, in the blood coloured brick." There is

a sudden upthrusting cackle of geese in panic, the sound of which brought home to him a stack of faggots he had seen blown high by a grenade, each stick separately stabbing the air in a frieze, and which he had watched fall back, as an opened fan closes. So, while the geese quietened, he felt what he had seen until the silence which followed, when he at once forgot.

But there was left him an idea that he had been warned.

The shimmer of cataclysm about to erupt from cracks and fault lines and thin air is a recurrent motif, and the greatest danger is memory, with its ungovernable juxtapositions. Death, for better or worse, doesn't expunge anyone from the record, and Rose, conjured up by a glimpse of something, a sound, a resemblance, a word, a random association, repeatedly overwhelms Charley, toppling him out of the present moment, pervading his mind and senses and causing him to misinterpret simple information. And Rose's mother, Mrs. Grant, in a parallel state of extreme distress, now conflates Charley with her own younger brother, John, who was killed decades earlier during the previous war.

Delusion here is both a solace and a torment. And what is "delusion" when all orienting markings and indicators have been scrambled? Is memory loss a wound or a sealant? Is forgetting a betrayal or a portal, and what does it mean to "forget," anyhow?

While he was working on *Back*, Green wrote to one of his amours, Rosamond Lehmann, whose brother Jonathan was to become his editor at Hogarth Press, that he had "been blessed or cursed by a frightful surge of power & ideas.... The truth is that the present times are an absolute gift to the novelist. I see everything crumbling & growing all round me."

That twining interdependence of life and death is right there on the book's first page:

> For, climbing around and up these trees of mourning, was rose after rose after rose, while, here and there, the spray overburdened by the mass of flower, a live wreath lay fallen on a wreath of stone, or on a box in marble colder than this day, or onto frosted paper blooms which, under glass, marked each bed of earth wherein the dear departed encouraged life above in the green grass, the cypresses and in those roses gay and bright which, as still as this dark afternoon, stared at whosoever looked, or hung their heads to droop, to grow stained, to die when their turn came.

This high, poetic rhetoric and elaborate, chivalric imagery is matched later by Rose's voice when Charley eventually digs up his few, precious letters from her (which, following a perfect though insane line of reasoning, he cuts up so he can show pieces of them to a graphologist):

> "Stinker darling. I'm writing this lain in bed. Old mother Gubbins just got me my breaky. I sniff for my Stinker but there's

not a trace. I bet you wish you were here you old smoothie. Jim won't be home now till the end of the week. . . ."

His eyes filled with tears. These letters were sacred.

Green has a firm grip on the root from which hilarity and grief diverge. To a great extent, our attitude toward events—whether we see something as devastating or ridiculous, as unbearably painful or as just another of history's ludicrous exhibitions—is one of distance. Did the thing happen this morning or a thousand years ago? Did we read about it in the newspaper or *The Iliad*? Did it happen to you or to me?

And in *Back*, Green often conveys the queasy sensation of experiencing things from incompatible vantages—simultaneously at close range and at a remove, and from various angles. The planes of reality can't be fitted together any more than the splintered facts of Charley's world can be fitted together, and our minds have to rearrange themselves a bit to accommodate the jamming of perspectives.

Characters who seem harmless enough initially can take a sinister turn and then twist back into harmlessness. James—the Jim of Rose's letter, who we've realized was her husband—is an obtuse sweetie. Or maybe he isn't all that obtuse. Or all that sweet, either. Or, no, maybe he is. And Mr. Grant, Rose's father, amplifies unpredictably and alarmingly from pathetic and wheedling to sanctimonious and bullying. He comes as close at times as any of Green's characters to being intolerable, but it's his death that is the most frankly and movingly anguished moment in *Back*:

It was Mrs. Grant calling, so loudly that he could only just recognize her voice. "Gerald." "Gerald." And much more urgent, "D'you hear me?" "Oh d'you hear me, do speak." She was yelling now. "Gerald." After which the most frightful sobbing. "Gerald darling, Father, where are you?"; then, in a sort of torn bellow, "Father," then, finally, "Come back,". . . .

There are the characters who seem to emanate irrepressibly from mischievous potentialities of the universe. Mr. Middlewitch, for instance, whom Charley first meets at a place where they're both having artificial limbs fitted—who is he, really, and why is he everywhere? Is he just the annoying clown he seems to be, or is he, as Charley suspects, something more troubling? How is it that everyone else just happens to know him? And is Charley's landlady, Mrs. Frazier, a busybody, a specter, an oracle, or what?

The central puzzle is personified in Rose's half sister, Nancy, whom Charley, against mounting evidence to the contrary, insists is Rose. Does she actually look just like Rose? There are indications that she is thought to by a number of people—but there are also indications that she does only in the light of Charley's need for Rose.

Physical resemblances can be fugitive and treacherous, as we know, so Charley's painful conflating of the two women, his painful process of distinguishing between them, feels closer to home than psychosis, though certainly gentle, prudent, compassionate Nancy could hardly be more different from frivolous, manipulative, delicious Rose.

The locus of uncertainty keeps changing, and the book's frequent tone shifts intensify the destabilization. In addition to the sere atmosphere of Charley's isolation, incomprehension, and despair, there are some of the most voluptuous and exquisite descriptive passages to be found even in Green's work:

> Autumn was the season, most roses were dead. Petals that had dropped some months back and rotted, traces of a summer now gone, were covered by the brown leaves which even in this still air rocked down to lie deep on the ground as they walked, so that their feet rustled. Where a flying bomb had dropped recently, the drift of leaves was still green underfoot, the trees bare as deep winter. Then, just as they were passing this spot, the syrens set up a broken wailing.

Interspersed is the deadpan comic banality of daily life at the office where Charley has been given an important position, with its impenetrable wartime bureaucratese of acronyms and his invention of a disastrous foolproof, double-indexed filing system, the undeserving casualty of which is his secretary—poor Dot, who has been entirely unequipped to deal with Charley's murkiness.

And there is the inversion of a lyric interlude, when Charley brings Dot to James's (and Rose's) house for a couple of days in the country, and Dot somehow ends up in bed not with Charley but with James, and nobody can hear anybody else the whole weekend because of the American convoys thundering along on the highway outside.

The most extreme of these tone shifts—*breathtaking* in the sheer preposterous implausibility of its context—is a piece from a magazine that James sends to Charley in a moment of exasperation. When I first read it I took it to be a remarkable imitation of a piece of eighteenth-century French writing, but even more remarkably it turns out to be the real thing: Green's French was excellent, and he simply translated a section of the *Souvenirs de la marquise de Créquy*, a semi-fictional memoir that he was reading, and tossed it into the book.

"Read, mark, learn, and inwardly digest," the rather oafish James scrawls on the cover, and mails the magazine off to Charley. Written in a silken, courtly style, the outlandish piece describes how a young noblewoman faints when she encounters the double of her dead lover.

It is the third time we are told a story of someone who faints at the sight of a double. The second is the critical episode when Nancy first opens the door to Charley, who faints at what he believes to be the sight of his dead Rose. And the first is when spooky Mrs. Frazier, going on and on to a distracted and nervous Charley, says:

"Once you start on coincidences why there's no end to those things. I could tell you a story you'd never believe but it's as true as I'm here," and she at once began a long tale. He hardly listened.

He could not explain it to himself, but the fact that old Mr. Grant knew Middlewitch made him deeply suspect. He even asked himself what he suspected, only to find that he could not think.

He saw round and round it in his head.

"So I said, 'it's the same person,'" Mrs. Frazier was bringing the story to an end. "'Look out,' I said, 'I'm going to faint away,' I said, and she came forward to take me by the arm. For they were as like as two peas," she finished, with a glance of triumph at Summers.

From this hall of mirrors, through which fleet masked figures appear and vanish and doubles are triply reflected, there can be no easy escape. Identities coalesce and detach, coalesce and detach. Where is the true image and which are the distorted reflections?

Correlating Green's personal life with elements of *Back* could use up a lot of someone's time. Rosamond Lehmann was not Green's only girlfriend whose name incorporates "Rose," and one of Green's other very serious girlfriends was named Mary, a name that also belonged to Dig as well as to her sister, strangely enough, who was known as Miss...and so on. And then there is the more substantial matter of Green's faceted psyche. But someone's time is no doubt more meaningfully and enjoyably spent sifting through the book's self-contained splintered vision than puzzling over the stains of biography—sifting through the book's profound mysteries, its torn webs of fate and identity.

Back received a generally poor reception when it was first published. Naturally, those who might have looked forward, for instance, to a reprise of the visual bliss of *Loving* or the careering exuberance of *Party Going* were bound to be disappointed. A review in *The Spectator* by Kate O'Brien, Treglown tells us, "summed up the dominant reaction when she warned people off this 'small, grey, personal book: very sad, very narrow... greyly and coldly misted in small, mad sorrow.'"

An odd response, it seems to me, for a book that's streaked with red, that requires the reader to continually reinterpret its events, that revels in clashing styles. But maybe the ashes of war obscured the vividness and scope of the book's delirium.

Naturally the reception of *Back* was highly distressing to Green, though he had early warnings even when he submitted the manuscript to Jonathan Lehmann, who, as Treglown writes, "expressed dissatisfaction with every aspect of the book... including its basic premise." Lehmann and Green crossed swords over the text, but "Leonard Woolf took Henry's side in the quarrel, and the book was left with its muddles and inconsistencies intact...."

Treglown goes on to mention some of these specifically, such as the repeated assertions that Charley is getting a good night's sleep "for once." "Bewildered frustration is involved in reading Green at such moments," Treglown says, "and critics since the Lehmanns have found various ways of explaining why this seems an essential part of his work's value."

Insofar as I could be considered a critic, I suppose I'm joining in when I say that I don't even see the problem, as the book is essentially the story of somebody who must reconstruct from fragments and obsessive, misconceived, thwarted reenactments, a viable and integrated way to be. And years later, in his *Paris Review* interview with Terry Southern, Green himself simply dismisses the issue out of hand, proposing that if a novel is alive, "of course the reader will be irritated by discrepancies—life, after all, is one discrepancy after another."

After being tossed wildly about over the course of *Back*, we are put at ease on its last page, when Green tells us that Charley and Nancy will have "a happy married life." But our ease doesn't last long. Falling over it is the shadow, in the stunning meta-sex scene of the final paragraph, of the trials by which that happiness will have to be won.

It's typical of Green to leave us with more than we realized he was giving us and to conclude with a concealed reminder that the end of a novel is a highly artificial conceit, that in life stories have no end at all. In fiction, the narration generally just furnishes a resting point and sounds a fanfare: The End, we are told, and content ourselves with that expedient.

But Green's books tend to open up when you close them and come forth with whole new flowerings. *Back* is possibly the most eccentric of Green's extremely eccentric novels—though the gorgeous, enigmatic *Concluding*, his next novel, is certainly a contender—and *Back* is probably his harshest. But it conveys potently and with great delicacy the fragility of our sense of wholeness. We put it down in a dazzle of refreshed gratitude for whatever good fortune we happen to have and also with a heightened awareness that we are only a hairsbreadth away from disaster.

—DEBORAH EISENBERG

BACK

A COUNTRY bus drew up below the church and a young man got out. This he had to do carefully because he had a peg leg.

The roadway was asphalted blue.

It was a summer day in England. Rain clouds were amassed back of a church tower which stood on rising ground. As he looked up he noted well those slits, built for defence, in the blood coloured brick. Then he ran his eye with caution over cypresses and between gravestones. He might have been watching for a trap, who had lost his leg in France for not noticing the gun beneath a rose.

For, climbing around and up these trees of mourning, was rose after rose after rose, while, here and there, the spray overburdened by the mass of flower, a live wreath lay fallen on a wreath of stone, or on a box in marble colder than this day, or onto frosted paper blooms which, under glass, marked each bed of earth wherein the dear departed encouraged life above in the green grass, the cypresses and in those roses gay and bright which, as still as this dark afternoon, stared at whosoever looked, or hung their heads to droop, to grow stained, to die when their turn came.

It was a time of war. The young man in pink tweeds had been repatriated from a prisoners' camp on the other side. Now, at the first opportunity, he was back.

He had known the village this church stood over, but not well. He had learned the walks before he turned soldier, though he had met few of those who lived by. The graveyard he had never entered. But he came now to visit because someone he loved, a woman, who, above all at night, had been in his feelings when he was behind

3

barbed wire, had been put here while he was away, and her name, of all names, was Rose.

The bus, with its watching passengers, departed. In the silence which followed he began to climb the path leading to those graves, when came a sudden upthrusting cackle of geese in panic, the sound of which brought home to him a stack of faggots he had seen blown high by a grenade, each stick separately stabbing the air in a frieze, and which he had watched fall back, as an opened fan closes. So, while the geese quietened, he felt what he had seen until the silence which followed, when he at once forgot.

But there was left him an idea that he had been warned.

Propping himself on his stick, he moved slowly up that path to the wicket gate between two larger cypresses. He felt more than ever that he did not wish to be observed. So he no longer watched the roses. As if to do his best to become unseen, he kept his eyes on the gravel over which he was dragging the peg leg.

For there was a bicycle bell, ringing closer and closer by the church, clustering spray upon spray of sound which wreathed the air much as those roses grew around the headstones, whence, so he felt, they narrowly regarded him.

Which caused him to stop dead when a boy of about six came, over the hill on a tricycle, past the porch; then, as the machine got up speed, he stood to one side, in spite of the gate still closed between the two of them. He sharply stared but, as he took in the child's fair head, he saw nothing, nothing was brought back. He did not even feel a pang, as well he might if only he had known.

Charley was irritated when the boy, after getting off to open the gate and climbing onto his machine again, shrilly rang the bell as he dashed past. Then the young man started slow on his way once more. And he forgot the boy who was gone, who spelled nothing to him.

For Rose had died while he was in France, he said over and over under his breath. She was dead, and he did not hear until he was a prisoner. She had died, and this sort of sad garden was where they had put her without him, and, as he looked about while he leaned on the gate, he felt she must surely have come as a stranger when her time came, that if a person's nature is at all alive after he or she has gone, then she could never have imagined herself here nailed into a box, in total darkness, briar roots pushing down to the red hair of which she had been so proud and fond. He could not even remember her ever saying that she had been in this churchyard, which was now the one place one could pay a call on Rose, whom he could call to mind, though never all over at one time, or at all clearly, crying, dear Rose, laughing, mad Rose, holding her baby, or, oh Rose, best of all in bed, her glorious locks abounding.

Oh well this would never do, he thought, and asked himself where she could be. For there was a large choice. While the church was small, this graveyard gaped deep and wide, densely stacked throughout its rising ground with mounds of turf and mottled, moss grown headstones. And, as he was forever asking himself things he could seldom answer, and which, amassing in his mind, left a great weight of detail undecided, the next question he put was, what he could say if a woman came while he searched, if she were to observe that he was lame who was of an age to have lost a leg, in fact what he should do if seen by a village gossip, who might even recognize him, but who, in any case, would have her sense of scandal whetted, so he felt, by a young man with a wooden leg that did not fit, searching for a tomb.

He thought how Rose would have laughed to see him in his usual state of not knowing, lost as he always was, and had been when the sniper got him in the sights.

Indeed, if he had not come such a distance, from one country at war to another, then home again, he might well at this minute have turned back. But as it was he went in the gate, had his cheek brushed by a rose, and began awkwardly to search for Rose, through roses, in what seemed to him should be the sunniest places on a fine day, the warmest when the sun came out at twelve o'clock for she had been so warm, and amongst the newer memorials in local stone because she had died in time of war, when, or so he imagined, James could never have found marble for her, of whom, at no time before this moment, had he ever thought as cold beneath a slab, food for worms, her great red hair, still growing, a sort of moist bower for worms.

Well the old days were gone for good, he supposed while standing by a cypress, holding a briar off his face. The rose, rocking from it, sprinkled held raindrops on his eyes as, with the other hand, he poked his stick at two dwarf box trees which had obscured what he now saw to be a marble pillow. He had time to read the one word, "Sophie," cut with no name or date, when his glance was held by a nest the walking stick uncovered, and which had been hidden by thick enamelled leaves that were as dark as the cypress, as his brown eyes under that great ivory pink rose. Changing hands with the stick so the rose softly thumped his forehead, he pushed past to lean, to feel with a hand. But the eggs were addled, blue cold as moonlight.

He wiped his fingers. Paper crackled in a pocket, to remind him of the wire, "Report to Officers Rehabilitation Centre Gateacres Ammanford by 20 hours June 12th." It was now the thirteenth. He supposed they would not shoot a chap because he had not gone, nor, out of spite, make him pay for the new limb waiting there numb and numbered in a box. "E.N.Y.S." it was signed. More letters standing he did not know what for.

The prisoners' camp had flowered with initials, each inmate decorated his bunk with them out there, to let it be known what he taught. Such as "I.T." which stood for Inner Temple, at which Marples, this very afternoon perhaps, was still teaching Roman Law. The idea had been to make the clock's hands go round. And now that he'd come, he told himself, all he was after was to turn them back, the fool, only to find roses grown between the minutes and the hours, and so entwined that the hands were stuck.

His felt thoughts began to wander. Of course he was lucky to have a job, his seat kept warm. There were plenty still over on the other side would give the cool moon to stand in his shoes. And they would get on with it if they were here, not spend as he was doing a deal of money on travelling to old places. Then there was the coupon question. What should he do? All he had was this suit he stood up in, which he had bought, and which the tailor had not delivered, but had kept safe till he got back. The rest was looted. Oh, he was lost in this bloody graveyard. Where could she be? Rose that he'd loved, that he'd come so far for? Why did she die? Could anyone understand anything? Perhaps it would have been best if they had killed him, he felt, if instead of a sniper's rifle in that rosebush they had pooped off something heavier at him. Rose would never have known, because she had died some time about that identical week. God bless her, he thought, his brown eyes dimmed suddenly with tears, and I hope she's having a jolly good rest.

Then he found it was raining. He must have stood there so lost he had never taken in the first few drops. He started to drag as quick as he could for the path, to shelter in the church porch. But he had to go sideways, brushing against cypresses, getting his neck scratched once or twice, having roses spatter in his ears because he could not lift his leg properly, and did not wish to pull it over the green, turfed graves, to scar them with the long souvenir he had brought back from France.

Misery kept his mind blank until he turned the porch. Then he had a bad shock when he found who was sheltering before him. For of all people, of all imaginable men, and fat as those geese, was James. They stared at each other.

"Why good Lord," James was saying, "why, Charley, my good lad," he said. Speechless, Charley looked over a shoulder to find whether this widower had been in a position to see where he had been searching for the grave below. "Why, Charley, then they've sent you back. Good Lord, am I glad to see you, man."

"Where've you been all this time?" James began once more, as Charley still found nothing. "In Germany?" he went on, not waiting for answers. "Why it must be all of five years. Now how are you?" and he pump-handled Charley who had said not a word. "They often tell us, 'Wait till the boys come back.' Well this is it, isn't it?" James asked. "I mean you're really home for keeps, for better or worse, richer or poorer, aren't you? And what's it like with the enemy? I suppose they put you in hospital, what? How'd they treat the boys, Charley? Pretty rotten I shouldn't wonder, when all's said and done. Well you haven't come back to much I can tell you. My, but I'm glad to see you, man."

"It's my leg," Charley explained. He drawled rather when he spoke.

"Yes, well there you are," James said.

"There it is," Charley agreed. One of those pauses followed in which the fat man's upper lip trembled.

"Well I'd never have guessed if you hadn't mentioned it, bless my soul I shouldn't. Never in the world. But they do marvellous things in that line of country now, or so they tell me. Medical science comes on a lot in a war, you know. I often say it's the one use there is in such things. Terrible price to pay, of course. But there you are."

"You're right there," Charley said.

"But look, how on earth were you going to have a bite to eat? Bit difficult these days, you know, what with the B.R.N.Q., the V.B.S. and the P.M.V.O. Since the war started, no, I'm wrong, it was after the invasion of Holland and all that. Well now we haven't even got a village bus. They still send the children in to school, of course the C.E.C. see to that, though the whole job is run very inefficiently in my opinion. But you'll come down now and take pot luck with me, won't you? As a matter of fact we've begun a pig club in the village. P.B.H.R. it's known by, everything's initials these days. Only time the people in these parts have got together within living memory. So there's a piece of ham left over. Tell you the truth I haven't started the ham, not yet. Oh and I expect we'll find a little bit of something to go on with."

"Thanks very much."

"Don't mention it, old man. Least one can do, if you know what I mean. No, but you'll be really welcome, Charley. You got my letter, didn't you? Must have been about the time you were taken prisoner. It's made a big difference. But then there's a lot of changes these days, and there'll be many more I shouldn't wonder. Lord yes. But this'll be a damn good occasion to start that ham. Why on earth didn't you let me know you were coming?"

Charley muttered something the other could not catch.

"I know," James went on, "I realize how it is. I remember after the last war when I got home." He described a visit he had paid, which meant nothing to Charley.

There was a pause.

"Now they've hit it with one of their damned bombs," James continued. "But, look here, you didn't happen to run across my nipper on his bike, did you? He'll get soaked through in this rain." It was teeming down, with the sound of a man scything long grass. As James went on talking, and almost at random, for this had been a shock to him as well, Charley did not catch a word because of what had been revealed.

He was wondering if his face had gone white while his stomach melted, for there had been more than a question between Rose and himself, at the time the baby was on the way, as to whether it could be his own.

He was appalled that the first sight of the boy had meant nothing. Because one of the things he had always hung on to was that blood spoke, or called, to blood.

So the child he'd had to step aside for was Ridley; poor kid to be called by such a name.

Now he wanted to sit down. Then his guilt made him listen to what James was saying, in case the man had noticed. But James was going on just the same.

Finally Charles was altogether taken up by a need to see the child a second time, to search in the shape of the bones of its face for an echo of Rose, to drag this out from the line of its full cheeks to see if he could find a memory of Rose laughing there, and even to look deep in Ridley's eyes as though into a mirror, and catch the small image of himself by which to detect, if he could, a likeness, a something, however false, to tell him he was a father, that Rose lived again, by his agency, in their son.

Wrought up into a sort of cunning, he waited for a break in the fat fellow's conversation. When this came he said so calmly that he was surprised,

"What time d'you lunch, James?"

"Look, old boy, there's one or two things I must do in the village first. You make your own way down to my place. In the meantime," he went on, in the same voice, "it's over here, follow me." Charley began to drag after, unsuspecting. But he could not go fast, with the result that he was far behind when James halted to doff his hat at an object. "See you later," James called, as he made off. Charley hobbled along. Then, behind the cypress where James had uncovered himself, there lay before his eyes more sharp letters, cut in marble beyond a bunch of live roses tied in string, and it became plain that this was where they had laid her, for the letters spelled Rose. So Charley bowed his head, and felt, somehow, as if this was the first time that he had denied her by forgetting, denied one whom, he knew for sure, he was to deny again, then once more yet, yes thrice.

ROSE'S parents, Mr. and Mrs. Grant, were still at Redham, one of London's outer suburbs. They had known, and liked, Charley as a possible husband to their only child some time before she was married to James. Mrs. Grant, in particular, had had a soft spot for him because of his great brown eyes. So, when old man Grant heard that Charley was back, he phoned up to ask him over for the evening.

He met Charley in their front garden.

"You'll find a wee bit of a difference in the wife," he said, once the first greetings were over. "It's merciful in a way perhaps, but I wouldn't know. You see she doesn't remember so very well as a rule, nowadays. What it may be is that nature protects us by drawing a curtain, blacks certain things out. Rose's going as she did was a terrible shock to her naturally. So I thought I'd better warn you to carry on as though you didn't notice. Just in case."

"Of course," Charley said. It was a blue and pink late Saturday afternoon. Once more he felt how grand it was to be back.

"Although this does bring you to wonder," Mr. Grant was saying. "Nature's cruel, there's no getting away from her laws. She won't let up on the weak, I mean. When the doctor went into it with me, his idea about Amy was it might be nature's way to protect her by letting her forget. I didn't say much. You can't argue with them, Charley boy."

"You're right there," Charley said.

"Yes, I expect you'll have found that over your leg. But you can set your mind at rest, no one would tell if they hadn't been told." He nodded his white, old head, up and down. "Isn't it a glorious evening? Where was I now? Yes, well, I took leave to doubt that doctor.

Nature's cruel I said to myself, you can't expect mercy in that quarter. So d'you know what? I'll tell you. I thought maybe it wasn't the best thing for Amy to forget Rose."

Charley coughed.

"Well, once you begin to lose the picture of this or the other in your mind's eye, it's hard to determine where things'll stop," Mr. Grant continued. "I knew a man once, in the ordinary run of business, who started to misremember in that fashion. Wasn't long before he'd lost all his connections. Even came to it they had to shut him away. Because when all's said and done you can't go on like it, can you? So I tried talking to Amy about Rose."

Charley wondered how he could get out. He looked around him. But he knew he was back now, all right.

"No," Mr. Grant continued, "nothing I could say was any use. And then I went into things. You see my firm has put me on a pension, now I'm retired, and once the housework is done, which doesn't amount to a great deal, there's not such a lot to do but think. Well, we're not so old as all that, thank you, Amy and me. I mean there's a few years usefulness in us yet, what with the work I do unpaid on the H.R.O.N., and Amy who's still fit enough to go down to the A.R.B.S., and put in a few hours each week. So I said, 'Gerald,' I said, 'you've got to get a move on. It mayn't be the best thing, not by a long chalk, for her to forget her own daughter.' Mind you, Charley, she doesn't even know her grandson now. And, as a woman begins to age, the toddlers play a great part, Charley boy, or they should do, that's only human nature after all. So to cut a long story short, I made up my mind I'd call on Charley Summers. Not that we wouldn't have been glad to see you, any day. After what you've been through. You mustn't misunderstand me, please. But just to find whether she would…" and his voice trailed off as, turning his back, he began to move towards the house. Charley sullenly followed. "So don't be surprised if you notice a big change," Mr. Grant ended over his shoulder, in so loud a voice that Charley was afraid.

But how dead selfish of the old boy, Charley felt as he stood in the porch of their villa while Mr. Grant shouted for his wife. After all, here was a man who had no need for coupons, who couldn't have to buy anything new. Because surely he had done enough, Charley thought, once more coming back to himself. When all was said and done he had risked his life, lost a leg, spent the best years of his prime in prison behind barbed wire, and, now that he was back, they had a use for him as a guinea pig on Rose's mother.

Mr. Grant shouted again.

"I'm coming dear," she piped in a quiver, and there was Mrs. Grant, too neat, scuttling down the stairs. She came straight on, never hesitated, flung her old arms round Charley's neck, went up on her toes to do it, and sung out "John, John," twice.

"No it's not John, dear, it's Charley, back from the war," Mr. Grant announced at her towered white head of hair, which she was leaning on Charley's neck as the young man lightly touched her elbows.

"They are very cruel to me, John," she said. From her round cheeks he found that she was crying.

"Now dear, this is Charley Summers," Mr. Grant repeated.

"Don't you worry," Charley mumbled.

But she would not have it. She was most natural.

"John, to think you're back at last," she said.

"There you are," the husband explained, "she thinks you're her brother who was killed in seventeen."

Charley hardened his heart.

"Why my little baby brother John," Mrs. Grant exclaimed in rather a happier voice and stood back, laying hands gently on his forearms. She looked yearning into his face. She was much too neat. But for two tear drops under the chin, and a wet run to each from out the corners of her eyes, which were intensely bright, everything was mouse tidy, except it seemed her wits.

"Now Amy," her husband begged.

"But you mustn't stand here. I don't know where my mind is, I'm sure," she went on, preceding him into their parlour. As he sat down he felt she did not seem so sure of him after all. In fact he did not like the way she shaped, complaining as she now was that it must be the war, that ever since the Russians gave up she had felt tired. "This terrible war," she ended, and screened her eyes with a hand as if he were seated opposite nude.

"Look dear," the husband said, "you rest yourself while I go fetch our tea. I shan't be a minute," he explained to Charley, who did not want to be alone with her, who opened his mouth to ask him to stay but was too late, as happened so often.

"So cruel," Mrs. Grant murmured, once they were alone. There was then a silence while she still held a hand on her eyes. Charley asked himself if it was safe for them to be left together, and then for no particular reason remembered that he had forgotten to buy the tie he'd meant to get in the morning.

"You're not John, are you?" she said, when he looked up.

But he did not have to answer because her husband came back just then, wheeling the tea trolley. "Here we are," this man genially announced. "John always had cream with his," she said, her eyes on the small, half empty jug of milk, "Oh, but of course, I forgot," she went on. "You're not, are you. It's my memory," she explained. "Sometimes I get a bit tired."

Mr. Grant began to pour. "Seems queer," he said to Charley. "Rose always used to do this. D'you remember?" Charley remembered, but he did not say so. "Insisted on it way back in the days when she had her hair in pigtails. Made such a commotion that we had to let her. This is Charley Summers, dear," he said briskly to his wife. "Surely you recollect him, Amy? Used to come to tea in the old days,—and she wore pale pink bows in the plaits," he added, his mind turning a corner. There was a pause. When he spoke again his voice was flat. "You know him I'll be bound," he said. "It was Rose he used to come down and see, and now here he is to pay a call on her old people."

Charley sat silent, kept an eye on his empty cup.

"Why you aren't eating," was what she answered. "I'm sure I get so bewildered sometimes." The young man glanced at her to find she was offering him cake. "You must excuse us, you know. We live very quietly, oh so quietly."

"I hear you do work for the A.R.B.S., Mrs. Grant," he asked.

"Yes, dear, dear, and what a business that is. Sometimes I think it will be too much for me, Mr. . . . , Mr. . . . , so stupid, I'm afraid I didn't quite catch your name."

Charley noticed that she never seemed to address Mr. Grant directly.

"Charley Summers, dear," Mr. Grant said, brisk.

"Of course. Mr. Summers. You know we've had some terrible Zeppelin raids round about, lately. Some have been in daylight as well, so daring don't you think Mr. . . . , Mr. . . . ." He looked at her. When she saw this she dropped her eyes quick, and put a hand on her mouth as though about to belch.

"She will insist it's the last war," Mr. Grant explained in a normal voice.

"Of course," Charley said.

"How's things over in Germany these days?" Mr. Grant enquired, ignoring his wife. "I expect you had a pretty rotten time, eh? What I say is, I can't see any end to this lot. But I mean, did they treat you badly? What part were you, anyway?"

Charley felt the old man was almost being sharp with him. He supposed it to be irritation at his life partner. But the nausea, which had recently begun to spread in his stomach whenever prison camps were mentioned, drove all else out of his head.

"Rather not speak of it," he replied, indistinctly.

"I'm sorry, Charley boy. You don't want to pay any attention to us old folks," he said. "The plain fact is, we're past it. You'll find out as you grow older. You seem to lose grip somehow. Worst of all is, you don't seem to notice. But the hard part must have been the ladies, eh? Because it's not natural to be without them, after all. And then not even seeing one. Why, you must have been in a pickle," he ended with genuine sympathy, unable, it seemed, to realize how odd, or, if you like, how charming this was in him to speak so in front of his sick wife.

"Might I have another cup?" Charley asked Mrs. Grant.

"Why, whatever am I about?" Mrs. Grant said, bright, as she snatched his saucer. "You mustn't heed me," she went on. "I've been so forgetful lately. You'd never believe."

"But you aren't eating, Charley boy," Mr. Grant told him. "Yes, it must be rotten for a young man in those places. Unnatural. But then there's a deal in life you don't understand at the time. You'll find that out later. Why, sometimes, when I've done the housework and seen to Amy here, I just sit where I am, and remember. That's what she's missing. Because it's not all bad what's happened to you. Not by a long chalk."

"Who are you, then?" Mrs. Grant unexpectedly asked.

"Why he's Charley Summers, dear," Mr. Grant replied. "You remember him," he said, with confidence. "He used to come in to see our Rose. Yes, it does feel a long time, eh Charley?" But the young man did not reply.

"Everything's initials these days," the old man said, abruptly changing course. "You can't even pay the public house a call of an evening any more. Of course you go there just the same, but it's an anniversary of the Home Guard being stood down that takes you, or the H.R.O.N. having a reunion, and so on, and so forth. I'll wager it strikes anyone as a bit different to come home to," he suggested. Charley merely said it did.

"And how d'you manage with your coupons?" Mr. Grant went on, while his wife seemed to recollect herself behind the hand she now held over her eyes, "Do they give you a supply so you can get a stock up?"

"There you are," Charley said, thinking about a dressing gown.

"I suppose it's what you could term necessary," Mr. Grant commented, "but it's damnable, boy, in a free country such as we were supposed to be. To think of a man like you, who we should all be grateful for, having to pass through that rigmarole makes you ask yourself what we're fighting to finish, doesn't it? I could tell you tales would make you really wonder. Why, down at the B.D.S. offices, there's a man in charge who, before the outbreak, if I'd gone to him holding a few potato peelings, he'd have eaten them out of my hand right before my face, that same individual is sitting behind a telephone and it's ivory coloured, who I knew in the old days when he was with Thomsons, a despatch clerk, that's all he was. Well now, if you should want anything, he's the man Charley. From a toothbrush right up to a typewriter. And sitting there just to say no. As a matter of fact, with Amy in the state of health she's in," and his wife did not flinch, "as things are with her, the doctor gave a prescription for a bit extra of this or that, or whatever it might be, and I had to go down to George Andrews, because that's the man's name, to get him to countersign the diet sheet the doctor had made out. You could never imagine the time I had with him."

"Is that so?" Charley said.

"You aren't John, are you?" Mrs. Grant objected, between her fingers. But Mr. Grant saw fit to let this pass.

"Yes, if I was to tell, you'd never believe," he said to the young man. "This, that, and the other," he said.

"Then who are you, then?" Mrs. Grant asked quietly.

"Now, dear, don't take on so," Mr. Grant said. "You've forgotten, you don't remember, that's all it is. Yes," he continued to Charley, "men I wouldn't have engaged as office boys when I was in charge of the department, lording it over us now, heads I win, tails you lose."

"What are you doing here?" Mrs. Grant demanded, looking at Charley between her fingers, and cringing.

"He's come to take a cup of tea with us, dear," the husband said. This time he glared. She did not notice because she never took her eyes off Charley.

"I don't like it," she muttered.

"I'm very sorry," Charley Summers said to Mr. Grant.

"Just pay no attention," this man replied. But it was not to be as easy as all that, for Mrs. Grant took control by throwing herself back into the sofa to thrust her head into one of its soft corners, from which she began to shriek, muffled by upholstery.

"Amy, stop that this minute," Mr. Grant said firm. "You're not a child after all. It's just the habits she's been getting," he explained to Charles. "It'll pass in a moment, you'll see." Upon which Mrs. Grant took her nose out of the arm and the back, and screamed, not very loud. Charley saw his chance.

"I really must be getting on," he said.

Mr. Grant was remonstrating, "Now Amy," as though with an awkward child. He had gone to sit beside his wife, who had hidden her face again, and he was patting a shoulder. Charley thought she moaned something, but he could not be certain. In any case he was on his way. And Mr. Grant called to him,

"But wait for me, Charley boy," he begged, "I won't be a minute. Now mother, there. By the road, out of sight. I've something I must tell you," he ended, to Charley's back. And Charley waited behind a tree, dreading a renewal of those small shrieks and cries. He heard no more however, and, after ten minutes, he saw Mr. Grant hurrying down the path.

He was very sorry, he told Charles, and it had not been much of a welcome back after his experiences abroad, he said. But he knew Charley would not mind, the doctor had decided they ought to try it. Now that they'd made the attempt there was nothing to be done. Perhaps rest and quiet would put her right. Charley said he was not to worry. Mr. Grant said it was white of him, to which Charley, marvelling at his own falseness, replied that it was the least he could do.

"Well, matters are like this," Mr. Grant made an end. "I never was one to saddle another with my troubles, but there was just the chance everything might come back to her, in which case she could've had a good cry on your shoulder, and you wouldn't have known the difference. But I'd never have brought you all this way for nothing," he said. "I've a surprise for you. Go to this address," and he gave Charley a number in a street, "and you'll find someone who knew Rose. She's just the age Rose was, maybe a month or two younger. She wants to meet you. She's a widow."

Charley did not even consider it. He thanked Mr. Grant, and made off fast for the District Railway.

When he got out at the other end he followed a strange girl with red hair the best part of three miles, back to what may have been her home, without trying to strike up an acquaintance.

ANOTHER morning, in London, in which he worked, Charley ran across a man by the name of Middlewitch, whom he had met, in July, at the Centre where he had been to have his new leg fitted.

"Why," this gentleman said, "it's Summers, isn't it, my companion in arms and legs? I'm just off to get me a bite of lunch. D'you know that place across the street? Funny," he remarked, as he piloted him through the traffic with a chromium plated arm under his black jacket, while Charley dragged the aluminium leg in a pin striped trouser. "Before the old war we'd be going to have a coffee about this time. Now we've to dash into some place before all the grub is gone. 'Les grands mutilés,' that's the name the French have for us, and it's good enough to get to the head of any queue out there. But not in this old country. Not on your life." He laughed with real pleasure. All this time Charley had not said a word. "Here we are," Mr. Middlewitch explained, diving into a gap before the bar. "What's yours?" he asked. And, before he could expect an answer, this man was getting hold of John, the head waiter, to keep a table for two, as well as greeting acquaintances in the crowd. In this way he had ordered a couple of double whiskies before enquiring what Charley might like better. Summers hardly ever touched spirits.

"Here's luck," Charley said, to speak for the first time.

"All the best," Mr. Middlewitch replied. He offered a cigarette with his good hand, then went into an elaborate drill to light a match. "I can't bother with lighters," this man explained. He put the box up under an armpit, to dab with a match at the millimetre of sand paper that was left exposed. But the barmaid dropped every-thing she was doing to give him a light. "Thanks Rose," he said.

It gave Charley a jolt. He had not been paying attention. He looked, but the girl was fair haired.

"Well," Mr. Middlewitch said, as he turned this way and that. "And how's the world been treating you? You know I wish they wouldn't do what she did. Light matches for one, I mean. But it can be a sight awkwarder at more intimate moments, eh? Lord yes. Mine squeaked the other day, just when I was putting it round her fattest bit. And a bloody sight more awkward for you I shouldn't wonder. Never fear though, they like it."

Mr. Summers quacked a laugh.

"Women are extraordinary," Middlewitch went on, in a loud voice. "There's my sister in law, now. So quiet she makes you ask yourself if by any chance she knows what's what, but then, as they say, still waters run profound. But to get on with what I was saying, I remember the time they were married, and the usual jokes got fly-ing. It's seven years back now. She sat there as though she had no idea in a million what it was all about. And afterwards the same, mind you. You know how things have a way of cropping up. In the ordi-nary run, I mean. Well whenever there's anything the least bit rude, not dirty, mind, but a trifle on the risky side, she sits there like she was miles away. Yet the moment I got back repatriated, and they had a little do in my honour, she was on at me the whole evening. I thought at first she had changed, for with all respect to Ted (that's my old lady's other boy), she never seemed to be what I'd call a pas-sionate woman. Now I've seen more of her, I'm dead certain she's just the same as ever. No, it's women's curiosity, Summers, there you are. Wanted to know what we did about girls all that time behind the wire. Kept on coming back to it, too. Did I feel embarrassed, and I'm not a man who colours easily! Then Ted, when he saw I was getting a bit hot under the collar, he chipped in as well. Gave me an insight into their married life for the first time, I can tell you. If you follow me, there was something in how they backed each other up, so as to make me speak out."

Charley cleared his throat. He had a faint glow from the whisky, was beginning to enjoy himself. He was thinking that, in another quarter of an hour, he would be liberated, free to talk. Because he had something, a sort of block in his stomach, which, in the ordinary way, seemed to stand between him and free speech. He looked at his empty glass. "Have another," he said.

"Thanks, I will. Extraordinary meeting you like this," Mr. Middlewitch replied. "No, it's curiosity," he went on, "they're the same as cats, when you scratch with your finger under the newspaper, which have to come and see what you're about. They're like this. They know you've lived the most unnatural damned life through no fault of your own for years, so want to get under your skin. Because it wasn't only Yvonne. Practically every girl I know had a go at me. Turned it to very good advantage, too, I did, on more than one occasion, I can tell you."

Charley grunted.

"Perhaps that's what they intended," Mr. Middlewitch said. "You never can be certain. There's that about the little ladies, you never know, not even afterwards."

"It's not only the women," Charley rather surprised himself by bringing out, as he paid for his round of drinks.

"Oh that other kind, men like that," Mr. Middlewitch announced, "I've no time for 'em. Sticking their noses into other people's private affairs like one of those horrible little dogs, poms they're called, aren't they, that go snuffling and yapping at every bit of dirt on the side. But you're one of the quiet ones, Summers. They must go for those big eyes of yours in a big way, the ladies, I mean. What about a bite to eat now? John has the table ready, they look after me in this little place. Yes," he said, and it appeared as if he spoke only out of civility, for his voice was entirely free from any note of interest, "I'll bet you could tell a true story or two on that score. But I know your type," he said, looking round the dining room for acquaintances, and he waved a hand, "I know your type," he repeated. "Mum's the word where you're concerned," he said.

After Charley had asked for beer and had been overruled, his host making the point that, when there was whisky, it was a sin not to drink it, he ventured on a remark.

"It's funny your mentioning what you did just now," Charley said. "I had an experience just the other day."

"I know your sort," Mr. Middlewitch replied, hardly listening, still on the look-out round this crowded room for old mugs, or pretty faces.

"Done nothing about it," Charley continued. He took a long pull at his whisky and soda, then warned himself he'd be drunk in a minute.

"Have you met old Ernest Mandrew?" Mr. Middlewitch demanded. "He's a big noise these days."

But Charley, like any very silent man, was not to be put off once he had begun.

"Asked me to come down to see them," he drawled. "Parents of a girl I used to meet. Wasn't much of a party. But as I was leaving the old man up and slipped me an address. Just like that. You see I was friends with the daughter, who's dead now." Here he paused. Then out it came. "Had a child by her as a matter of fact," he boasted, denying Rose a second time. "Yet there he was, giving me the address of a widow." Charley took another gulp, leant back unburdened.

"A widow?" Mr. Middlewitch echoed. "Oh boy. I say, remind me to go across to Ernie Mandrew when we're through, will you? I've got a bit of news will interest him, only I'm so damned forgetful these days. What were we saying?"

But Charley, for the time at any rate, had had his say. He was staring at the glass he held. His face, it is true, was very sad, but his mind was a concentrated blank. He felt the relief in his stomach.

Mr. Middlewitch glanced at him.

"Yes," he said, "we all of us came back to what we didn't expect. There's a number of people dropped out in everyone's lives. I'm not sure, but they do seem a long time over our soup."

He tried to catch the waitress several times, while Charley looked about, well satisfied.

"A widow you said, eh?" Mr. Middlewitch began once more. Summers nodded. "Dark or fair?"

Mr. Summers had never considered this.

"Red," he replied, from habit.

"Oh boy, a redhead."

"At least I don't know. Haven't seen her," Charley mumbled.

"Haven't seen her still?" Mr. Middlewitch echoed. "Then you must be getting your oats, right enough. Of course, I grant there's a lot of it around. That's only human nature, with the numbers of men there are overseas. But a redhead with freckles, I don't understand you, man?"

Charley was not to be drawn. He sat there, smiling.

"Well, any time you feel like," Mr. Middlewitch continued, "just pass over that address to me. I can't say I've a lot of free time on my hands, but no doubt she could be fitted in, at a pinch. I don't doubt at all, really."

As the waitress brought their soup, he ordered two more whiskies.

"Steady," Charley said.

"Well it all comes out of E.P.T., doesn't it? Carry on. Don't stint. Lord knows we've done without more than Scotch these last few years. Reminds me of the first girl I saw, when I got off that Swedish boat they sent us home in. You know, the first ordinary girl. She was a wizard blonde."

If Charley had not had the whiskies he might have let this pass, but as things were he said, "Ah."

"Well, I mean to say," Mr. Middlewitch took him up, sensing a response at last. "After all those years without a taste of it, nothing but men, getting to realize there's damn all in human nature, don't tell me you didn't find that out, that there's not a man, when you get down to bedrock, isn't a twirp through and through, well then, to step off that boat of repatriated maniacs gone a bit crazy for having been released, and then to see a blonde out shopping, or whatever she was about, and free as air, I ask you. There was such a howl went up I thought the dock buildings would blow down."

"And her?" Charley asked, becoming talkative.

"She never turned a curl. I've often thought about this since. She was used to it, you see. Very likely she might be the dock superintendent's daughter, anyway she seemed to have the run of that place. You on to what I'm getting at? All the hundreds of thousands of service men coming and going in a port. Well, I mean, it's war isn't it, *c'est la guerre*. Makes brutes out of women."

"Certainly does," Charley agreed.

"Why, there's no question but," Mr. Middlewitch said. "When we were over in Hunland, thinking of home, didn't you and I imagine summer evenings and roses and all that guff, with a lovely little lump of mischief in the old car of course, but most of the time we were like kids dreaming for the moon, and perhaps for a little accident to happen to them with a girl. And what happened when we did get back? Why, we got stinking tight, old lad, and catted it all up."

"That's right, we did," Charley agreed again, who had not got drunk particularly.

"And why?" Mr. Middlewitch asked. "Because we found everything different to what we expected." He pushed his plate of soup away, as though in disgust. Then he laughed. "Though I wouldn't have been doing that with this grub out there," he said.

Charley leant forward, but kept his eyes on the glass. His blood was soaring under the whisky.

"My girl died while I was out there," he said, "the one I mentioned. I've been down to the place they buried her but everything's different."

"That's just what I mean. Yes, there you are. That's it. But, boy, are there compensations, eh? Not but what I fancy you should take a grip on yourself, Summers. We've been through it. We know. So I can speak to you as I wouldn't to my best friend perhaps, just because you don't know me from Adam, and I don't know you. You see, I've kept in touch with some of the lads from our lot, and one or two have drawn their horns in, gone inside of themselves, if you follow me. Now that's dangerous. All you're doing is to perpetuate the conditions you've lived under, which weren't natural. Well, my advice to them and to you is, snap out of it."

"Of course," Charley said, and looked at him unseeing. He'd hardly heard.

"My God, but they're being a long time with our bunny," Mr. Middlewitch replied. "You'd think they had to take it out of its hutch, kill it, get the skin off, cook the little blighter, and then dish him up, by the time they're taking."

"I went down to the graveyard and, damn me if I didn't run into her husband," Charley told him.

"That must have been awkward," Mr. Middlewitch agreed. "What happened then? Did you cry with your two heads together over the monument? You speak as if you knew the lad."

"He's all right," Charley said, seemingly a bit daunted. "We had a bite to eat after." Mr. Middlewitch did not notice the reaction.

"And you had a bit of a chat? Compared notes eh?"

"No," Charley said. He frowned.

"I remember I was in a situation like that once," Mr. Middlewitch explained. "Very awkward too. It was soon after I left school, and I'd got in with a girl about my own age in the same road. Of course there was nothing to it, we were kids, see. But she went down with something or other, I forget, I believe it was meningitis, that can be a terrible thing, and when she died I had to spend most of every evening for weeks on end comforting the mother. Nice bit of stuff the mother was as well, but I was too young in those days to tumble the way the wind lay. Not that I wasn't well developed for a boy mind you."

There was no response from Summers.

"No, it's the opportunities missed that get you down as you grow older," Middlewitch went on, with the wisdom of his prison camp. "Take this rabbit before us now. If I'd ever known I was to have so much coney, why I'd 've never cancelled those steaks I used to in the old days, thinking a heavy meal at this hour did me harm. I went regular to the old George at the corner of Wood Lane, which is blitzed down, because most any day you could get a portion of rabbit there. If I'd known then what I do now. But that's life."

As for Charley, he did not care by this time what he was eating. And, when Middlewitch called their waitress for cheese and coffee, Rose was no more than a name to him. All the girls at this place were called alike. He concentrated, greedily, on the widow Mr. Grant had mentioned.

"Shall I give her a tinkle?" he asked into the silence that had fallen, in a sighing covey of angels, above their table.

But Mr. Middlewitch was bored. "Tell you what," he said, "I'll take you over and introduce you to old Ernie. He might do you a bit of good one of these days. What's that we were saying? Ring her? My dear good lad, do no such thing," he said. He had forgotten his earlier advice. "Drop in, boy. There you are. Then they can't say no. Because women are practised on the telephone. Drop in unexpected, that's my advice, drop in," he said.

MRS. FRAZIER sat beside Charley, in front of a roaring fire, in the bed sitting room he hired from her.

"No coal, no nothing," she remarked. She was about fifty and thin.

He grunted.

"Enjoy this while you have the opportunity," she said, "take what pleasure and comfort you can, because who is there to tell what may befall. When these new bombs he's sending over, turn in the air overhead, and come at you, there's not a sound to be had. One minute sitting in the light, and the next in pitch darkness with the ceiling down, that is if you're lucky, and haven't the roof and all on top. But as to our coal, that's certain. 'Coal?' my own merchant said the last time. 'Coal, Madame? Never heard of it.' And you don't catch a sound when they crash, everyone that's had one, and come out alive, speaks to that."

He sat vaguely wondering about chances of promotion in the office. Then about his coupons.

"Which is quite different from the last war," Mrs. Frazier continued. "And what a difference, oh my lord how different. Always heard them coming in the last war, and so gave the men time to cast themselves flat. I remember Mr. Frazier telling me. But of course in your case you didn't have long to form a judgement. They took you prisoner within a fortnight of your landing over on the other side, as you informed me. So enjoy this scuttleful while you may," she ended with relish, "for there's not another in the cellar. I said to Mary, 'Let Mr. Summers have it, Mary,' I said, 'We owe him that for all the poor man's been through.' 'And what about your own fire, Madam?' 'Why I'll sit with Mr. Summers, Mary, and see the last fire out we shall have this winter for the gentleman.'"

She said this with an easy mind, who had a ton and a half stowed safe in the other cellar.

She chanced a look at those great brown eyes. He continued to ignore her. But his expression was very pleasant.

"I can't make up my mind why you don't go out more often," she went on. "At the age you are as well, and after what you've been in. Find a young lady I mean," she said.

He gave a happy laugh.

"Laugh?" she asked. "You may laugh but I'm serious."

He did not take this up.

"Now Mr. Middlewitch," she said, looking into the fire, "that was another kettle of fish, with that man. Why I never had one like it. In the end I was obliged to tell him. Well, I mean to say."

"Middlewitch?" Charley asked. "Who works in the C.E.G.S.?"

"Oh I couldn't be certain, I'm sure," Mrs. Frazier answered, but she then gave a description which agreed exactly. "Perhaps you've met each other in the way of business?"

"Same man," Charley said.

"Why I often wonder what's become of him."

"Didn't know I knew him?" Charley enquired.

"Every year you live the world shrinks smaller," Mrs. Frazier replied. "Fancy you knowing Mr. Middlewitch. I didn't intend anything. It's only that some are different from others. I believe it really was that he thought he'd suit himself best near the Park, in Kensington. Took a fancy to run before breakfast, or suchlike. Whichever way it was, he left here. Paid what was due quite all right. Oh yes, there was nothing of that sort about the gentleman, even if there was a bit too much of the other. You understand I wasn't altogether sorry to see the back of him. But I wish the gentleman well, oh yes, I wish him quite well. It was a Mr. Gerald Grant recommended Mr. Middlewitch."

Charley was so surprised he spoke sharp.

"Elderly? Lives out at Redham?"

"The same," Mrs. Frazier answered. "Now, of course, you do know him. Why, he recommended you. Very lucky you were, too, even if it is me that says so. If you hadn't had your experiences I shouldn't wonder but I might have refused."

"Of course. I forgot," Charley mumbled.

"I daresay you think it's a lot of nonsense," she said, looking at him with open irritation, "but, when you've been back a while longer, you'll find conditions very different to what you remember of when you went off. Decent flatlets are hard to come by these days. There's not many roofs left in this whole town, for one thing. So, when Mr. Grant rang me, I said, 'It's not another Mr. Middlewitch, is it?' 'Oh no,' he said, 'as different as chalk from cheese.' Because that man. Well I'm a married woman, I'm as broadminded as most, but that gentleman's love life defied description."

"Never knew the two were acquainted," Charley explained, aghast.

"What is there strange in that?" Mrs. Frazier enquired, irritable still. "Once you start on coincidences why there's no end to those things. I could tell you a story you'd never believe but it's as true as I'm here," and she at once began a long tale. He hardly listened.

He could not explain it to himself, but the fact that old Mr. Grant knew Middlewitch made him deeply suspect. He even asked himself what he suspected, only to find that he could not think.

He saw round and round it in his head.

"So I said, 'it's the same person,'" Mrs. Frazier was bringing the story to an end. "'Look out,' I said, 'I'm going to faint away,' I said, and she came forward to take me by the arm. For they were as like as two peas," she finished, with a glance of triumph at Summers.

"Good lord," he said, not taking it in.

"But you want to brisk yourself up," Mrs. Frazier went on. "There were plenty like it after the last war. Sat about and moped. Of course it was understandable, but then most things are, and when all's said and done that's no credit to anyone, to mope," she said. "Yes, it draws sympathy, going on like that does, but not for long. There's the rub.

Well I mean no one can be expected to put up with it, not for ever. You want to go out and find yourself a nice young lady. There you are."

"Talking of resemblances," Mr. Summers suddenly began, and he was still staring at the fire. "Children, and their fathers and mothers. Would you say they looked like?" he enquired.

"Nothing in it," Mrs. Frazier said, favouring him with yet another long glance of interest, "nothing at all." She went into a detailed account of nephews and nieces, while he thought of Ridley. And then blamed himself that he did not think oftener of Rose.

The telephone rang down in the hall, cut Mrs. Frazier short.

"I'll go," he offered, for he was willing. Curiously enough, it was for him. Odder still, it was Mr. Grant wished to speak.

"And Mrs. Grant?" Charley asked.

"Mustn't complain, mustn't complain at all," Mr. Grant replied. "When you come to consider, there's compensations in not remembering, as I dare say you've found, eh Charley?" His voice was thin. "No, but what I meant to ring you about was this. Did you ever call round on that little lady I mentioned? I'll tell you why. You're one of the diffident sort, unsure of yourself. I'll be bound you've done nothing."

"It slipped me," Charley admitted.

"Look," Mr. Grant said, "I'm older than you. I can put forward things that perhaps you would never allow from a man your own age. I didn't altogether make that suggestion just casually as you might say. There was a reason behind."

"Well thanks," Charley answered.

"That's all right," Mr. Grant ended.

When Charley got back to his room Mrs. Frazier spoke of rising prices. "Why," she said, "they rose, they've rose..." and the words, because he had not paid attention, the words pierced right through. He held his breath for the pain to which he had grown accustomed, particularly in Germany, he waited for it to break over him, as he sat isolated by Mrs. Frazier's voice he did not listen to as she rasped on. For he was as sure he would feel the ache as he had, on his one early holiday before the war, been certain that he would hear a cuckoo each walk he took, each occasion he passed an open window. It had been the right time of the year for cuckoos. And now, it seemed, was autumn, for he felt nothing at all at her mention of Rose. Nothing. He was amazed. He blamed himself. But he felt nothing whatever.

"No warning," he brought out in surprise at this new condition in himself, cutting across the landlady's tideless flow of talk.

"A warning?" Mrs. Frazier echoed, agitated. "I never heard the sound. It can't be our syrens, then."

"My mistake," Charley Summers told her. "Talking to myself again."

She watched him. He was quite unconscious, with a bewildered look on his face.

"Speaking to yourself?" she asked. "Now Mr. Summers, you want to watch out. Not at your age. Why," she said, "your voice rose," and again, as this word came through, he not even experienced guilt. "You spoke loud," she said. "Take care, you can do that when you get to my age, but for a young man like you, well..."

There was a silence while he sat there, avidly listening now.

"Take the price of flowers," Mrs. Frazier continued, back to what she had been discussing, "tulips, daffodils, chrysanths, even violets of the field," and Charley waited, waited for another sign, "why, they're out of all reason, they're black market charges right in the light of day. It's wrong," she said.

"There it is," Charley encouraged her. She thought that, when in the end he did regard you out of those great eyes, they seemed to grow from his head, and float in the air before your own. She was actually breathless with them.

"Yes well..." she tried to go on, then hesitated. But her subject carried her forward. "Yes, you say that, you're like all the others, you take it for granted," at which, still thinking of his girl, he smiled, her last remark seemed so absurd. "But you do nothing, the next pay day you'll go in and buy her a bunch; when you find her, that is, which you won't by sitting here listening to me. I tell you, when I saw the prices they charge round the corner, my gall rose," she said, and he heard Mrs. Frazier no more. He fastened on this word. Once more he waited. But he felt nothing, nothing at all.

Rose was gone.

So he was in a mood to look about, when S.E.C.O., a government department in charge of the contracts on which he was working, found him Miss Dorothy Pitter as his assistant.

The other girls in the office had had to do his typing as and when they could, on top of their own work. Through the weeks that he was losing Rose they were continually saying to him, "When is this new one expected?" Or, "Don't S.E.C.O. take a time?" He was popular because of his leg, but the office was critically short of staff, and he could not always find a typist to stay late. As a result he could hardly trust his ears when, a few days after this last talk with Mrs. Frazier, a member of the counting house met him one morning to say, "She's in."

Then, as he went to his room and saw her, he had once again the experience inseparable from government procedure, he had before his eyes the product of a prolonged correspondence; that is, first the discouraging replies, followed by official consent to there being a vacancy, after which a notification that the vacancy would be filled, then, at last, the name of a person to be directed to fill it, then, finally, that wait, a deadly pause of weeks, before, without warning, these letters, these forms and the reference numbers bloomed into flesh and blood, a young woman, with shorthand, who could type.

She was fair, rather untidy. She seemed absolutely null and void. But he was so pleased to see her, he got almost talkative.

"Well, Miss, it's been quite a time," he said.

"I don't know about that," she said. "They had me out of where I was working before you could say Jack Robinson. And not a word to warn you."

"That's strange," he said. "They told us they were sending five weeks ago."

"That's S.E.V.E. all over."

"We're under S.E.C.O. here," he said.

"S.E.C.O.?" she gave a little scream. "Are you sure there isn't some mistake?"

"Oh no Miss," he said, and showed her the papers. He'd kept them, as a sort of talisman, on top of everything else, in the left-hand drawer of a kitchen table they'd given him for a desk.

"That only shows," she exclaimed. "It's been going on for weeks, you can see from the dates here, and there's me been doing everything so I could get forty-eight hours leave, to visit my mum up north."

"You've got your mother away?"

"Yes, she's evacuated with some relations near Huddersfield. You wouldn't think they'd miss me for that little time, while I was changing jobs, would you?"

"There it is," he said. "But we might be able to manage you the trip. We do a deal of travelling around."

"D'you really mean it? Why," she almost grumbled, "that would be nice." She did not seem to want to go now. "What are you on here?"

"Process plants for parabolam," he replied.

She did not know what this was, so she tried him out.

"Why, fancy that, with me that's been on penicillin."

"On the production side?" he asked.

"I was in the lab," she said. "With the card indexing. But I've never worked with one of those," she complained, pointing to the two long and narrow steel cupboards that flanked his desk, to the system he had installed, and which had kept him sane throughout the first re-flowering of Rose.

"That's my visible system," he explained. "If you'd like to draw up your chair," he went on, and did this for her. "It's like this." He could always be glib at his work. "We're a firm of engineers and we've no factory, it was burned to a cinder in the blitz. So we have to get everything we do made out," he said. "Everything, down to the last nut and bolt. Well, of course, in times like these, when each engineering firm's got more on its plate than it can manage, we'd be out of business if it wasn't for the Government thinking we're so important that they make other companies turn out our work for us. So we get S.E.C.O. support, which is pretty high, as you've found yourself, for a start. We do all the designing and drawing, and we're responsible for the performance when the finished plant is installed. Also it's our end of it to follow up the stuff while it's being made, to see that things don't get behind, or that the Admiralty, or M.A.P., doesn't nip in ahead and put ours back in the list. So everything that we order goes onto these cards, one card to each item, with the due date for delivery, and who it's to go to."

"Oh dear," she said.

"And there's the index. And here's the cross index. The whole thing's visible. Tell at a glance, I don't think. It may seem loopy to you but this is the one way our particular job can be done."

"I see," she said, while he sat back, having talked too much for him. "I wonder if I could meet one of the other girls," she said.

"I say, you must excuse me," he begged. "You want to know where to put your things?" And he took her out to the friendliest typist, in the Board Room office.

It was a great relief to have her. The main advantage was, it let him get back to his digs at a reasonable hour each night, and that at a time when he had got over Rose, that is to say when he could keep quite a bit relaxed. But he found he never seemed to do much in the evenings, all the same. He had explained it by making out that his staying sorry for himself about Rose, and his being overworked, prevented him going off free at nights. Yet now that he was so much freer, he seemed rather at a loose end.

So he began to look about him. Even in the office; in spite of the saying, "Never on your own doorstep."

It began one afternoon, over the tea and bun at three thirty, as they sat side by side.

"I wonder if you'd mind," she said. "I get so muddled. What is what we're doing for?"

He took a sip. "Steel," he replied.

"Oh, they make steel in them, then?"

"No. Parabolam," he told her once again. "Used in special steels."

"Sounds strange," she commented, and sniffed. She was drearily untidy, but there was something there, he thought.

"What's parabolam, then?" she asked, to keep the ball rolling.

"Comes from birds' droppings."

She looked at him, surprised. "Here," she said, "you wouldn't be having me on, by any chance?"

"Word of honour," he said. She waited.

Like any silent man he talked technicalities freely, once he got started. "It was an accident," he began, "like it was with stainless steel, when the heads were on an inspection round the foundry yard and one of 'em spotted something he'd noticed before, a bit of bright scrap through the rain. So they had it analysed, and there you are. Now it's what you cut your meat up with."

"Well, I never knew that," she said.

"It was exactly similar with parabolam," he went on, "only this time it was birds' droppings. The swallows used to nest under the staging, where they charged the furnace. One day the foundry manager had all the nests cleared out, together with the filth below. And the labourer he gave the job, was too tired to take the mess down, he shovelled it in with the charge into the cupola. And what came out with their molten metal was so hard they couldn't machine the casting."

"I can't hardly believe you."

"Well I may have been exaggerating a trifle. Anyway, they all got to work and it was isolated. In the end, they discovered there was a higher percentage of what it takes where sea birds roost. So we ship it in the raw state from South America, and the stuff is burned in those retorts we buy from Dicksons. In burning, a gas is released, which is treated in the catalysts. From there the vapour passes to those cooling chambers, that come from the A.B.P. people, and then the cold gas deposits its crystals onto what you won't believe, you'll think I'm play acting, onto ordinary common or garden laurel leaves they place on those long racks which Purdews make us."

"I know a girl named Laurel. Hardy we call her."

"I knew one called Rose." Each time he said her name he noted he felt nothing any more, so much so that he hardly bothered to watch himself these days. He went on. "After which the leaves are washed, and it's got to be laurel because of the chemical properties in the leaf. Then we take the water out on a Bennetts evaporator. And bob's your uncle. Sells for £250 a ton into the bargain. That's roughly the lot. If you wanted it in detail you'd have to question Corker."

Corker was the technical director who designed this plant.

"I'd never ask him in my life," Miss Pitter said, with reverence.

"He's mustard," Mr. Summers muttered, relapsing into silence. But he watched her. In the five minutes they had before the phone began to ring again, she could get no more out of him.

There definitely was something, he thought.

That night, she came from the girls' washroom just as he was on his way out of the office.

"What's it like in the air?" she asked.

"Don't know yet," he said.

"Oh, you are comical," she laughed, and was really amused. He began to feel excited, nervous in his stomach. He told himself he had never been like this before the war. She was complaining about something in the office. He did not pay attention, he was noting his inside. They came to the bus stop.

"No one here tonight," she said. He did not answer.

"One of the girls told me you had the M.C.?"

"Me?" he asked. "Not me."

She waited. He said no more. They got on the first bus.

"But they said you'd been a prisoner of war?"

"That's right."

"It must get you right down, being cooped up like it?"

He made no reply. She gave in.

"What number is this?" she asked, when they stopped.

"A nine," he said.

"Gosh, I don't know what I'm doing, I'm sure," she cried. "See you tomorrow," and was gone. He thought about her that night as he lay awake for hours.

The next day, at the first opportunity, she began again. As she started she asked herself, "Well what's the odds?" After all, she knew she was quite uninterested.

"That was queer, my getting on the wrong bus with you, wasn't it?" she said. She was leaning against the card index system. "Since mum's been evacuated I've caught myself doing daft things, really, ever so often. It's the loneliness."

He looked at her.

"Not that we don't have good times at my hostel," she went on, "but mum and me, we were good companions. You know, got on together. Not like mother and daughter at all."

"Yes, that's it," he said.

"'Dot,' she'd say, because that's my name, Dot and no comma, 'What's on round the corner?' and with that we'd drop whatever it was we were doing, and go out to the movies. But she couldn't stand the bombing."

Charley was spared any necessity to reply because the telephone began to ring. It kept on pretty well all day.

And he began to notice.

He was not frank about it, he shied away in his mind, but there were her breasts which she wore as though ashamed, like two soft nests of white mice, in front. Their covered creepiness, in this hot summer, nagged him. And, every time he looked, he felt she knew, as she did.

Most of the working day she sat at his side marking up the cards, or turning up references as he phoned the suppliers. Often, she had to lean across to get at the second cabinet. He began to take in her forearms, which were smooth and oval, tapering to thin wrists, with a sort of beautiful subdued fat, also her hands light nimble bones with fingers terribly white, pointed into painted nails like the sheaths of flowers which might at any minute, he once found himself feeling late at night, mushroom into tulips, such as when washing up, perhaps.

He dreaded getting into this condition.

Or sometimes, while he dictated, it was the softness there must be on the underside of her arms which caught his breath, and that he remembered after, and then the finished round of muscle, where the short sleeves ended, as he read out to her, "Their ref. CM/105/127 our ref. 1017/2/1826," because he would not leave the girl to copy these from the correspondence on her own.

Prison had made him very pure. His own name for all this was lust. It shook him. But he did nothing whatever about it. Perhaps because all of her seemed a contradiction. Those arms came out of frocks that did not hang properly, from below untidy hair her blue eyes were sharp, yet worried, and also too self sure; her legs were quite customary, yet the arms were perfect; and ever more uneasily he watched those breasts.

He imagined he could see her arms without her noticing, so he was more open with these. But he did not touch.

Her arms built great thighs on her in his mind's eye, while she might be asking him, "About those needle valves in stainless...," made her quite ordinary calves into slighter echoes of what he could not see between knee and hip, as she might be saying, "Now those break vacuum cocks...," but which, so he thought, must be unimaginably full and slender, when she wanted to know where the "accessible traps" came from, white, soft, curving and rounded with the unutterable question, the promise, the flowering of four years imprisonment with four thousand twirps. And he would lift his great brown eyes, and say, "They come from Smiths," while she wondered, "Are my stockings straight, I wonder?"

It made him ashamed the way he felt about her.

But this was the sole promise there was in being alive. Hopelessly turned over to himself, as well as conscientious to a degree, so careful in his work there were occasions she could have shrieked at the way he wrote, time and again, to the same firm holding them to the last promise they had made, so careful with his words, tactfully nagging, letter after letter, never leaving them alone, so Dot was the only carrot in front of his nose, because he found of an evening, when he got back, that he barely existed, lived in a daze now that Rose was over.

Sometimes he would dream of red-haired fat women. But they were not at all like Rose.

As for Miss Pitter, she sniffed when one of the girls back at the hostel asked how her new place was shaping. "I don't know what they took me away from my old job for," she said. "This is a Fred Karno war, if you ask me. And the man I work with is dippy."

She never mentioned his great big eyes.

Nevertheless, she began to get involved with the card index system. The main thing was, she found it dead accurate. She had thought Charley so wandering, the first few days, that she at once did a check through with the order book. There was not an item wrong. Then, as fresh orders were issued each day through the drawing office and she had to enter up the particulars on the cards, together with the details of what had been delivered, which she took from the advice notes, she began to be more and more frightened she would make a slip. Without knowing, she was becoming enslaved by the system.

Until one afternoon it occurred.

He was on the telephone as usual. He was speaking to Braxtons. She turned the card up, on which she had marked the number of items already delivered.

"Is that your ref. BMO/112?" he asked. "Summers, here, of Meads. It's in connection with our order number 1528/2/1781. We want those joint rings you promised this week. To go to Coventry."

He waited. He laughed. "No, we shan't send you there," he said. He waited again. He closed his eyes. He always did this when hanging on for an answer.

"What?" he said. "We've had 'em?" He looked at her. She was surprised at herself. Her heart had given a great jolt. "Oh no," she couldn't help saying. "What date?" he asked into the receiver. "Well thanks, old man, I'll give you a ring back."

"September the 10th," was Charley's reproach to her.

She went out to search through the files. Of course she'd had a bit of a bust up with Muriel, the night before, at the hostel. But when she found an advice note from Braxtons for the joint rings in question, and saw that she had not initialled it, and, therefore, that she had never seen the thing, and, consequently, that Mr. Pike, the chief draughtsman, must have kept it back on purpose—when she came into his room again she leaned her head on that beastly green card cabinet, and cried.

This upset Charley, because he thought someone might be getting at him by tormenting her. Anyway he felt the whole thing was a shame. So he got to his feet right off and clumsily kissed one of her temples through a drift of yellow hair. But he did not put his hands up. She warmed a bit, blamed herself aloud for being silly, and said no more.

Yet he found that anything so simple as placing his head against a woman's, was not so ordinary in practice. For he stood gawping there, like an Irish navvy. He had forgotten what it was like. The last time had been such a long while back.

He got much more that he had not remembered.

He was, for the moment, saved from greater torture by the telephone ringing once again. But when the office closed that night he thought he would walk home, rather than take a bus, so as to see girls, the day's work done, as they made their way back through streets.

So it was that he found himself, by chance, within a few yards of the address Mr. Grant had given.

The door was open.

He went in. He climbed stairs. He began to regret it.

Then he was outside an inner door, on which was written her name. Her name was there on a card.

He read her name, Miss Nancy Whitmore, in Gothic lettering as cut on tombstones. He noticed the brass knocker, a dolphin hanging by the tail. He ran his eye over this door which was painted pink. The wall paper he stared at round the door, was of wreathed roses on a white ground. He looked again. Someone had wiped the paint down so often, it was so clean that the top coat was wearing thin. In the moulding round the panels a yellow first coat grinned through at callers. And her card was held in place by two fresh bits of sticking plaster, pink.

With a melting of his spine, he felt she must be a tart.

The moment he realized this, his first idea was to go, to come back another day perhaps, but to get out of it for now.

Yet he knocked.

She opened, almost at once. He looked. He sagged. Then something went inside. It was as though the frightful starts his heart was giving had burst a vein. He pitched forward, in a dead faint, because there she stood alive, so close that he could touch, and breathing, the dead spit, the living image, herself, Rose in person.

WHEN HE came round, he was flat along the floor with his head rested on an object. Curled up above, on a chair, there was a tortoise-shell cat that watched him, through great yellow eyes with terrible black slits. He knew no cat. It meant nothing. He could not make out where he was until he tilted himself, to find Rose kneeling at his head, which was in her lap. Then he remembered.

"Darling you've dyed your hair," he brought out, proud to be so quick, for the room was dark. Apart from this one detail he knew it was all right at last, was as it had been six years back.

"That's better," she said.

He rested. He lay on. He was content. He felt his blood flow all over the inside of him. There was just one point; her voice sounded rather changed.

Her moon cool hands were laid about his temples. The cat shut its eyes and dozed. And he shut his.

"Take it easy," she said. Again the voice which had changed.

"Darling," he murmured.

"That's enough of that," she said, but although she spoke sharp it barely came through to him, in his condition. Because this, he felt, as he now was, must be what he had been waiting for these years, the sad soldier back from the wars.

"Why?" he asked, absolutely trusting her, and still shuteyed, and in a humble voice.

"You're telling me," she said.

He began not to understand. He looked. He saw the cat was there no longer. A kettle was boiling. He tilted again. Her dear face did not even seem to belong, he thought. But he knew it must be all right.

"Here," she said, reaching for a cushion. "Put this under you."

He shut his eyes again. He sighed in deep content.

"Have a quick rest now, then get to hell out of here," she said, rising to her feet.

He heard this right enough, but thought she was joking. When he shakily sat up to be fetched a kiss, he found she was gone, that she was next door in the kitchen.

He dragged himself off the floor, and sat on a chair because he did not feel so good. He was empty, and ill, and the room began going round once more, with the cat, which had come back. Still, he found he could focus after a few minutes. He watched it settle down opposite, start to wipe the side of its mouth.

Then he watched the opening to the kitchen. He thought he was stronger, and he had so much to ask Rose he did not know where to begin.

She came back with two cups of tea. Except for the hair, which was black, she was now exactly like again.

"I was only making myself one when you came," she said. He half rose, but his hands shook so badly she put his down on the table.

"Doesn't seem possible," he started. He stopped. There was something he could not fathom in her face, as she watched over the rim of her cup.

"What exactly is the matter with you?" she asked.

Then he knew what it was. She was an enemy. She couldn't have heard about him. She thought he had given her up. Everything must come all right. But he dreaded it so, that he could not bring himself to speak.

"How you people manage to dress as you do," she said, in a hard voice, at his city suit. He thought "Oh what have I done? She's out of her mind." His mouth went dry as he realized, next, that she was completely self-possessed. He reached for his cup. He did not know how he would be able to lift this. He tried to take heart because she had given him a saucer with it.

"That's right. Drink that, then go," she said.

"My God," he said as he dropped it. He had been afraid he would. "Now look what you've done," she said, and rushed out into the kitchen for a dish cloth. "Here," she said, throwing this. He mopped at his trousers. "And what about my covers?" she asked. He stumbled to his feet, began dabbing at the chair.

"Rose," he said low, his back still turned to her.

"What's rose?" she asked frantic.

Then he had another thought. That she'd lost her memory, same as her mother. He knew he must take things slowly. He worked on the chair.

"Think it's all right now. Terribly sorry," he said.

"I don't know what to make of you," she complained, but in an easier voice. The suit had taken all he had spilt.

"Careless of me," he said, with such a hang dog look she must have felt sorry. Perhaps it was to hide this up that she said, "I expect there'll be a drop left in the pot."

He sat on. When she came back with another cup, this time without a saucer, he said,

"I'll get you a replacement."

For a moment she did not understand this phrase, which came from the jargon of production engineers, but as soon as she realized he meant to buy her a cup and saucer in place of what he had just broken, she put her foot down hard.

"You won't, thank you," she said. "I wouldn't want you in here a second time, thanks very much. Not to get to be a habit. I'd never have done this, only I happened to know Mr. Middlewitch was in across the landing."

"Middlewitch?" He spoke out in real horror.

"Now then," she said, beginning to look frightened.

"Middlewitch?" he repeated, absolutely bewildered.

"Just because I give you the name of someone who lives in these digs, don't you start wondering if you'll strike lucky twice," she said.

"Me strike lucky?" he mumbled.

"It's rationed now, you know," she insisted.

This was too much. He almost laughed he was so frantic.

"That's rich," he said.

"What's rich?" she wanted to know. "And cups aren't easy to come by these days, either," she went on, "though I'm not accepting anything from strange men, you can be sure of that," she said.

She sat there, looking. She was cold, cold with hostility.

"Middlewitch, who's with the C.E.G.S.?" he asked, clutching at the straw, but suspicious.

"You drink yours up, then go."

"Not before you tell me if it's the same."

There was a long pause while he watched her. He could tell nothing new from her face.

"I wouldn't know," she said at last, but so cautiously that he could tell it was the very same.

He put his cup down with care. His hands were much steadier. Middlewitch was something to hang on to.

"Don't you know me at all?" he asked. Putting this question, however, was so dreadful that he again began to tremble all over.

"Now, don't you start," she said. She looked really frightened.

"Oh dear," he said. There was another pause.

"D'you do this for a living, then?" she began, almost as though to give herself confidence by making awkward conversation. But he gave no answer.

"It's getting cold," she said of his tea, it must have been to hurry him up. "I'm telling you."

"I've seen Ridley, Rose," he said. He watched her as he spoke, as a dog sits up for a bone.

"There you go, more riddles. And who's Ridley?"

He looked at her idiotically.

"Don't stare at me," she said, looking more frightened than ever. Then she gave way. She explained.

"It's not the first time," she said. "Why don't you take things as they come, and get out of here?"

"Not the first time?" he echoed, gaining confidence.

"I've had people stop me in the streets. Who hasn't anyway? I suppose I've a double somewhere in this town all right. Though why I'm telling you I can't think." She smoothed her skirts.

"My dear, you've lost your memory," he said, trying to smile.

She shot out of her seat.

"Here," she shouted, "d'you want me to call the police? I've had about enough of this. Who d'you take me for? Anyway, why aren't you in the Army? I'm not your dear. Who d'you fancy I am?" She had gone over by the door, and was holding it open. "Or d'you want me to fetch Mr. Middlewitch? He'll soon make up his mind how to put you to rights."

"Yes," he replied, braving it out, the colour coming back to his face. "He knows me."

She bit her thumb.

"He's not in," she said, suddenly like a small girl. "That was to get rid of you."

Charley sat down, put his head in his hands, almost defeated now he had won his point.

"You haven't been keeping watch here, by any chance?" she asked, as if she were shy. "Until you know who's in and out? Oh, you're a worry. Now will you go?"

He sat there hiding his face.

"Now what?" she said.

"You say you've been mistaken for someone?" he slowly asked.

"Well, who hasn't?" she said, half on the landing.

"Lately?" he asked.

"No," she said, "not for ages."

He looked at her again. He became excited.

"That's exactly it," he said. "That's what I'm after. So you haven't been taken for her lately?" What he meant was, it must be all of five years since Rose was said to have died, in which time she could have been forgotten. It did not make sense, but he hung on to it.

"What's that got to do with me? And who are you any way?" Yet she shut the door, possibly because he looked so queer, and came back in the flat. "It's I should be making enquiries about you, I fancy," she said in a strong voice. "Coming in here, fainting right in my arms. I shouldn't wonder if I hadn't strained my side when I tried to lift you." She came right up to him. He could not bear her near, like this. He hid his face a second time.

"Oh Rose," he mumbled, "how could you?"

"Here we go once more," she said bright. "What did you say your name was?"

But he made no reply.

"I'll have a real laugh with mum over this."

"You won't," he said.

"That's the limit," she said, loud. "Look I'm fed up, thanks." She moved away from him impatiently. "Will you stop telling me? Who d'you think you are to say how I'll laugh with my own mother?"

"You could. I hadn't thought." What had come to him, was that this might only be too possible, mother and daughter both suffering, as they must be, from lost memories. In that case they might very well, the two of them, twist their guts inside out with laughing.

"Thanks a lot," she said. "Now will you please get along. I don't know where we're coming to with the war effort, but I can't find time to nurse strangers."

He sat on, his head in his hands. He could not face it.

"All you want is a good feed," she said. "You try the Army. A month or two in that, and you'll be as right as rain."

"I'm discharged. I lost my leg. I wrote you."

She opened her mouth to reply, and by the look on her face he was going to catch it, when her eyes followed, down one of his legs, the creased cloth which lay as this never does over flesh and bone. It silenced Miss Whitmore.

"They repatriated me in June," he mumbled.

It came over her that he was going to cry.

"You've been a prisoner, then?" she asked.

He did not answer. He was quite still.

"Well, I mean," she said softer, "you're back now, after all? Must be a change after what you've been in. Look," she said quite soft, "there's nothing terrible about this, is there? I mean there's others have come up to me in the street, respectable people mind, and have fallen into the same error. And when I've put them right they've always gone off about their business. I mean, be reasonable," she said. "I had to close the door just now so you couldn't be seen in the state you've gotten into. Why don't you just pull yourself together, and go?"

"Did they call you Rose?" he asked. She knew he was watching her again, desperately. And she could not look at him, or reply, because they had indeed. So she just stood there.

"It was your father sent me, Rose."

Again she could not speak.

"Mr. Grant, Rose," he said.

She whirled herself round, turning her back on him, so he could not see her face. He took what he imagined to be his advantage.

"You wouldn't deny him, Rose?" he softly asked.

"What is your name, then?" she said in a low voice.

"Charley Summers." He spoke confidently.

"Never heard of it," she answered right out, turning round. He saw this was the truth, yet there was something here he had never seen in Rose, that he hadn't ever known of her, and it was shame. Then he realized she was now so angry as well that she could not stoop to a lie. "What?" she said, "You come along, you play some dirty trick to get in, pretending to faint?" and she stamped her foot, while keeping her arms rigid at her sides, "Then you bring his name up?" she said, in a voice breaking with rage and something else, "Him?" she cried, "Why you aren't a man, a real man would never do a thing like that. And how did you ferret his name out?" she shouted. "What is he to me? What've I had in my life from him, from Mr. Grant?" and she burst into tears, spreading a small handkerchief to cover as much as possible of her mouth and eyes.

"Rose," he said, shocked, "you've forgotten yourself."

She cried uglily. He did not dare go near. When she was a little recovered, she turned her back on him once again.

"Now look what you've done," she stammered. "Won't you be content? Now won't you go?"

"Rose darling," he said, "you're not yourself."

"I'm not your Rose," she wailed, crying noisily once more, "and I never was, nor ever could be. Oh I rue the day that man had me, was my father," she mumbled. "Didn't give me his name," she added, cried noisily, then began blowing her nose. Charley stood apart, absolutely flummoxed, yet a bit triumphant.

"But your mother, Mrs. Grant," he said, archly.

"That's enough," she shouted, "that's enough. You don't suppose I let you in here to talk over my affairs, do you?" She had taken him by the shoulders. She seemed beside herself. "Come on out of it." Her face was terribly twisted. But she did not look at him. She hustled him out. The last thing he saw before she slammed the door shut was her cat, tail up, treading the carpet, treading the carpet.

He stumbled out in the street. He walked for hours. This time he did not look at the girls who passed.

HE LOVED Rose desperately and despairingly now.

He gave the office a miss next day. He did not even ring them to say he would not be in. They were surprised. He had always been so careful in the few months he had been back. But they let him be.

He left the lodgings at his usual hour for going to work so that Mrs. Frazier did not know; his bed, which had been an unquiet grave all night, disclosed nothing to the maid, Mary.

He fled Rose, yet every place he went she rose up before him; in florists' windows; in a second-hand bookseller's with a set of Miss Rhoda Broughton, where, as he was staring for her reflection in the window, his eyes read a title, "Cometh up as a flower" which twisted his guts; also in a seed merchant's front that displayed a watering can, to the spout of which was fixed an attachment, labelled "Carter's patent Rose."

For she had denied him, and it was doing him in.

A woman behind said, "They're like flies those bloody 'uns, and my goodness are they bein' flitted." Then he saw Rose as he had once seen her, naked, at sunset, James away, standing on the bed which was so soft it nearly tumbled her down, laughing and flitting mosquitoes on the ceiling above, and with her hair which, against the light, on the edges of it, shook and trembled in a flaming rose.

He rushed off so he should hear no more, and in trying to go fast he limped exaggeratedly. Rose that he'd loved, and who could not be explained.

"Lost 'is leg in the war I'll bet," another voice came, and he knew

Rose as she had been one afternoon, a spider crawling across the palm of a hand, the hair hanging down over her nose, telling him how many legs they had, laughing that red spiders were lucky, dear, darling Rose.

He got so that he did not know what he was about.

When he came to once more, it was still the same day and he was gazing into a tailor's, at a purple overcoat, worrying about his coupons. What had brought him back, sharp, was a song oozing out next door, from a wireless shop, a record through loud speakers of "Honeysuckle Rose." He felt extreme guilt that he could have forgotten her again. Then, for the first time, that he must get hold of old Grant. Because why had that fiend out of hell sent him on the visit? They could not all be out of their minds in that family? So they had used him as a guinea pig once more? It was vivisection? And Rose must have good reason for acting as she did. Wasn't for nothing that she'd sent him packing. It was Grant's fault.

There was a queue before the telephone booth, and, as he came up, the girl within was just coming out. He did not know what he was about but he went to the head, said to a man with white hair, who was the next customer, "Excuse me won't you. A favour. Just back from Germany. Repatriated, wooden leg," and went in. As he dialled the Redham number, he saw this man calm the others behind. He knew it because they were all looking down at his limb, yet he had no idea of what he had just done. Indeed his impression was that he had been standing his turn in the queue for hours.

However, when Mr. Grant answered, Charley did not find himself so glib. It was rage cut him short. While the old man said "Hullo," all Charley could get out was, "I say," twice. At last he did manage, "Summers speaking."

"Oh it's you, my boy," Mr. Grant returned. He voiced this acidly. "Most unfortunate," he said. "The fact is, mother's not so well this morning. I'm expecting the doctor any minute. So you went to that address after all," he continued. "I must say I did think you would respect my confidence." At this Charley gaped into the receiver. "It's the least I'm entitled to," Mr. Grant went on, "or that's my opinion, and we've got a right to our opinions, you know, oh yes. Because I particularly asked you not to say where you got her address," and Charley thought, you lying bastard, was even about to say it, but he listened instead. "Now, my boy," Mr. Grant was continuing, "that's just what you did do, and the moment you got there. Look, this is the doctor. I must be about my business. But I must say—yes I'm coming—it was—oh well, good day to you." And Mr. Grant rang off.

"You bastard, you bastard, you bastard," Charley began to shout down the dead line. Then someone tapped on the glass. It was the man with white hair, who just shook his white head.

The next thing Charley knew he was by a church. He found himself reading a poster stuck up on the notice board outside, which went, "Grant O Lord," then said something about a faithful servant. The first word shook him. He cried again, "The bastard," right out loud.

Then he connected Mrs. Frazier with the house at Redham. It came to him that he must at once put this to her, that she was in league with Mr. Grant. That it could only be white slave trading?

He looked about for a taxi, damn the expense for he had no time. He ran across traffic at a cab moving the other way, and, as he went, it was like a magpie with a broken wing, he flopped along, but the flag was down, the taxi taken. He straggled back to an island. He leant on one of the posts that bounded it, stabbed with a finger out of his closed fist at each cabby passing. A policeman began to watch.

But then he got one.

After he had given the address, he leant forward in case he should see Mrs. Frazier shopping, although he was more than a mile outside her district. Because he could not wait.

It was only about the third time in his life he had taken a cab.

When he got back, Mary, the maid, thought she was out after the rations, and explained where to find the fruiterers Mrs. Frazier had told her she was off to, the rumour today being that there had been a special delivery to Blundens. He limped towards this shop. He was beginning to look very untidy, very staring. Then he saw her, a thin dark monument, the landlady, halfway in the queue.

When he got up to her he had nothing to say that he could get out. He stood dumb. As usual, she talked first.

"Why, Mr. Summers," she exclaimed, "what are you doing on a weekday? Don't tell me one of those dreadful new bombs has brought your place of business down about your ears?" She spoke in mincing fashion, so as to impress the others in this queue. But every one of the women had her eyes fixed on the veg, watching for what she wanted to be gone, finished before it was her turn to be served, watching with eyes that seemed to pin down prizes in the shop's open tea chests, pin them with long pointed pins of steel the length the eyes were from these cherished beans, or peas, or harico vers, or, more terribly, watching for what was not displayed, for what those already served were carrying off in covered shopping baskets. What that was not one of the others knew because no one had been told for sure, as they stood hoping for the extra special under the counter, a dwindling stock of something unknown to them which they sought after, with steel cupidity forged in their old eyes.

"Now if you had gumption you'd pass to the head with that war injury, and do my buying for me," Mrs. Frazier said, arch. "If I was to tell you were my nephew, back from Germany with what you've got, I dare say they'd let it go, just the once," she said.

"I never," he brought out. He had forgotten the phone booth.

"Why, Mr. Summers," she warned him in a low voice. "Why you're not quite yourself. And look at you," she added.

"Look," he said, averting anguished eyes. Why, she thought, he's like a dumb animal. "Most important," he stammered. "Rose's . . . , Rose's . . . ," and he could get no farther. He kept swallowing.

"Roses," she half whispered, when he could not go on, afraid the queue might take notice. "What about them? You won't find many now, and the price. They grow those under glass. The shrapnel's got the most of that, Mr. Summers."

"No," he said, "it's Mr. Grant . . . ," and he could not finish.

By now she was afeared, almost.

"Look Mr. Summers, not in the street," she said. "I can't discuss private affairs while I'm in the middle of my business, thank you."

"I've got to ask this," he said, quite clear. His brown eyes were on her now. She thought no, they're black. "Did he lose his daughter?" he managed, in a sort of gasp.

"I'm sure I wouldn't have any idea. Now why don't you let Mary fetch you a nice cup of tea, at home, till I'm ready. It's the strain," she said in a louder voice, perhaps for the others. "I get like it sometimes."

"No now," he said.

"What? With me only four from the shop?"

"I must," he said. He was whining.

"Why you'll have a treat tomorrow when you take the cover off the dish. I don't know I'm sure, only Mrs. England passed the word there was a special in at Blundens. Mr. Blunden is always good to me."

"Most important," he said, quite clear. "About the daughter. How d'you know she died?" His voice was rising. One by one, those nearest began to click those yards long hatpins back inside chameleon eyes. They turned from what might be in the shop, from what was unseen, onto what might be in this young man, click click they went at him, and Mrs. Frazier noticed.

"I can't have this," she said firm, "not possibly. I'm a respectable married woman I'd have you know. And I couldn't say what became of his daughter. How would I? We were never related," she said. "But if you don't think to ask him, there's Mr. Middlewitch," she said to rid herself of Charley Summers. It did the trick.

"Middlewitch," he stammered, with renewed dread. And made off fast.

When he got to the next call box, he rang this man at the C.E.G.S. But he was out. Then Charley walked a great distance unseeing. Until he found himself by a park. He awkwardly sat under a tree. He collapsed at once into deep sleep. And, when he woke some hours later, he was a little recovered, but so sad and excited he could hardly bear it.

It was the last good sleep he was to have for some time.

HE WENT back to the office next morning. He had only been gone a day. Watching himself in a mirror in the lavatory, because he always washed face and hands the moment he arrived, he could see no change. It was a shock that he did not look different.

"Oh there you are," Miss Pitter said. She was made harsh by the relief she unexpectedly felt at the sight of him.

"Yes," he said.

"I thought perhaps you'd gone off to Birmingham, then when I looked in your engagements, there was nothing," she went on, still sharp. "And yesterday we had that special batch of reminders."

He did not reply. He was pawing through his mail.

"Oh, and Purdews phoned," she said with relish. "They've had the Admiralty down. Those trays are put right back. Their Mr. Ricketts is very sorry but they've had to sign an undertaking. Number something priority, he said, way in front of ours."

He passed no comment.

"I explained you weren't here," she went on to get some reason out of Charley, "I told him you'd had to go to Birmingham. And then I tried to get any kind of a promise, I mean about when we could expect the trays, or racks, or whatever you call them," she interpreted herself, quite unnecessarily, "and d'you know what? He just laughed. Quite the comedian."

She was leaning now on one of the card indexes, gazing at the top of his head. He went on handling the post. She lowered a forearm down along the green steel front, perhaps so he could notice. But he didn't.

"Is anything wrong?" she asked.

He looked at her. There was something dreadful in his eyes. She saw that. She wondered the more.

"No," he said. "Why?"

"I only asked," she said. "So I told him you'd be bound to ring back when you got in, when you did come, I mean. I know I shouldn't, but I do get worried," she lied, because she must find out what was up.

He lowered his eyes again to the mail. There was a pause. She powdered her nose.

"Because I'm not fretting to be left alone with this lot," she said, and gave the card indexes a sour look, "with you away ill or unable, not little Dot, thanks all the same," she said.

She did not know him well enough to ask such questions, but she couldn't leave things where they were. He had been so dependable. It had come as a shock not knowing where he was yesterday, and now doubly so on account of his eyes. Yet she told herself it was only she would not be left alone with those cards if she could help.

"What were you doing yesterday? Did you go out with a girl, and celebrate, or what?" she said.

He gave her a frightful look, which she misinterpreted on purpose.

"Is that what a hangover is, then?" she trilled. "You know I've never had one of those. Of course I've been a trifle dizzy now and again, but not enough for mum to spot when I came in. And what mum doesn't notice where I'm concerned is nobody's business."

He sat on. She could see he was not pretending.

"Just two glasses of port," she said, "and something went through my nose right up to my head, I suppose it was the fumes rose . . ." she said, then fell silent as she saw the spasm pass across his face.

"Are you all right?" she enquired.

"A bit faint," he said.

"Put your head between your knees, then, while I get you a glass of water." He sat hunched there. When she came back she said,

"Well, all I can say is, after seeing the effect it's had on you, that

I'll pass it up," she lied, referring to the hangover she pretended to suspect.

"Thanks," he said. He did not drink the water. She was silent for a bit.

Before she could begin again the telephone bell rang. He picked up the receiver, put it to his ear and waited.

"That you Dot?" asked Corker's secretary.

"Yes," he said.

"Oh Mr. Summers. Good morning Mr. Summers. Mr. Mead says can you spare him a moment."

"When?" he said. "Now?"

"Yes please. Thank you," she said, and hung up. Mr. Corker Mead was the boss.

"Corker," he told Miss Pitter in explanation as he walked out.

"Gosh," she said, and meant it.

Mr. Mead waited. He had expected Summers to be several days absent. Every morning a little list of those who were away was put on his desk, first thing. It surprised him to find that young Summers was back. For he thought it likely these young men coming home from the war might be a bit wild for a period, it would only be natural. He had considered the matter, foreseen that. He had even had a little talk prepared for Charley, who was the first to return. And now Corker was ready to deliver, even though the lad had only taken a day. For Corker was mustard.

"Good morning," he said. "Sit down. Well how's everything? Cigarette?"

"We're late with the first plant," Charley said, hopelessly. "We're nine weeks overdue."

"That's nothing these days," Corker said. "We can stand it. No, I meant in yourself?"

"I'm O.K." Charley said.

"That's fine," Corker agreed. "Bit difficult, I shouldn't wonder, for you young fellows, after what you've been through?"

Charley did not answer. He was looking at the photo of Mrs. Mead on his chief's desk. She had a goitre.

"Though, mind you, the war's not been a surprise in this. The civilians have had their share, this time," Mr. Mead went on, keeping strictly to what he had thought out. "Yes, we've had our share," he said.

There was no reply.

"Would you fancy a few days off?" he enquired, with no trace of sarcasm. "Takes time to settle down I shouldn't wonder."

"No thanks, Mr. Mead."

"Sure? Because you'd be welcome. Well don't worry your head too much over that contract. You're doing quite nicely, Summers. That's all. But give us a ring next time."

Again Charley said nothing, left without another word. That was one point Mr. Mead did not like about the little talk. The other was, that he had not called him sir.

Miss Pitter nervously waited back in their room.

"Well, you do look down," she began, at his face, when he came in. "He didn't give you the sack, surely?" she asked, to be playful. But he ignored her.

"You were only away twenty-four hours, when all's said. But in any case you've got your full six months, I mean you're entitled to that, aren't you, after discharge from the army?" Her voice was more serious. She could not make him out at all. "They must keep you the full six months," she ended.

He said nothing. She lost interest. Then he did a thing he had never done. Taking up the receiver he said, "Excuse me. Private business."

"You'd rather I went out for a minute? Why sure."

But she remembered the cupboard outside, from which you could hear anything in this room. She thought he was going to ring his girl, in which case there might be something that rated an eavesdrop. She shut herself in, unobserved.

He began hurriedly speaking.

"Middlewitch?" he asked, "Middlewitch?"

"Middlewitch that you? I say about Rose...," then his voice stopped. If she could have seen him, she would have noticed he kept swallowing hard.

"Charley Rose?" Mr. Middlewitch returned. "Ran across him the day before yesterday. We were talking about you. Why? D'you want him?"

"Charley Rose?" Mr. Summers stammered, and with a sigh Miss Pitter left the cupboard. After all it wasn't very nice to listen to someone else's private conversation.

"Must see you some time?" Charley managed to bring out.

But Mr. Middlewitch had pretty well had enough of Summers. In his shrewd opinion Charley was moonstruck. That time they had lunch together the man hardly behaved as if he knew what to do with his knife and fork, even. Here and now, on the phone, it was worse than ever. Long crazy silences. And not ten o'clock yet. So he said,

"Why, my dear old boy, what a question. Any day you choose. Look, I tell you what. You ring me up next week. I'm a bit snowed under, just at present. Why, what on earth's old Charley Rose been doing?"

"Not Charley Rose," the voice came back, and seemed to be short of breath, "Rose," it said.

"Got to go now. You give me a tinkle next week," and Mr. Middlewitch rang off then. And he forgot.

So MIDDLEWITCH, in one manner or another, managed to avoid him. It was harder for Mrs. Frazier to keep out of the way. But she was no help, for she seemed to know so very little. All she would admit, when he got at her, was that she had never met Rose, that, years ago, she was acquainted with Mr. Grant, who had recommended Middlewitch, as he had recommended Charley. No more than that.

His work at the office began to suffer seriously.

Then, one afternoon, while Dot was doing her best to keep him straight with the correspondence, he again saw this whole thing as a whole. What he saw was that, somehow or other, Rose had, in fact, become a tart, gone on the streets.

Once he realized, everything seemed to fit. And he made sure he must deliver her.

He did not hesitate, he shot out of the office while Miss Pitter was in the middle of what she was saying. He did remember to mention he had a call to make. And then, with what he considered to be extraordinary cunning, he bought a cup and saucer to take along, intending that this should be his excuse when she answered the door.

He hurried. The shop girl had liked his eyes and wrapped the china up. He took this off while he was still on Miss Whitmore's stairs. He knocked, carefully holding the crockery to his chest. Surprisingly enough she was up and in. She opened.

It was Rose again.

He forgot the plans he had made.

"It's about me," he said in haste, "about myself," he explained, slipping past her.

"No you don't," she said. "Not now."

"I can't help myself. I'm desperate."

"Well so am I, that is whensoever I see you. So get out." She held the door ajar, behind.

"I brought the cup and saucer," he said. But it was probably the look in his eyes, like a dog's. Anyhow she seemed to soften.

"Right," she said. "Thanks. Now then be off." She spoke as though she did not mean to deny him.

"Had to do this," he explained.

"There's no more tea," she replied. "I'm short."

He took heart at these last two words. But she had the door open yet. He felt and felt what to say. He said nothing.

It did the trick. She shut the door.

"I can't make you out," she said. "What is the matter with you? Why don't you come out with it? Not that that will be any use," she ended, her voice hardening.

They stood facing each other.

"Look we've got to do something over this," he began.

"Over what?"

He could not go on.

"Are you proposing to have another of your turns?" she asked. "Well, I suppose you'd better sit then." He took a seat.

"Oh Rose," he said.

"Here we go round the old mulberry bush," she answered. "But at least this time you can't do any damage now you're seated. I hurt my side with you, you know."

"I'm sorry," he mumbled, obviously taken up with just gazing at her. She became quite gay.

"I'm crazy really, that's what I'm like on occasions." She lit a cigarette. "There you are, a stranger I've never seen but once, and then how, and here's me entertaining you. What d'you think?"

He thought nothing. He took out a handkerchief, sat watching his hands as he dried them.

"Now what about if I ask one or two questions since you are here," she said. "Just for a change? How did you get this address?"

He muttered a request to her not to be angry with him, keeping his eyes down.

"No, go on," she said. "That other day you caught me bending. It doesn't mean a thing. Why should it?"

"Mr. Grant," he explained, as though guilty. He was terribly confused.

"Well?" she asked. "What about my old dad? And what is he up to, sending you? That is, if you're to tell the truth?"

"Then he is...you are...?" and he could not go on. He was looking at her in a way she could not understand.

"Why stare at me like that?" she said. "Don't you smoke?" He shook his head.

"Here, what is the matter with your leg? Were you really wounded?"

"Oh yes," he said, eager. "Out in France."

"Then d'you know him? My dad, I mean?"

"Of course I know him," he replied, suddenly abrupt. "Why I tell you..."

"All right, all right," she interrupted. "I only asked, didn't I? Because I thought it might be old Arthur up to one of his larks."

"Arthur?"

"Arthur Middlewitch of course. You made out you knew him, last time."

"What about him?" he wanted to be told. He was getting angry.

"All right, don't upset yourself," she said. "You think I'm Rose, don't you?" she said.

All he could say was, "What?"

"Because I'm not, see. She was my half sister."

"Half sister?"

"Were you very much taken up with her, then?" she enquired, as though making conversation. Probably she did not want to appear too interested, but he was beyond taking in niceties. He began to dry his hands again.

"You're not," he said, low voiced.

"Hark at him," she said with amusement. "Yes, you all fall for it hard."

"All fall for it?"

"Well you don't suppose you're the first, do you? Still, I expect we're most of us alike, it's natural after all to consider you're the only one on earth. That's something I had to unlearn very early, I can tell you."

"And James?" Charley asked.

"The widower? Why bless me, no. It would be a bit of a surprise for him, though, wouldn't it, if I dyed my hair red?"

He was disgusted, and showed it.

"And the name I have is my mother's," she added.

He obstinately stared at her.

"It's not very nice having a double, practically a half twin if you like," she went on. There had actually been very few to come up to her who had known Rose, but plainly it was not for her to give this away just now. "I've had trouble over it, all right. The first time I did listen." She laughed, and seemed to be going over this in her mind's eye.

He saw everything a third time. She was a tart, and her father had sent him to redeem Rose because his hands were full at Redham. It was Rose right enough. But how different with the war. The troops must have been the cause? Made brutes out of women, that's what Middlewitch said.

"I had a time with him," she commented.

"Who's that?" he asked, run through with jealousy.

"Here," she said coming back to Charley. "No names, thanks. No, I consider, being as I am, the dead spit of another, that I've a responsibility, I'm not like the common run. But I don't give names away," she said, again with what seemed to be pride. "Only my father's," she admitted, wryly. "But then what has he done for me to thank him?" she asked. "No, I'm a special case," she said.

He looked at her. He wondered if, later on, he would be sick all over the carpet.

"I had such a time with the man I mentioned just now that I had to make a rule," she went on. "To protect myself. I never admitted it again. Or hardly ever. Till you came along. It was your fainting did it."

"Did what?" he demanded through his nausea.

"Why tricked me into admitting, of course," she said. "What else?"

"I don't know what to think," he brought out, nauseated. Oh how she could, he cried in his mind, his Rose that he'd loved?

"Come as a bit of a shock to you, hasn't it," she said. "Take no notice. The first two years are the worst." She actually laughed.

"Rose, listen here," he began, with a stronger voice than he had used. But she broke in.

"Look," she said sharp. "You aren't sitting pretty here except on one condition. You'll drop all this Rose stuff, or, if you can't take it, stay silent. Otherwise out you go, this instant."

He stayed silent.

"I'm a respectable girl," she said.

He said nothing.

"Even if I am living alone because my mum's been evacuated. You ask anyone here. They'll tell you about us."

He remembered he had been informed that whores had old women who took the money and who called the police, got help if need be. She was in that kitchen this minute, most likely.

"Yes it's a bit awkward in my position," she began again. "I mean everyone has their own life, that only stands to reason, and here's me has two, my own and someone else's."

He felt she might be trying to tell him she was sorry. He took heart again.

"Yes," she went on, "I've a responsibility. You know why I did what I could for you the last time?" She paused. All he could remember was, she had chucked him out.

"Because this has hit you hard," she explained. "You never put that faint on, I could tell. So I didn't send you packing like I should. I've a responsibility."

"A responsibility?" he asked.

"I've just said," she told him. "Although it's none of my fault, I've got to be fair. If a man really mistakes me for another I have to let him down in a decent fashion. I can't laugh right in his face, not straight off, any old how."

"I see," he said.

"You don't, from the looks of you," she replied. "Oh all right, take your time. You'll get used to it. Don't mind me. Be easy now."

"Has Mr. Grant sent many to you?"

"Here," she said harsh, "what are you insinuating? I told you before I won't have his name mentioned, ever again." He had no recollection of this. He assumed that he must have forgotten, as he had with Mr. Grant's request not to disclose how he got her address.

"I rang him up," she said. "I told him. 'This is the first time you've done this,' I said, 'and let it be the last. Haven't you been enough trouble all my life?' I said. 'And now if you're to start sending people round, what will the others think? Why I'd be hounded out of these rooms.'"

"What if Ridley came?" he suddenly asked, with the air of a man who has produced the unanswerable, who is bringing the whole house of cards down.

"Her little boy?" she enquired, absolutely unmoved. "You know I've often and often wondered. Why, it would be cruel, wouldn't it?"

"You've said it."

"I'm not too sure I like your attitude," she complained. "Of course that would be cruel, but not my fault? I can't help looking as I am, can I? Which is at my father's door."

He did not wait to consider this. He must have thought he had her pinned.

"But if Mr. Grant sent him?" he asked. His face flushed, and it was plain that he was trying to hold her eyes with his own. She became agitated.

"Why, he'd never," she cried. "Why, it wouldn't be right. He'd never dare." She was truly indignant. "When the little chap thinks his mother's away with the angels? I dream of it sometimes. Running across him in the street, I mean. Perhaps his grandma takes him up round the shops with her. I often wonder, wouldn't that be awful if we met. But then it couldn't be my fault, after all."

"Whose then?"

"Why my dad's of course."

He now realized that she must be out of her mind, which would account for the change in her voice, and manner. He became terribly sad. Oh, this was not the old Rose, at all.

"That's what makes me do it," she explained.

"Do what?" he murmured.

"Aren't some men dense?" she said. "You don't suppose I'm talking to you, like I do, because I've nothing better, surely? I'm a working woman. I wouldn't want to offend, of course. But as I told you before, I consider I have a duty by you and the others. Only when you said that my dad sent you, then I had to turn round at once. You see that surely?"

He felt he had best humour her.

"Yes," he said.

"And you seemed to take it so hard I was sorry for you, and here we are," she said.

He had a wave of self pity.

"It's affected my work," he muttered.

"You don't want it to do that," she said. "You see, I've thought more about this than you can ever. If you like to put it that way, I've been brought up with the problem. It's chance, that's all, nothing more than bad luck. I've known since I was sixteen."

That she'd leave the husband she had not yet seen, the unborn child, he cried out in his mind. He was sickened by it.

"What?" he said.

"Are you going queer a second time," she wanted to know. "I mean about my half sister, naturally. They all say we might have been twins. What d'you think?"

"There's no telling you apart," he said, back to his idea of humouring her.

"Yet it's funny I never felt anything when she was ill, like twins are supposed to feel, you understand. Then of course we were never real ones. Still, it makes you wonder, when I tell you we came within three weeks of one another. The old devil," she said, with a hint of admiration in her voice.

"Did he send Middlewitch?" he asked, jealous again as soon as Mr. Grant was mentioned.

"Of course not. I said, didn't I?"

"How did you come across him, then?"

"I'll not have these questions. What's come over you? I've a life of my own, haven't I? It's not my fault, is it? And if I'm being nice to you it's only that I've the responsibility. Even if he did send you along so things wasn't natural, like crossing one another in the street."

He began to hate. He saw her, yet again, as a tart, and could not bear the idea of these men having her, night after night having the old Rose.

"Oh no?" he brought out, bitter.

"What do you mean, thank you? I don't quite fathom how I'm expected to take that, do you? Besides, I'll tell you something. Just because you're crazy, and a bit knocked off balance when you're with me, you're not entitled to pass remarks."

"I'm sorry," he said.

"Wanting to know where I'd met Arthur Middlewitch. The sauce."

The one thing he could not have, was for her to send him away. If she believed she had a responsibility, in the state she was in, then how much the greater was his own.

"Forget it," he said. And, with a great effort, he returned to his normal manner of speaking, "Bit awkward for the rest of us, you see. The dead come to life," he said.

"You are cheerful, aren't you?"

"Bad about Mrs. Grant, isn't it?" he began. "Loss of memory can be a terrible thing."

"I don't want to hear about them, I've already told you."

"Sorry," he said. "I can't seem to keep off the subject."

She moved impatiently in her chair. "I've got my own life, as I mentioned before," she explained. "It's not exactly cheerful for a girl, is it, to talk of someone losing their memories when I'm a sort of walking memory to other people, complete strangers in every case? It's only natural I suppose, but you men, that used to know her I mean, with her red hair you all talk about, I suppose you're dead easy to think only of yourselves?"

Suddenly frantic, he looked about for the bed, to torture himself with the sight. She must have guessed, and guessed wrong, because she drew her skirt down over her knees, although she had not been showing too much leg, or no more than is usually shown.

"You'll have to go in another minute," she said, "and that's meant to mean what it says."

"I'll go now before...before...," but he could not finish. He rushed out, grabbing his hat, and slammed the door.

"Was there ever any girl as unlucky as me," she wondered. "But I like his brown eyes. Oh well that's all over, and I shan't see him again, thank God," she thought.

THE NEXT morning, after about the worst night he had ever had, he telephoned Mr. Grant. He did not bother to ask Dot to leave the room. She was all the more certain something must be very wrong when she heard him insist that he should meet Mr. Grant the same evening. He even fixed the time he would be there. And it did not help him, she noticed, for his work still suffered terribly all day.

When Charley got out to Redham, straight from the office, he found Rose's father hanging around in the front garden.

"She's better," this man began at once. "Mother's much better to-day. Tell you the truth I can't make her keep to her bed, she will begin running downstairs the whole time. So I shan't take you inside, if you'll overlook it. Not after the recent occasion."

He said this in such a way as to make it appear that he blamed Charley for the last visit, when Mrs. Grant had been so upset to see what she understood to be her brother John. And Charley found himself tongue tied.

"So I presume you've come to apologise, my boy, eh?" Mr. Grant said, walking up and down past Charley on the small patch of lawn. "But there, we mustn't blame you young fellows. I know. You've been through a whole lot, and we all ought to be grateful. What's more you're not looking too fit in yourself. Gone thin. Lost weight? You want to take things easy at first, believe me. I've no doubt it's the food. You've been on starvation diet out there so long that, when you are back, even the little we get is too rich for your stomach. I shouldn't wonder if that wasn't it."

But Charley, as usual, was some sentences behind.

"I'm sure I'd never . . . I mean, if I'd known, I'd not have let Mrs. Grant see . . . ," he mumbled, to protect himself from the unexpected charge of its being his fault that he had made Mrs. Grant so much worse.

"Don't give the matter another thought, boy," Mr. Grant said. "It was partly my error, I'll confess. When I'm in the wrong, or not entirely in the wrong because things aren't often black or white, life's not so simple as you'll find when you grow older, no, when I consider I've been the least bit in the world to blame, then I'm the first to admit the fact, that's me. But giving me away to Nancy is a different kettle of fish altogether." And he halted before Charley, who, in confusion, lowered his eyes.

"I can't understand that even now," Mr. Grant accused, staring at him.

"I never . . ." Charley tried to begin, only he looked so guilty it encouraged Mr. Grant.

"Now see here, my boy," he said, "I'm older than you, I've had more experience. What I'm going to tell you will be of benefit in your job. Never divulge a confidence. That's all. Never. I've had men come to me in business, competitors, who've let something drop which if I'd liked was not less than putting a hundred pound Bank of England note right in my hand. But what they'd done was in confidence, mind. They just used those few words to start with, that changed the whole conversation from a useful tip to something sacred. There you are. And it's paid me. Many's the time, even when I couldn't see what value there might be. I still kept silent. For why? Because it was a trust."

A voice quavered from the house. "Gerald," it called twice, thin and fretful.

"We'd best keep out of sight," Mr. Grant remarked, leading the way out of his front garden. "We don't want Amy to have another of her turns."

Once they were behind the tree, where he had given Charley

Miss Whitmore's address with no word about keeping the source dark, Mr. Grant began to lecture again. The injustice of all this absolutely silenced Summers.

"Mind, I appreciate your coming down, though of course you can't tell how difficult it is for me to get outside the house, even just for now, with Amy in the condition she's in. We all have our troubles, right enough. The only difference there may be, lies in how much we talk about 'em. There's another truth for you. No, I appreciate it that you felt you had to say you were sorry. Shows you have the right stuff in you, Charley boy."

"I'm sorry, but . . .," Charley said, and Mr. Grant interrupted him.

"I tell you it pays hand over fist, keeping a confidence. That's what life's taught me."

"But why did you send me?" Charley got out at last.

"To be a bit of company for her, of course," Mr. Grant said, as though it was the most natural thing in the world. "She's living alone now. She had her husband killed out in Egypt, and changed her name back. She's a plucky little thing," he said. "Because what you have to remember, Charley boy, is that you're one of the lucky ones. You're back. I know I reminded myself of that, come the finish of the last war, when I couldn't seem to understand at certain times, just after I got out of France. You see I trusted you. It's not everyone I'd give her address. And I trust you still, if I may have been mistaken in one respect. Don't you younger fellows ever think of others? There's that little lady been alone now for close on two months, ever since the fly-bombs got so bad. Of course I thought of you."

"When did she marry, then?" Charley managed to ask.

"While you were in Germany," Mr. Grant answered, bright. "That's all the life they had together. In 1943 it was. They had three leaves, then he was gone. And once he was killed it seemed to turn her bitter towards me. Life is like that sometimes."

A bigamist, Charley thought. Would this awful thing never stop? His jealousy got hold of him again.

"There's Arthur Middlewitch living right across the landing," he said, so bitterly there was no mistaking it.

"Middlewitch?" Mr. Grant cried out. "Who's with the C.E.G.S.?"

Charley was beyond an answer.

"How do you know?"

"She told me," Charley said, with a sort of satisfaction.

"Are you acquainted with Arthur Middlewitch?" Mr. Grant enquired, cautiously.

Charley did not reply, which seemed odd to Mr. Grant.

"Do you know him, then?" he repeated, sharp.

"He was where they fitted my last leg."

"And you took him along to her?"

"Me?" Charley brought out, with such disgust that the older man could see he had done no such thing.

"I should hope not and that's a fact," Mr. Grant agreed. "It's true I recommended Arthur to your landlady, the same as I done for you. There's a number of you young fellows I've served a good turn when I had the chance. That's what we're here for, after all. But not that man for Nance. You'd hold a funny opinion of me to think I'd introduce them. Because you might as well confess up. That's what you're supposing, isn't it?"

"Well…"

"I may have been mistaken in you," Mr. Grant said, as if wondering aloud. "It's not often I am, but then no one's infallible, you can't have all my experience without you learn that. But what sort of a man d'you take me for? The things Ann Frazier told me, after he hadn't been in her house above three weeks, opened my eyes, I can tell you. To send a chap of his bent along to a decent girl? If I were a younger man, I'd knock you down for it." He had become truly indignant.

"I didn't send him," Charley said, behindhand again.

"And I never thought you did. Maybe I'm a bit inclined to leap to conclusions," Mr. Grant said, in a more amenable sort of voice. "Things aren't easy," he went on, "not now particularly. What with Amy, and me not being able to leave her for an instant, I'm liable to dash at things. But she should be warned. She's only young after all. She hasn't much experience. Someone should tell her the sort of dirty hound the man is. She's so sore with me at this moment she'd never listen. But I'll wager you told her, eh Charley?" Mr. Grant was almost pleading with him.

"I didn't get the chance."

"That's bad, Charley, that's bad, yes. Mind, I'm not blaming. I know. Look, someone must have the job, and it can't be me, just now, as things are between us."

"She won't listen to me, Mr. Grant."

"When you get to learn as much of their ways as I have, my boy, you'll never say anything so definite about women. There's no man can tell one way or the other. Not one. But she's got to be warned."

Charley was sharp enough to see where this was tending.

"I doubt if she'd see me a third time," he said.

"What's that?" Mr. Grant enquired, at his most suspicious. "And has she a reason?"

Charley could not answer.

"I may have been wrong about you," the unconfessed father went on, "but surely not in this way, Charley boy? You never offered her an incivility?"

"I did not."

"Well, all right. I knew better than to think it. What was it, then?"

"I fainted away," Charley said, ashamed.

"Oh but you mustn't let a little thing like that upset you. Good Lord no. Of course I realize it's awkward at the time. While we're on this topic I could tell you a thing or two, little mishaps which have come to pass before my very eyes. Lord yes. But you'll mention it when you get back, eh, Charley boy? You'll do that for me, surely?"

"It'd come better from you."

"There you are, don't you understand?" Mr. Grant said, with impatience. "You're the very man has made it impossible for me to speak. Because, as I keep on telling you, she won't see me since my confidence was betrayed. It's a long story, but she's funny that way."

"I see," Charley said.

"I can rely on you, now, can't I?" Mr. Grant asked, wheedling.

The one thing Charley knew was, he did not wish to see the girl he still took to be Rose, ever again. He considered she had dug her knife too deep into him and turned it too often, by being the same in so many ways. And, after all, who was Mr. Grant to ask favours on top of having done him this injury, which he would never get over, not if he lived to the end of his life. Because from the moment he had seen her, a painted tart, from the moment this man here sent him, Charley considered he was as dead as if he were six feet down, in Flanders, under the old tin helmet. So he couldn't help himself, he spoke right out.

"I'd have thought, if anyone should tell her, it would be her own father," he said.

Mr. Grant was flabbergasted. The boy spoke as though near to tears. What had the kid done? Fallen in love? But what was Charley doing, knowing about him and Nance? He began to get as angry as Summers already was.

"Who told you?" he demanded.

Charley stayed silent. It was all he could do, now, not to hit this old man.

"I've a right to know, haven't I?" Mr. Grant shouted, quivering with rage, his voice rising high until it was like his wife's.

"She told me herself," Charley said, truthfully.

"Good God," Mr. Grant yelled. They stood there, careful not to look at one another.

"Who would you be if you weren't?" Charley mumbled.

"Who would I be if I wasn't," Mr. Grant echoed, choking with anger. "What are you insinuating? This is what comes of offering a kindness. And I have to stand here in my own front garden, or nearly, and listen to this? You must be mad, boy. That's it. What you've been through has unhinged you. Mind, I'm denying nothing," he said, with a lunatic sort of leer. "Why should I? But when you reach my age you'll realize that some secrets aren't our own. God bless me and I should think so, too."

"I don't know what you mean," Charley said, glaring straight at him as he said it. Was being a tart so secret?

"Have you no delicacy?" Mr. Grant demanded. He was actually hopping from one foot to the other.

"Delicacy?" Charley asked, soft with contempt.

"That's what I said, delicacy," Mr. Grant took him up. "Don't you know the meaning of the word?" As if in comment, there came again from the house his wife's voice, calling "Gerald," twice. "Where we might even be overheard," Mr. Gerald Grant added.

"Don't make me laugh," the young man said, and left.

Charley walked off anywhere, so blind with anger he did not know where he was going.

IN HIS good nature, for he was a kind-hearted man, James decided he would look Charley up when next in London. He thought Charley, who had been such a friend of Rose, would be glad to see him for old times' sake, and besides he was touched that Charley should have come down to find her grave the moment he was back from Germany. Her dying, which he was forgetting, had been the saddest point in his life. Summers was a link between them.

Because Mrs. Grant was now too queer to travel, and Mr. Grant insisted on her seeing the grandson at least every six months in case she remembered, the next time James was to bring him up for two nights, he wrote Charley. He said nothing of the boy, only that it would be grand if Charley could come along that evening.

When Summers got the letter, a day or so after his scene with Mr. Grant, and at a moment when he was arguing in himself whether he should see Rose just once more, if only to warn her against Middle-witch, he saw what he took to be his opportunity to clear the matter once and for all. He also realized it was his duty to bring Rose and her husband together again. If it worked, then she would be saved from the life he was sure she led. So he sent word that he would be round at the hotel by tea time.

It was a bad shock that Ridley should be present, and at first Charley did not attend to James he was so busy in the quest of a likeness to himself, this time, in this boy who might be his own but who, unknown to him, was nothing to do with him at all, except in so far as he was a reminder of his Rose. For in point of fact Rose had been mistaken, perhaps on purpose. In any case she had never been definite as to when she started the child. But Summers thought he now knew the boy was his, and looked for an echo of his own face in those cheek bones, whereas, immediately after he got back, he had searched for a return of Rose, of whom, now he thought he had found her, he wanted nothing more to remind him, much less the curve of a lip, or its corners when smiling.

At the same time he knew it would be too drastic to confront Ridley with Rose. He also had the idea he would keep this somehow up his sleeve. So, while James was running on with the usual questions, and making great cautious, anxious play with how ill he found Charley looked, Charley had become occupied with the manner in which he could get the husband away to meet the wife, thereby to prove what he now took to be Grant's ignominy, for, in the last few days, Charley had even come to believe that the father was sharing the daughter's immoral earnings, possibly because Mrs. Grant's illness came so expensive.

"So I thought I'd look you up, old man," James was saying for the third time, "for old times' sake," he said, "and see how you were looking after yourself, after your experiences, I mean. Because I didn't think you looked too grand when you were down my way, you know, old chap."

Ridley sat opposite, right back in an armchair, his head sideways along the back, eyelashes thick as a hedge, watching the people in the corner. Summers thought the boy wouldn't be so bored if he knew about his mum. And he held it against James, that this man had let Rose get away.

"Something I want to show you," he brought out at last, with great difficulty.

"Why, of course," James agreed at once, but Charley was looking with significance at the child.

"Right you are," James said. "I say, Ridley," he went on, "I left my handkerchief in our room. You remember which that is, don't you now? You'd never believe what a bad memory he has," James said to

Summers, like a woman, "there are times I send him for something, and he forgets all about it while he's on the way. It's 56. You won't lose that will you?"

"What, now?" Ridley demanded rude.

"If you wouldn't mind, old chap. Your dad wants to blow his nose."

At this Ridley looked full at Summers, so that this man's heart jumped right up into his neck. Charley dropped his eyes, but not before he had recognized contempt in what he took to be his son's.

"Oh all right," the boy said, and slouched off.

"Lord, he reminds me at times of his mother," James began when the child could not hear. "He's got just the way she had when she didn't want to do something. D'you catch it now and again? But you wanted to ask me? What is it?"

"A certain person," Charley said, distracted.

"Why, my dear good lad," James said, looking about him. "Where? Not in this lounge, surely?"

"Only ten minutes off," Charley said.

"Someone we used to know?" James asked, as though suddenly talking of a brothel.

"They're usually in about now," Charley said, because he could not explain.

Meantime Miss Whitmore, who would soon be off to her work, was feeding the cat and worrying about her mother. Now that her mum was evacuated, Nance came under the heading of mobile labour, which is to say that, if the Ministry officials got to know she was alone, she could be sent anywhere in England, even be put in uniform and packed off where the Japs might get at her. Of course she had not told the Ministry when her mother went, who had bought her own ticket and agreed not to claim the evacuation money, to save Nance from the consequences. But, all the same, the girl was worried. Her mum was on her own, having quarrelled some years back with Mr. Grant, and if anything should happen there was only herself left. So the girl did not want to be sent away. Besides they were comfortable on what she made each week, and the small bit Mr. Grant still contributed every Saturday. And the day before, one of her friends said she'd had a visit from the officials. Oh, they'd been perfectly polite of course, nothing anyone could take exception to, if it wasn't that they'd more or less forced their way in, as if to search the premises. And they'd explained it was only that the country was so short of mobile women, so they were driven into coming to people's homes, now their records had been lost in the bombing. Yes, they'd made themselves pleasant, and been perfectly respectful. But then Ellen had her mother, large as life. What would she do herself if they came here? She'd been so nervous all day she'd hardly been able to sleep, waiting for the knock on her door.

She was just saying aloud to the cat, "And what'd become of you, Panzer?" when there was the knock, like a rap right on her heart. Her mouth fell open. She covered it with a hand, as Mrs. Grant had done.

Charley had easily been able to persuade James to come along without having to tell him who, or what, he was to find. One of the reasons was that James did not want to lose sight of Summers. At one time he could have thought Charley was seeing too much of Rose, but he now found Charley would be the main link left with the happy days which were fast slipping into the past. Also he considered him affected by his war experiences.

As he rang, Summers got behind so that, when she answered the door, her heart pounding, all she saw was the stranger. She took it very hard.

"So it's come," she said, dead white, and made way.

Charley naturally imagined this to be her reaction at being exposed. He could not understand, but he felt desperately ashamed of his part in bringing them together again. And, as James moved forward, Charley wished once more that he could be unseen.

But of course, the moment Miss Whitmore saw Charley she knew the stranger could not be a Ministry snooper, and she was so relieved that she grew angry.

"So it's you, is it?" she said.

With acute dread and anxiety Summers slowly raised his eyes to James' face. He was terribly frightened to see on it the last expression he had expected. So that he was made to feel crazy. For James stood, just watching, polite and lost, though his upper lip trembled.

Then Charley knew he was back in a trap.

"What is it now?" she asked him.

He could not answer.

James thought the best thing was to introduce himself.

"I'm James Phillips," he said, quite ordinarily.

"Rose's husband?" she said. It was obvious that she was profoundly shocked. "You?"

"That's right," he said, with what seemed to be complete calm. "Why, did you know her?"

There was a pause. Charley listened to his heart thumping.

"I'll tell you what this is," she said then, violently, yet as if searching in herself. "It's not proper, that's all."

"What?" Charley said. He could not believe his ears again.

She turned on him. "Bringing this man here," she shouted, and slammed the door shut, so she could not be heard on the staircase. "Think of it. Him that's met his wife naked in bed with him, and you bring him along to me. Oh, it's not proper," she repeated.

Mr. Phillips had gone rather white in his turn. But he kept his temper.

"I don't see that you're at all alike," he said with truth and absolute conviction.

But Charley was beside himself. They must be playing some frightful game, and he blamed it on her. He remembered her bigamy that, as he thought, Mr. Grant had spoken of.

"All very well acting the innocent," he said, trembling all over, "but you've been married, haven't you?"

"You swine," she yelled, coming up to him. "You keep Phil's name out of this, d'you hear? He died fighting for you," she shouted and, bringing her hand up, she slapped his face hard, and it hurt.

"Here, that's enough of that," James said, pushing his way between them. But the harm was done. Charley sat down, quick, in the chair over which he had spilt the tea on another occasion, covered his face with his hands, and began uncontrollably trembling. "Died for me?" he kept on repeating.

"He's been out in it, too," James said quietly. "He's just been repatriated."

She burst into tears.

"What's a girl to do?" she wailed.

Mr. Phillips thought he was the most hurt of them all. Everything considered it was he who had been widowed, who had to look after their son, who could only show the boy microfilms of his mother. And what was this about? The girl was not like his Rose, quite apart from her dark hair. Certainly she did not behave in the least like. But he said gently,

"Well, my word, this is a party I mean to say..."

"Never knew such filth existed," Charley muttered recovering.

"That's plenty now," James objected.

"Well it's right, isn't it?" Charley Summers asked.

"You're not yourself, Charley, old man," Mr. Phillips said. "And I'm thinking there's the little lady we should apologise to," he added. "My dear, this is the war. Everything's been a long time. Why only the other day in my paper I read where a doctor man gave as his opinion that we were none of us normal. There you are."

"I'm not your dear," she answered. "And I'm not his lost one, as he seemed to imagine the last time." She showed, by her look at Charley, who it was she had in mind. This direct reference to Rose, and to Charley's possible relations with her, was too much for James. Yet he still remained polite.

"Well I've got to get back now. I've someone waiting for me," he said. He closed the door gently behind him. And his last words made Miss Whitmore pity herself the more. She began to cry again, this time quietly, and with zest.

Charley felt ten years older, cynical as never before.

"What filth," he repeated, as though from a great height.

She cried on.

"The end of my life," Charley said, thinking aloud. "That's what it is. I'm finished," dramatising it.

Still she cried.

"Well, I'm off, Rose," he said. "You'll not see me again, now."

He got up to make his way out.

"No, don't go," she said.

He waited. She blew her nose vigorously.

"I'll have this out with you, if it's the last thing I do," she began. Apparently she had got over her rage with him.

"What can you say?" he asked, helpless.

"It was what Mr. Phillips told me about your having been out there as well," she began. "Maybe I've misjudged you. Were you blown up or what?"

"I was not."

"All right, a girl can only ask, can't she? And when she finds a man making a fool of himself, perhaps ruining his whole life, it's only natural if she wants to put him wise, even when that man is a cracked stick like you. After what you've done to me I'd be justified in just showing you the door, now wouldn't I?"

"What have I done?" Charley asked, injured. He would not look at her, and wore an absurd expression of dignity.

"Bringing Mr. Phillips like you did. How d'you suppose it makes a girl feel?"

"Up to some low game, the two of you," Charley muttered, beginning to get frantic.

"Being the man you are, I didn't suppose you'd get it. Why, you're so proud you can't see out of your own eyes. If it wasn't for that thought, I doubt if I'd be sitting here trying to get the truth. No, it was a dirty wrong to bring that individual to me, to be reminded of his own son's mother. It was vile."

She spoke with dignity, while he thought of her as a dirty double crosser. Actually she was intensely proud of the terrible likeness to her late half sister, and had been ever since she first learned of it. Then he had another idea which flooded all over him, he was so sure it was right.

"You're in this together," he shouted.

She burst into tears again. "All right, I've tried, haven't I?" she brought out between sobs and hiccups. "They ought to lock you up. Yes, well then, go now as you said, and I never want to see you more."

He went. It was not until the room was empty of him that she remembered to be afraid. For she saw he must be a shell shock case, and dangerous.

THE WHOLE thing had been so unpleasant for James that he decided to put it out of mind. But the evening he got back from London he picked up one of the literary reviews his wife had liked, and to which he had kept up the subscriptions after marriage while hardly ever reading. And he came on a translation which seemed so close to Charley's situation that he thought he would forward it, even though he was sore at the man. Accordingly he wrote on the cover "Read, mark, learn, and inwardly digest," signed his initials, drew attention to the story with a cross, and sent the thing to Summers, whom he forgave the moment he had posted the packet.

Meantime Charley had gone sick. He told the office he had 'flu. He kept to his bed. What he thought of himself was, that he was going to lose his reason.

When Mary carried up the thick envelope, he recognized this review as one that used to lie about in the old days, missed what James had written, ignored the date, which was recent, and, uninterestedly, turned over the pages until he came to the cross with which James had marked the place. His heart gave a twist. Just for a moment he thought it must be an old kiss from Rose. Then he asked himself why it could have been sent. Finally he was not even going to look through the thing, he felt too ill, when his eye caught a bit about a girl fainting. So he turned back to the beginning, and went into it, as it is printed here:

"From the Souvenirs of Madame DE CREQUY (1710–1800) to her infant grandson Tancrède Raoul de Créquy, Prince de Montlaur.

"I must tell you about Sophie Septimanie de Richelieu who was the only daughter of Marshal de Richelieu and the Princess Elizabeth of Lorraine. She was far more sensible of the honour that was hers from her mother's side of the family than she was of her father's ancestors. Indeed she did not always bother to hide this from her father, for which he occasionally gave her a rap over the knuckles.

"Septimanie was indefinably gracious. You could say she held a mirror to all that was the France of old days. She was a mixture of wit, of manners, with a sense of tradition, yet always absolutely herself. She had exquisite ways. She had a kind of full dress elegance but underneath there was all the time a hint of the dreadful death in store for her so soon. She was tall and lithe; she had brown black or grey eyes according to the mood she was in. There have never been eyes like hers to show changes of mood more brilliantly or, for anyone lucky enough to be under their spell, to make a gift of such a magical effect.

"My grandmother thought to marry her to the son of Marshal de Bellisle, the Count de Gisors. This young man was in his day what you are going to be we hope, the best looking, the finest, and the most lovable of them all. But Septimanie's father did not think a great deal of the family. 'Really,' he said to my grandmother with malice, and this is to show you what sort of a man he was, 'the two young people can always meet after Septimanie has a husband.' And so it was that, against her will, Septimanie became Madame d'Egmont.

"Her husband Casimir-August d'Egmont Pignatelli was the most reverential, silent, and most boring of men.

"Thus it came about that Mademoiselle de Richelieu, my very dear friend, became Countess d'Egmont, with all that this means, and that is, as we have the simplicity and good taste to say nowadays, that she had married into a family which was one of the best connected in Europe. In other words she was a Princess de Cleves and of the Empire, Duchess de Gueldres, de Julliers, d'Agrigente, as well as a Grandee of Spain by the creation of Charles V, and therefore on the same footing as the Duchesses of Alba and Medina-Coeli, who are of course the first ladies in Europe. I could run on for four pages more with the titles belonging to the great and mighty house of d'Egmont, which is descended in a direct line from the Reigning Dukes de Gueldres, and which the great aristocracy in all countries has had the mortification to see die out for want of an heir. And afterwards it was always said that this was Mademoiselle de Richelieu's fault.

"However Madame d'Egmont got on quite well with her husband. No more than that. And, in the meantime, a marriage was arranged between a Mademoiselle de Nivernais and Monsieur de Gisors. But the young man was killed a few months after the ceremony.

"So the two lovers never had the chance to meet after Septimanie had a husband.

"But Madame d'Egmont could so little forget him that she fainted if his name came up in conversation. This actually happened when the Prince Abbot de Salm purposely named him, and the young woman was taken with appalling convulsions on the spot; after which all decent people shut their doors to that wicked old hunch back.

"Now there was at this time an old man, a member of the well-known family de Lusignan who, if no one knew him by sight, was at least familiar to everyone by name. He was called the Vidame de Poitiers. It was generally understood that he vegetated away in a great house, but he was never seen because he was so extremely eccentric. So you can imagine the Countess d'Egmont's surprise when one day she had a letter from the Vidame asking her to be so good as to pay him a visit, in order that he might put before her a matter of some importance. He said he could not wait upon her in her own home as he would have wished because, as he put it, he was not 'transportable'; a phrase which, as things turned out, and if you have the patience to read your old grandmother to the end, was, as you will come to realize, ever afterwards of significance at the Richelieu's.

"Madame d'Egmont did not want to go, but rather unexpectedly her father the Marshal insisted, and she had to give in.

"So one afternoon she started off, in her carriage with six horses, only to find the outriders did not know the way because no one went there any more. But she arrived at last and when she was shown in at the door she found, without giving the least idea of it from the outside, that the Vidame's house was nothing more or less than a kind of dream palace. Used as Madame d'Egmont was to the elegance of her father's residence, and to the magnificence of her great uncle, the Cardinal's, mansion which is unequalled, she was amazed at what she now saw. The entrance hall and marble staircase were stately with statues and evergreen shrubs, the antechambers were full of liveried footmen drawn up in two ranks, all the saloons were of an unparalleled grandeur and led to a long, high gallery in the form of a winter garden along which, under a vault of orange, myrtle, and flowering rose trees she was escorted towards nothing less than a sort of rustic retreat raised above floor level. Even the steps up were formed out of the trunks of forest trees, with a handrail of gnarled branches. She was left to climb this alone, and she found herself in a sort of elegant cowshed, in which was an old gentleman fast asleep on a little bed, with his head carefully wrapped up. Madame d'Egmont felt dreadfully embarrassed. Then, while she waited for the Vidame to come out of his sleep, she looked about. The walls were whitewashed, and there actually were five or six cows feeding peacefully in their stalls. A few pieces of simple furniture were between his bed and one wall. She particularly noticed that everything was spotlessly clean. All this affectation of a peasant simplicity in the centre of Paris, and in a palace, began to amuse Madame d'Egmont. She sat down on a little cane-bottomed chair to wait. After a quarter of an hour she coughed, then she coughed louder, until at last she threw modesty to the winds and coughed as loud as she could, enough to make her spit blood. In the end when she saw it was no use, and that the old gentleman would not wake up, she thought it would be comic to go away without saying anything to the Vidame's page who was waiting for her below.

"We were all waiting for Madame d'Egmont at the Richelieu's when she got back. While she was telling us, and we were in shouts of laughter, her father the Marshal unexpectedly came in. All at once he began working his little mouth and shutting his eyes, a sure sign that he was displeased. 'Countess d'Egmont,' he brought out in his nastiest voice, which is saying a great deal, 'in my opinion you should not have behaved as you did before a man of his age, as well born as he, ill as he is as well. I advise you to go back no later than tomorrow morning.'

"'Alas Monsieur,' she replied, making her voice, that was always so soft, even softer, and turning on him her eyes which literally enchanted you, and which, on this occasion, were half appealing and half malicious, 'but how am I to set about waking the gentleman?'

"In the end Madame d'Egmont had to agree, after which the Marshal tried to change the conversation without, however, being able to hide his anger. As soon as he left the room, which he did at the first opportunity, Madame d'Egmont complained that she thought he was being most frightfully difficult. She said it would prove to be almost impossible to avoid laughing in the Vidame's face, and that in any case she would find herself with the old man in the undignified position of a little girl who has played a trick. But then she went on to put her real reason, which was that she had been overcome by a presentiment of evil, that evil must result from a second visit to the Vidame.

"The second time she visited him she found the old gentleman sitting up in bed. But he seemed very poorly, so much so that with a real feeling of horror she realized he could not have long to live. However he did not appear at all embarrassed by what he had to tell, and set about it at once, and quite methodically.

"After thanking her in the most respectful way for calling on him, without referring to the previous visit which he had slept through, Monsieur de Poitiers handed Madame d'Egmont a bundle of old letters from the late Count de Gisors addressed to himself, and begged her to read them. She found, poor thing it nearly suffocated her, that they were all almost entirely about herself. The Count de Gisors wrote of her so passionately, as she told me afterwards, that she felt as though her heart were in a vice. But there was also mention of an unhappy child his father, the Marshal de Bellisle, had abandoned, and for whom the young man desired the Vidame to do what he could. 'I shall not come back, I am sure of it, I shall not come back from this war,' he had written in the last letter, 'and I call on you to look after Severin, that I may die easy at least on that.'

"Madame d'Egmont cried her heart out for some minutes by the old man's bed. When she was a little easier the Vidame opened his eyes which he had kept shut all this time.

"'Madame,' he said, 'he for whom you are weeping, and whom we both regret, had no secrets from me. For he left behind him a young fellow, of about his own age, who is his double.' The old gentleman went on that this boy, Monsieur de Guys, was believed to be the natural son of the Marshal de Bellisle. Finally the Vidame said he wished to do something for this young man, because he did not think that he himself had long to live. He desired Madame d'Egmont, appealing to the love they both had for the dead Count de Gisors, to take certain bearer bonds and, as soon as he himself passed on, to hand these over to Monsieur de Guys. He explained that this was the only way to circumvent his creditors and heirs at law, and begged Madame d'Egmont not to say a word to anyone, repeating once more that she was the only person left whom he could trust. Madame d'Egmont reluctantly agreed to do as the Vidame asked, subject to certain safeguards with which I do not propose to trouble you, and within five or six days the Vidame had died.

"About this time the Queen of Portugal departed this world. There was a Memorial Service for her at Notre Dame. I had to attend in waiting on the Royal Princesses, although I certainly owed no obligation to Louis XV, or his court, for which, if I may do so without seeming too proud, I thank God in His mercy.

"The Queen of Portugal had actually, and even obviously, been put away by poisoning. Nevertheless Madame d'Egmont, as she told me, felt obliged to make an appearance at the ceremony because, through her husband, she was a Grandee of Spain. As such she had the right to take her place in the front rank, with the wives of the Dukes. But, when I came up the aisle with my Princess, the seats reserved for these Duchesses were almost empty. There was only a shapeless bundle, not fully under control, which must have been Madame de Mazarin, then a sort of gatepost, so stiff and immovable it could only have been the Duchess de Brissac, and last, a little bat-like creature in perpetual motion, flinching and fluttering throughout the ceremony, which told us this was no less, or more, of a person than the Countess de Tessé. I could not see a soul in the least like Madame d'Egmont, and I had told my Princess, whose train I was carrying while my aunt de Parabère bore mine, to look out for her, explaining that no one could mistake Madame d'Egmont. It was a real disappointment for the Princess Louise and the rest of us. Because Septimanie curtseying in the full glory of Court dress was unforgettable. I have only seen two women do it to equal her. One was Queen Marie Antoinette, and the other (saving the respect due to a Queen of France), Mlle Clairon of the Comédie Française.

"After the Absolution, at which the Princesses and peeresses are never present, we were told, when we got back to the Archbishop's, that Madame d'Egmont had been taken ill as she came up the aisle, and that she had cried out as she was falling.

"I found her waiting for me at home. She was deathly pale. She could only just speak. All I could get out of her was that, as she was about to take her place by the catafalque, she thought she had seen the Count de Gisors. 'You won't laugh at me will you?' she begged, 'I saw him, I know I did, and it almost killed me.'

"I told her that Monsieur de Nivernais had spoken of a young private soldier exactly like Monsieur de Gisors, and that it was probably this man who had been on guard at the catafalque. Septimanie burst into tears. 'Don't you see, it must be Severin his younger brother,' she sobbed, 'the boy I'm to give the Vidame's legacy to. I promised. Now that I have to see him again I'm terrified.'

"From this point onwards you will not find me so well informed, my child, and I confess to you that it would ill become me if I were. However, Madame d'Egmont did tell me some months later, in an embarrassed sort of way, that she had summoned Monsieur de Guys, secretly, to a church. She had joined him on foot, without any of her servants, and had handed over the £10,000 given to her by the Vidame for that purpose. But I saw a blush on her forehead as she was telling me. I had an idea she wanted to say more, and that I was not having the whole story. But I was careful to do nothing to persuade her to go any further with me, for I feared she might find herself confiding, or even attempting to explain away, certain things that I should have been embarrassed to learn. Because I did not wish to encourage her in this affair, which in any case, I imagined, was over and done with. All I said was, I could only be surprised and vexed that she had met him in church.... My child, she lowered her great eyes at that, and bit her lip. Then I changed the subject abruptly. It hurt me to do this. But I could see she understood, and from that time on I saw less of poor Septimanie. Indeed it must have been five or six months before I heard tell of Monsieur de Guys again.

"I had gone to dinner at the Richelieu's. I remember it was the night of a great storm. The Marshal asked me if I meant to pay my respects at Versailles the next day, and dine with their Majesties. I told him I had planned to do so. 'My daughter ought to go,' he said. 'Which of you will take the other?'

"I had always had a very good idea that I was the person with whom he best liked his daughter to go out, and I thought I saw that the sharp old man had noticed how we were no longer quite what we had been to each other. What he had in mind was to put us in one carriage. He imagined this was all that was needed to bring us together again. We exchanged looks, and smiled, his daughter and I.

"As we travelled down to Versailles the next day in her state carriage, I thought I had never seen Madame d'Egmont in such brilliant looks, or more superbly dressed. She was wearing the family pearls, those on which the Republic of Venice once lent such a large sum to Count Lamoral d'Egmont, to finance the war against King Philip, and which were without price, they were so valuable. But I flatter myself her jewels were not the only ones to attract attention that day. For I had brought out the diamonds you will inherit with the family heirlooms. The moment she set eyes on them the Queen sent for me to get a closer view of the Lesdiguière diamond. It was then and there admitted that this was a far finer stone than any of her twelve Mazarin diamonds. Commander d'Esclots, my uncle, and who was making the circle, was so absolutely delighted that it was only after some little trouble that I could persuade him not to write to the Queen to thank her for what she had said. The good old man belonged to a generation when the least word from royalty was too valuable for anything. But he was the old-fashioned sort of Frenchman. He died without having been persuaded it could be a fact that Madame Lenormand d'Etioles had ever had an apartment in the Palace of Versailles, nor, above all, that she could, by any fantastic stroke of the imagination, have been ennobled under the title of Marquise de Pompadour.

"At State dinners in those days the public came quickly in by one door, and were hustled out by the other, thus making a quarter circle round the royal table. We were seated on the right of the King, near the door the public was let in by. Madame d'Egmont was next me, and last in the row. That is to say she was nearest to the flow of people.

"The first thing I knew was a kind of awkward murmuring, which was kept low, no doubt out of respect. Then, when I looked up, I saw the officer in charge of the King's Guard speak to a private soldier who was one of the public, but who kept on staring fixedly at Madame d'Egmont. He was a beautiful young man. His face and appearance, in spite of his rank, were brilliant, and would have graced anyone in the kingdom. Can you doubt who it was? But because I was not continually thinking about Monsieur de Gisors, and that I never wondered about Monsieur de Guys, I was not, at that instant minute, struck by how alike they were.

"I instinctively turned to Madame d'Egmont. I could not whisper on account of the hoops we were wearing, and the space, left in accordance with what was usual at Court, between the stools on which we were seated. Because the poor lady was so upset that it was plain for all to see. Her eyes were glazed, and she was even holding a fan half across her face (a thing which could not be done at Versailles in my day, for one never took the liberty of opening one's fan before the Queen, except to use it as a salver if one had occasion to hand anything to her Majesty). Meantime the young man, not bothering about the King's presence, and without paying the slightest attention to the officer in charge who was ordering him to move on, was frozen before the lovely Septimanie in her black Court dress. He was holding up the people behind by standing where he was, as well as getting in the way of the gentlemen waiting at table. He did not listen and knew nothing at all of it. In the end they were obliged to drag him from the room. Then it was that Madame d'Egmont could control herself no longer. She moaned. I felt quite desperate for her.

"The King, who, through the secret police, always knew everything going on in Paris, even to love affairs, his Majesty, at this moment, acted with that instinct for the right thing which ever distinguished and honoured him. 'Monsieur de Jouffroy,' he said to the officer in charge, loud enough to be heard by all, and turning his head in our direction without, however, looking at Madame d'Egmont, 'Monsieur de Jouffroy it must be the style in which our meal is being served has surprised him,' and then he added, bowing to the Queen, with an adorable smile, 'or perhaps he was lost when he saw her Majesty. Leave the young man alone, run and tell them to let him go in peace. At the same time I thank you for what you have done.'

"Madame d'Egmont sighed. She seemed relieved. She began to look a little better. But people had started whispering, and the Marshal de Richelieu could not forbear to glance angrily at her once or twice.

"I felt most miserably sorry.

"Then, as we got into our carriage to go away I heard, over on the side she was sitting, a deep, trembling, man's voice say, almost in terror, 'it's you—it's truly you.' I could not see who this might be, and I did not catch what Septimanie answered. All I know is she said no word on the drive back to Paris. In fact she did nothing but cry her eyes out the whole way.

"The next morning I was just going to the Richelieu's to see Madame d'Egmont when they came to tell me her father was downstairs. He was a cunning old man. No doubt he counted on catching me unawares, to surprise me into telling what little I knew. But Marshal de Richelieu was not the sort of person with whom I cared to discuss anything of that kind. Dissolute men of his type are invariably wrong, on these occasions. They imagine that any sympathy, which may be expressed for a person in love, must include tolerance of what, in this instance, was something unquestionably underhand. Then they cannot grasp ordinary, nice-natured good wishes. In fact they can never explain, to their own satisfaction, how there may be a halfway house between absolute austerity and open acquiescence. So they make the most abject mistakes about honest women.

"Accordingly, all I did was to tell him for quite half an hour about a tiresome law suit we had against the Lejeune de la Furjounières, at the end of which time he was driven away, as I had hoped he would be. It was a mistake on my part, as it turned out, because he became convinced that I had given his daughter up. And this at a time when everyone was beginning to talk, including the Grammonts!

"In the end it was Septimanie herself who came to ask if I would use my influence with her parent in favour of her Severin. What had happened was that his father, the Marquis de Bellisle, had had him thrown out of the army, and was proposing to have him sent for good to Senegal, where no member of the white races lives longer than twelve months.

"'Come,' Richelieu begged me maliciously when I sent for him, 'tell me more about your case against the Lejeune de la Furjounières.' I did not let him get away with that, and, once I had made him talk of Monsieur de Guys objectively, I soon saw, with his years old hatred of Marshal de Bellisle, to whom in any case he was senior, that he would not be averse to helping the young man. To cut a long story short he did what I asked, the boy stayed in France, and what is more I saw him myself. He could not have been more charming. Monsieur de Créquy came to love him like his own son, and my great aunts adored him. But, alas, one day, he mysteriously disappeared. There can be no doubt he was done away with. He was not heard of, or seen, again.

"Septimanie did not recover. She lingered a few months and then she died of a slow fever.

"All my life I shall never forget this twin attachment, these two extraordinary passions she somehow found a way to lavish on two men who were entirely different and yet at the same time exactly similar, on the living and the dead, on the brilliant Count de Gisors, and an obscure young man. Nor can I ever forget her last moments when, with both lovers gone, she seemed, as she in her turn lay dying before my eyes, to fuse the memory of these two men into one, into one true lover."

After he had read right through to the end, Charley said aloud, "Ridiculous story." Nevertheless, when he switched out the light, he had his first good night's rest for weeks.

THAT SAME day the following letter was in the post to Messrs. Mead, addressed "Attention Managing Director." It was read by Corker first thing next morning.

PARABOLAM PLANT

Dear Sirs,

When last autumn at the instance of the Ministry, Section S.E.C.O., we accepted your esteemed order no. 1526/2/5812 for 60 (sixty) size N.V. Rotary Extraction Pumps and 60 (sixty) size O.U. Centrifugal Feed Pumps, we pointed out both to your goodselves and to Mr. Turner of S.E.C.O. that we could only undertake this contract on the clear understanding that you would be in a position to urge through sufficient quantities of the pump body castings, which are to be in the secret acid resisting metal to your special requirements.

If you will refer back to the letters which passed between us at the time this order was placed, you will see that we covered in the correspondence exactly the eventuality which has now arisen, namely the non-delivery of these parts, which is seriously impeding our production programme not only for the pumps in question, but for all the other work passing through the particular shop involved, and which is on S.E.V.B., S.E.P.Q., and S.O.M.F. priorities.

Repeated appeals to your office (ref. C.S./D.P.) having had

no favourable outcome, we regret to inform you that we have today been instructed by the last-mentioned Ministry office, namely S.O.M.F. (ref. MIS/POM/1864), that we are to discontinue manufacture of your order until such time as we can be assured of sufficient supplies of the items in this special metal, so as to avoid setting up the lathes each time.

We are now seriously behind with our S.E.V.B., S.E.P.Q. and S.O.M.F. contracts, and unless we can get a clear run at these without, as at present, having to break off to machine the few castings we do receive from you, and we never know when these are coming in, we have today been warned that we shall seriously prejudice the war effort.

Regretting the real necessity we are under to write in such terms to so old and valued a connection as your goodselves, but the matter is right out of our hands.

Yours faithfully,
Robert Jordan,
Director, Henry Smith & Co. Ltd.

Mr. Mead sent for the files and for Pike, the chief draughtsman. Then he did some telephoning. After which he summoned Charley.

"Read this, Summers," he said.

Charley had realized there was trouble when they came for the files. Nevertheless, when he went through the letter, word by word, it dazed him. After he had finished, he just sat on. Corker waited. At last Charley said,

"I can't believe my eyes, sir."

"I can. I have to."

There was a pause.

"So do you," Mr. Mead went on. "Of course you do."

"Not from Smiths," Charley objected. He handed the letter back. His fingers were trembling. "It's not true," he added.

"Truth or lies, it's written here, Summers."

"Can't believe that of Smiths," Charley said. He felt betrayed on every side. "Not after what they promised."

"Take a good look," Mr. Mead continued, passing the correspondence in its folder. "Turn up your letter of six weeks ago to the foundry."

"Yes sir," Charley said, when he had found the place. "They couldn't get those castings right. Had a lot of wasters."

"What d'you want us to do? Kiss 'em?"

But, when this was suggested, such a look of distress passed over Charley's face that Mr. Mead tried another approach.

"Listen to me, lad," he started. "After five years of war, and all the S.E. this and thats which the Ministry have created to their own ends, everyone in this game is case hardened, punch drunk if you prefer it."

"That fourth paragraph of Smiths doesn't seem to make sense, sir," Charley broke in, misunderstanding the drift.

"What's that got to do with it? I've known Rob Jordan all my life, haven't I? We served our apprenticeship together. He thinks we don't want this job, that's all. And I must say, if I was in his shoes, I'd come to the same conclusion. What's happened here? He's got his own men chasing castings through the various foundries. And they're doing it right, they're going down themselves, not writing letters. One of 'em was shown this wet thing of yours. Rob told me so, I've just phoned him. Because it was wet what you wrote, sloppy. You don't want to encourage people to turn out wasters. You have to threaten 'em, when we've the priorities we've got at the back of us. What firm's supplying these castings?"

"Blundells."

"Then they showed one of his snoopers your letter. Look, don't worry too much," Mr. Mead said. "I fixed it with Rob just now. I gave him a ring. But do something for me, will you? Get back to your own room and write Blundells such a letter that will burn the fingers of whoever takes hold on it. Threaten them with the Minister in person if Smiths don't receive the balance, and in a month. Then go down, for God's sake see them. We shan't be too late yet. And Charley?"

"Yes sir?"

"Don't be in too much of a hurry to take things at face value. You were wrong about Jordan's letter. He was only covering himself in case he got the blame. There's just one other point. Keep lively. Don't think that everything's a try on because of this single instance."

Summers collected the files and the letter, and went back to his room.

"Read this," he said to Dot.

She skimmed through.

"Well, that's that," she said when she had finished.

"It's not, then," he replied, more violent than she had known him.

"If S.O.M.F. say so, I should think it was. We came up against them when I was on penicillin."

"Nothing but a try on," he announced.

"O.K.," she said, pert.

"Turn me up the cards."

On these cards were recorded actual deliveries of the parts from Blundells to Henry Smith and Co., together with brief particulars of the letters that had passed. He did not check the detail.

"I don't know," he muttered.

She stood there.

"Everything seems to come at once," he added, riding his feelings on a loose rein.

She said, brightly, that it never rained but it poured.

"The lying bastard," he cried, once more reading Mr. Jordan's letter, as if it had been a note from Mr. Grant.

"Well we can't expect the impossible, can we?" she asked.

"Look, Miss," he said, and he had recently been calling her Dot, "this letter's a try on, doesn't mean what it says. I saw that the minute I set eyes on it. I've had some lately. There was a time I believed everything I had under my bloody nose, like you seem to, but I don't now. Excuse me, of course."

"This has got you upset, hasn't it?" she said.

Then, without warning, he surprised himself by coming out with his own story.

"Well what would you say if a woman you'd known most of your days told you she wasn't herself? Not sick or ill I mean, but another person all at once." Because he had never before discussed anything outside the office, she was intensely curious.

"What?" she asked.

"No one will ever believe that," he said.

"Well I believed this letter, didn't I, which you saw through at once, or so you said."

"Which letter?" he wanted to know.

"Why the one from Smiths, of course, to do with those blessed castings. But you've had something on your mind, lately. You've been different."

This drew no reply.

"I'll say you have," she went on. "My mum always tells the world, 'If there's anyone to understand a person it's Dot.' Of course we have rather a wonderful relationship really, mum and me. Not like mother and daughter at all." There was a long pause.

"Back from Germany," he started, as though thinking aloud, then stopped, looking very queer, so she thought.

"Yes then?" she encouraged.

"A girl I used to know says she's not that girl," he brought out, with difficulty.

"The self-same girl?" Miss Pitter did not know if she mightn't laugh out loud.

"Dyed her hair," he explained.

"Well what about her handwriting? Has she changed that when she sends you a line?" Dot asked him, with what is known as a woman's intuition.

"Oh dear," he said. He had never considered this. "Oh dear," he said, in anguish.

Then the telephone went. For a time they were very busy. It brought him back to office life. As soon as there was a lull he carried Smiths letter, and the files, out to Mr. Pike.

"Can you spare a minute?" he asked this man.

"Read this, Mr. Pike," he offered, handing the correspondence over. Mr. Pike perused it, without in any way letting on that he had looked into the whole matter only an hour or so ago.

"There's two points I don't like, Summers," Mr. Pike began, then halted. He was like an owl in daylight.

Charley waited.

"This mention of parabolam, here, for one," Mr. Pike started, slow again, "and then his quoting your reference."

"Yes, Mr. Pike." A pause.

"Of course it's a try on."

"That's so." A long pause, while Charley waited.

"Which stands out a mile," the chief draughtsman continued at last. "Another thing. This is a secret process, Summers. We don't want any special metal associated with parabolam."

"No, Mr. Pike."

"And, you know, I don't care for their quoting your reference. That's nasty, that is. Right oh," he ended. "Thanks for showing me."

But Charley's feelings got the better of him. "You don't consider someone may have forged it?" he asked, on impulse.

Mr. Pike stayed quite still. Charley blushed.

"Silly I know," he said, "but I just wondered. Noticed some strange things lately. One of those handwriting experts could tell."

"The old man and Mr. Jordan served their apprenticeship together at the same bench," Mr. Pike said at last, to dismiss Charley. And, when the young fellow was gone, the chief draughtsman could not get down to his work. He was disheartened with the times he lived in. "They're coming back nervous cases, like they did out of the last war," he repeated to himself, and thought that, in that case, then everything was hopeless.

As Charley got back to his own room he found Miss Pitter bending to reach an object she had dropped. Seen from behind her short skirts were lifted, while she stretched, to show an inch or so of white flesh above the stockings. He noted that to have come upon this a few weeks back would have meant more than somewhat.

"It was plain as a pikestaff I'll be bound?" Miss Pitter asked.

"He agreed this is a try on," Charley answered.

"Yet that doesn't prevent his department holding out on us with the advice notes, so I can't keep our cards up to date."

He stayed silent.

"Oh well I don't imagine he does it on purpose, or I don't suppose anyone would, for that matter?" She had recently come round to thinking Mr. Pike rather an old dear.

He glared at nothing in particular.

"You are taking things to heart, aren't you?" Miss Pitter said, to be sympathetic. "Was Mr. Mead upset, then? I'll tell you what. You have a good night's rest and it will seem different in the morning."

He looked at her as though she were insane. Then his telephone rang. As soon as the conversation was over, and while she was marking on the appropriate card what he had just been told, he said, half to himself,

"How do I get her to write?"

"Don't you worry," she replied. "She's worrying her wits this very instant, I'll bet, to find an excuse to do just that very thing."

He gave such a cynical laugh that she turned round to look.

"Oh well, if you've quarrelled, that's another matter," she went on. "You can't expect her to run after you, can you now? A girl's got to keep her self respect, when all's said and done," she said.

"Self respect?" he echoed scornfully. The telephone rang once more. She could have kicked it.

"And no mention of parabolam from this time forward," he said to her, as he put back the receiver. "Even if I forget when dictating, don't take that down. Mr. Pike doesn't like it." Charley had almost escaped from his obsession. But she brought him back.

"I'll tell you something you don't care for," she replied, relentless. "The mention of her name." He started up out of his chair at this cruel shock, this searchlight on a naked man, but she went on. "Oh I've known for ages. It's Rose, Rose she's called, isn't it Rose?"

"No," he lied, and went straight out of the room to the lavatory, in case he should have to vomit.

HE USED to think that no one could ever take from him his trust in Rose which, when the time came, Rose had snatched away herself in a moment.

As soon as he was in bed of an evening, he would literally writhe while he remembered how they had been together.

He grew more and more sure this whole thing was a plot, like the affair with Blundells.

So he set himself one morning in the roadway, a beggar with his stick, to have a word with Middlewitch while the man was off for lunch.

He was more and more jealous of the relations he felt certain that Middlewitch must have had with Rose, and was probably still having.

Arthur saw Charley from afar. He knew it was a nuisance, but the chap was obviously in dire trouble. What they shared of the war, that is the experiences they'd each had on their own, was a bond between them, if only of aluminium, pulleys, and elastic. He thought there was nothing for it but to take Charley along with him.

So he greeted Summers exuberantly, and Charley, with bad grace, accepted the invitation he had hoped for, finding little to say at first while this man rattled jovial, patronizing tit bits in his direction.

"Rose, Rose," Mr. Middlewitch called to the waitress once they were seated.

"Reminds me," Summers said quiet. "D'you know Nance Whitmore?"

"My dear old boy? Why she lives across my landing. Grand girl Nancy."

"Used to be Phillips," Summers said.

"What did?"

"The name. Phillips."

"Is that so?" Mr. Middlewitch replied, uninterested. "Well it's a small world. Fancy you coming across young Nance. You've kept a bit dark about that, surely? You never told me, I mean."

And what about your not saying a word, Charley thought. He chewed this over in scornful silence for a while.

Mr. Middlewitch considered that Summers was looking very strange.

"Of course I haven't known her long," he said at last. "Only since I was felt hatted, and went to live in digs. Now Rose, darling, don't say it has to be bunny again. We've had a proper dose of that this week."

"Oh Mr. Middlewitch," she said. "Oh Rose," he gave her back. Both of them laughed.

Charley began to feel sick in spite of the whisky.

After more had been ordered Charley said,

"Her name was Rose."

"Whose name?"

"Rose Phillips."

"You're telling me a lot about this Rose Phillips, old man," Mr. Middlewitch complained, "but I've never had the honour, have I?" He was continually looking round the luncheon room for acquaintances.

"It's Nance Whitmore."

"What was her name, then, before she married Phillips?"

"Nancy Whitmore was Rose Grant."

"You're wrong there, old chap. Nance lost her husband in the war. He wasn't called Phillips. Then she changed her name back by deed poll. But her hubby was Phil White. Is that what you were thinking of? Phil and Phillips? He got his at Alamein."

This was more than Charley could stomach.

"What's the penalty for bigamy, even when the second husband's dead?" he demanded, choking.

"Bigamy, old boy? Why ask me? Never marry 'em, that's my motto. Best thing too."

"She's a bigamist," Charley insisted, almost draining his second whisky at a gulp. Middlewitch looked at him with disgust.

"Steady," he said, "steady, old man. I've known the little lady in question ever since I got back."

"Old Grant introduce you?"

"Gerald Grant? Here, what is this? If they know each other it's the first I've heard. And I suspect it's none of my business."

"She's a bigamist," Charley said. All this time he had kept his eyes on the table. Middlewitch took it for a sign that the fellow knew he was lying. "Now see here, Summers, you'll be getting yourself into a peck of trouble one of these fine days." Then he began to lose his temper. "And in any case," he went on, "I say damn a man who says what you've just done about a lady and doesn't look you in the eye as he speaks. Even if it is about a girl, and they're capable of anything. You can't tell me," he ended, appreciating the sally.

But Charley raised his eyes to Middlewitch for the first time, who could only stare at what was opened to him in them.

"I see," Mr. Middlewitch said uncomfortably.

"Well, there you are," Mr. Middlewitch exclaimed again.

Charley finished the whisky, laughed, and said, "Yes, there it is," with a sort of satisfaction.

"But look here, Summers," Arthur started, once something, he was not sure what, had begun to sink into him, "why she's straight as a die, you know, straight as a die. I'd stake my life on that. Nancy Whitmore. Good lord yes."

"Did you know about her son?"

"My dear good chap you're mistaken there, I can assure you. Why, after they've been in the straw they've a brown line down their little tummies. Well she hasn't, so what d'you know?"

"And how did you learn?" Charley brought out, in such a voice that Middlewitch swallowed, then, when he did reply, began to bluster.

"Why, I went swimming with her of course," he lied. "Last summer it was. Took the girl down to Margate."

"With mines on the beach?"

But Arthur had recovered himself.

"In the *Palais de Swim*, or whatever they call the place, naturally," he answered. "Look, you'll excuse my saying this, old man. You may even think I'm a funny sort of host. But let's change the subject, shall we? I mean the little lady's quite a pal of mine. It's strange. You've got the wrong side of one another some time, I know. But that's nothing to do with this chap," he said, pointing a finger at himself, "if you get me."

Then, through his rising, nauseating misery, Summers had, as he thought, a brain wave.

"A written apology is what she should send," he announced.

"O.K. Enough's enough. Now what's to follow? Rose," Arthur called to the waitress, his patience with the whole subject at an end, "Rose."

"Sorry," Charley said. "Suppose I'm a bit upset."

"I can see that, old man."

"Her name was Rose. That got me started."

"All right Summers," Middlewitch replied with unction, his position now Charley had weakened, "all right, but I can't use any other name for the waitresses, can I? Or call Nance by any other than what I know? See here, old chap. You sit on as you are. Simmer down." He laughed. "There's old Ernie Mandrew across the room I must have a word with. And while I'm away I may be able to get hold of Rose to bring us what's to come. You'll have another drink of course?" He got up and left.

He managed to stop their waitress. "Look, darling, I've got to go," he said. "See to my friend," he asked. "He's more than a bit queer, had a bad war," he added, "was repatriated, after me as a matter of fact. Fetch him another whisky, like a good girl. I shall be in again tomorrow. He's stuck on a girl called Rose. Bit of a coincidence, isn't it?" He went off laughing.

An hour and three whiskies later, Charley paid the bill and left. When someone else was put in Arthur's place, at their table, he had hardly noticed.

After Middlewitch got home that night from the office, he was still angry with Summers. As soon as he'd had a wash, however, he began to see the whole matter in a rosier light. The chap had had a rotten time. Girls like Nance should appreciate what Charley, and he, had been through. He would have a chat with her. If he went across now, she would not have gone to work yet. So he knocked at her door.

She did not open up, but called out to ask who might it be.

"Only Art," he said.

"Why Art," she said, letting him in. "There've been some queer customers around lately," she explained. "I'm in a state of siege now, I promise." She was laughing.

"Customers?" he enquired archly, as he settled himself in the best chair. "But Nance," he said, "you ought to watch out how you express yourself, or you'll be misunderstood."

"Well then," she replied, "don't you misunderstand for a start. You can't tell what I've had to sit here and listen to these last few weeks. And what's become of you in all that time? It must be months since I've seen you, Art."

"Oh I've been around, here, there, and everywhere, like the scarlet Johnny," he said. "And by the way, I came across someone who claimed your acquaintance."

"Go on? What colour was his hair? Ginger?"

"You're joking," he objected. "No, it was a chap with me, where they fitted us with our limbs. He was repatriated a bit later than me, as a matter of fact. Charley Summers' the name."

"You too," was all she said, and seemed disgusted. Arthur considered, perhaps this was more serious than he had thought.

"Look Nance," he said, rushing it, "you and me's known each other for some little time past. Strictly speaking this is none of my affair. He never told what all this was about. Charley Summers may be a queer card but he's straight as a die, Nance old girl, straight as a die. And he's been through a tough, rotten period. I've had some in those prison camps. You'd only to go in the guard room and sneeze in front of one of Herr Adolph's portraits, and it was off to the dark in solitary confinement, right away. They called it inciting the glorious Wehrmacht to revolt. Things may be a bit different, now they see the writing on the wall, but that's how it was when we were out there. He's had it Nance, *il l'a eu*, as our French cousins say. Now, maybe the old lad's done something to upset you, I wouldn't know. I couldn't get anything out of the man myself. But if he did, I shouldn't take too much notice."

She sat there.

"Have you finished?" she asked.

"Now what have I said?" he enquired, a bit daunted.

"Did you send that damned lunatic my way?"

"I?" Mr. Middlewitch cried. "Not on your life."

"That's all right, Art," she said. "But, you're a witness to the fact that, since Phil was killed and Mum went off out of these flying bombs, I've lived on here very quiet. I'm all right. I don't need company. Then someone tells this man out of Colney Hatch my address, and the way I am these days I daresn't open the door for fear it's him again. It's my nerves won't let me. The first time he came he fainted, and the next—oh well, you've said it, he's not normal."

"This is none of my business, Nance, you needn't tell me and I respect you for it, but things weren't easy for us chaps out there. Drop him a line like a good girl."

"Sakes alive, is that the time?" she cried. "I must be off or I shall be late." The next day she wrote Charley a note. All it said was, that she did not want to leave things tangled.

She was a good-hearted girl.

MISS NANCY Whitmore sent her note to Charley's business address, which Middlewitch had given her. By the same post there was a line for Charley from Phillips, who was the sort of man who forgave freely, for old times' sake. In his letter he asked Charley down over the August holiday, and said for him to bring a girl, though he added, as a wry joke, not the Miss Whitmore he had been taken to visit that once.

Phillips' letter was marked personal. Dot did not open it. But there was nothing of the kind on Nancy's envelope. Because of this, she read what Nancy had written. It looked to her like he must really be after this girl. She put it away in the middle of the day's mail. She was most curious.

As soon as Charley had washed himself and settled down to go through the correspondence, she watched to see how he took it when he came on Nancy's note. But to her amazement all he did was to laugh, out loud, triumphantly. He thought Rose must be disguising her hand.

Then, when he came to Phillips' letter, and read the invitation, he was so cynically amused to find the husband specially asking him not to bring the wife, that, because he felt particularly bright this morning, he said to his assistant,

"What are you doing over the holiday, Dot?"

"Me? Why nothing, as per usual, I shouldn't wonder."

"Care to come along to an old friend of mine in Essex?"

She was astounded. She took it absolutely seriously. She was so surprised she could have kicked herself, after, for what she said next.

"Well, this is a bit sudden, isn't it?" she brought out. He was embarrassed, because he saw she meant to accept.

"It's a lovely place, right in the village. Very old," he said, ashamed of himself. But he could not draw back, not now.

"Well I shall have to think this one out, I mean shan't I?" she mumbled. He could see her mind was made up. And he said, "Why not?" to himself. After all, life owed him something now. Then his phone rang, and they became submerged in work. He forgot Miss Pitter.

When he got back to his place that night, he had still forgotten her. He could think of nothing but his own girl disguising her hand. He went to the suitcase under the bed, and took out those five letters he had had before the war from Rose, which he kept in a big envelope. His hands terribly trembled. The letters were undated, in no particular order. What he wanted to find was one fit for the handwriting expert to compare with Miss Whitmore's screed.

"Darling Stinker," he read. "If you weren't such a stinking darling you'd go down to Redham for me and see the old dears. I didn't half get a moan from dad yesterday in our letter box. You know what I am about letter writing. My hubby says they can't ever have sent me to school so probably if I did write they couldn't read anyway. So be a dear old Stinker and go down and tell them how you saw their little Rose blooming over Whitsun. Got to rush now. From your Mrs. Siddons."

These letters put him in agony, they made him love her so. And he knew he could not send that one, it was too intimate. He started on the next.

"Dear Stinker. I must say I think it's a bit lop-sided your simply making up your mind you'd forget when I asked you especially to get me those mules we saw in the advert. Don't be a meanie darling. From Rose."

He knew he couldn't part with this one either. No stranger must ever see it.

"Stinker darling. I'm writing this lain in bed. Old mother Gubbins just got me my breaky. I sniff for my Stinker but there's not a trace. I bet you wish you were here you old smoothie. Jim won't be home now till the end of the week. Are you mortified in your silly old office? And don't you wish you were here with Your Rose."

His eyes filled with tears. These letters were sacred. After a little time he began on the next.

"My dear. Of course now I've got someone else to consider—I mean while I'm bearing baby, I've got to be careful I don't do too much haven't I, coming up to London and all that well you wouldn't wish for me to have a turn in front of all the crowd at the cricket would you. So you'll just have to be a patient old Stinker. No seriously the doctor says I'll have to watch myself and not get overtired and to put my feet up when I've half a chance. He's such a sweet old bear of a man. So not just yet Charley Barley. The next few weeks he says are the tricky ones. Keep your chin up. Your Red Rose."

They were too outspoken, he told himself. Because anyone could tell from this one that Ridley was his own child. Then he read the last.

"Dear Stinker. I must say I do think you might have sent on those things. If you could see me every hour watching for the postman, dear, I expect you'd do something about it now. But it's out of sight out of mind with you darling. So do be quick. Your ____' and she must have forgotten to sign.

There was not one of them he could let go. He put the lot back in the suitcase. Then he had an idea. He found his nail scissors, got the letters again, and began, without thinking, to cut those sentences out which he thought would not give him away. He worked fast, laying each snippet on a sheet of newspaper to which he proposed to paste the bits like a telegram. And this was the message from Rose that he scissored, almost at random, out of their love letters:

"Dear / go down to Redham for me and / tell them how you saw / those mules / coming up to London. / So be a dear / and go down / From Rose."

He felt he had been exceedingly clever, till, all at once, he realized he had destroyed, cut into ribbons, every letter he had ever had from Rose. Then he despaired, blaming himself. But he could think of no other way to get an expert opinion. And he knew Nance was really Rose. And, after all, that had killed her letters.

So, for the evening, he mourned the fact that Rose's treachery had destroyed the last there was left to him, the letters which, for all the months and years in Germany, had been what he was most afraid to find mislaid, or lost, when he got back.

Yet that night he slept very well for once, and did not dream.

IT RAINED all the August holiday. The Phillips' home, in which Charley had last known Rose, was on a main road just off the village street. Convoys of American army trucks shook the old house, the whole day. Often Dot had to yell to make herself heard. The three of them even had difficulty in getting across to the pub opposite, where darts, at times, were shaken off the pig bristle board. From out the darkness of their cabs the nigger drivers could be told only by their white smiles.

As soon as Dot and Charley arrived, James took her up to see the room. She looked brazenly at where she was to sleep. Because, she felt, she knew what she was there for. It was a double bed all right.

"Very nice I'm sure," she murmured.

"What?" he asked, for, with a noise like thunder, another line of heavy lorries was being driven past. She repeated herself, and moved to the dormer window which looked over the back. It had sounded crude to say that again.

"Where's Charley's room?" she then enquired, but he did not hear this either. She felt she could not put that twice, and to cover her embarrassment she traced Dot with a finger on the leaded window. She'd treated herself to a manicure up in town. Its nail was enamelled to the colour of wet flesh.

James laughed. "Oh well you know there's nothing very special, I'm afraid," he said. "In fact, I'm very much afraid." As he stood at her side she could risk a glance. She confirmed that he was staring at her hand. It was lucky, she thought, that she'd had them done over.

"Silly of me," she said, "but when I come on lovely old windows I always wish I had a diamond to cut my name."

He laughed once more. She thought he would be O.K., though as yet she had, of course, no idea at all how, or how much.

"We'll have to see about that," he replied, but extremely pleasant, nothing to take exception to.

"What?" she exclaimed, yet she had heard. "Scribble right over your beautiful old windows? I'm sure you'd wonder how I'd been brought up. The very idea. Why I wasn't serious, I should hope not indeed."

"Well, make yourself comfortable. I must get old Charley fixed up now," he said. "Then we'll have a bite to eat. It's only cold, but I've a little something laid out in the kitchen. See you directly," and he went.

There was nothing more that night, absolutely nothing. They'd had a nice supper, and weren't these country people all right for food. Then they'd gone over the way where they bought her a few drinks. They wouldn't have it when she tried to pay for a round. At last she'd said, "All good things must come to an end," looking at Charley as she spoke, so much as to cry it out loud. So they came back to the house with her, and she'd slipped upstairs, got into a smashing pyjama suit bought specially the day before, put out the light and, quaking with wonder, she'd lain there. She could hear them talk in the kitchen. And how they'd talked. Then they came up. And she'd wondered some more. Her own worst enemy would not have laughed at her that half hour. Even if it wasn't the first time, of course. But nothing. She was all ready, pretending to be asleep, spread out like butter on bread. But nothing. She knew it was Charley when he went to the bathroom. For just that minute it was delicious to wait. But what all this added up to, she felt at the time, was that these repatriated men came back very queer from those camps. So in the end she'd gone to sleep alone, unvisited.

The next day they'd done this, that, and the other, all very pleasant to be sure, but nothing in particular. Charley'd never come out of himself, he'd stayed just like he was in the office. The two men were thick together, though. The wife's name cropped up once or twice. Rose. She thought she could see where the land lay. This visit was a bit of for old times' sake, she fancied. Oh they'd made themselves very friendly, except to do out her own room they never let her help in any way. But, by the second evening, she'd made up her mind there was nothing to it, nothing whatever. Charley'd had her down to be gooseberry. Then, after another very enjoyable little party over the road, she went up early to get her beauty sleep, because it was a pity to throw away this good country air which was already doing things to her skin, and she was just dropping off when the door did open a crack, someone came in, into her bed even, the sauce, and, believe it, or not, it was that fat James, though everything had been so dark she hadn't known till after.

That very first evening, when Charley did not come, while she lay in bed as they talked downstairs, she had asked herself if he was being told something which kept him. He was and he wasn't. To tell the truth, he had forgotten that she existed.

There was a silence this first night after she left for bed until Mr. Phillips announced,

"Well here you are again then, Charley."

"Yes," Charley Summers replied. They were sitting opposite each other, over cups of tea.

"It seems a long time," Mr. Phillips said. Charley did not reply.

"I've put her in Rose's old room," Mr. Phillips explained. Charley looked at him, but the widower's face was bland. Then the man went on, "Who is she?"

"Works with me."

"You London office people get all the fun and games," Mr. Phillips said. "But don't wake Ridley, will you?"

"Doesn't he sleep any better than his mother did, then?"

"Yes," James replied. "She was always complaining about that, wasn't she?"

"Well I mean," Charley loyally objected. "It's rotten if you can't sleep." He was surprised to find he could be cold once more, while speaking of her, cold.

"They get more than they realize," Mr. Phillips said.

"No way of telling."

"There is if you're stretched out by their side," Mr. Phillips answered cheerfully. "Many's the time I've listened to her snore, when she's told me the next day she hadn't slept a wink all night."

"I didn't know," Charley lied, delighted that he could talk easily of Rose. He couldn't now imagine why he had got himself into such a state about her handwriting. All of a sudden, or so he thought, she was dead to him at last. She was really gone.

"The doctor seemed to think it affected her resistance at the last," James went on. "I didn't undeceive him. You see she'd complained of not sleeping ever since I brought her here."

"I couldn't drop off when I first got back. It was the quiet."

"You weren't having raids out there, not all the time, surely?"

"Sleeping alone," Charley explained. "After twenty to a room."

"What did the Army doctors say?" Mr. Phillips asked.

"They're all trick cyclists now," Charley said. "Best not to undeceive those merchants either." Then his mind turned to Mrs. Grant. "Did the family come down when she lay dying?" he lazily enquired, free as air about Rose.

"Her old mother was too ill and couldn't be left."

"I see," Charley said.

"Or so that old bastard Gerald made out, anyway. I say, my dear lad, I hope I haven't gone over the line. In-laws and all that." He felt, entirely without jealousy, as though Charles and he had shared Rose.

"Don't mind me, Jim. He's poison."

"Right then, we know where we stand. That man's always up to some deadly work. Poor soul, it's really no wonder she's as she is today, Mrs. Grant, you know."

"You're telling me."

"Well, that's a real relief, Charley old boy. Because I felt a bit of a worm in front of you, letting fly like that about him."

Charley looked at Mr. Phillips. Everything had changed, yet it was no different. They had sat on so often after Rose had gone to bed, so many years back, saying much the same.

"Lot of water's passed under the bridge," Charley commented with a trace of disgust, as though speaking of the sewage system.

"It was terrible when it happened, poor old girl," Mr. Phillips said. "Ridley was the worst part. Must have come as a shock to you, too. One of the first letters you got from home?"

"There it is."

"Life has a funny way of getting back at us, sometimes." Phillips spoke as though he'd had one wife after another, each of whom had lived just three months. "But d'you mind if I ask a question? Why did you take me along a few weeks ago to meet a certain person?"

"Then you did notice a resemblance?" Charley asked, showing the embarrassment in his voice.

"Not the slightest," Mr. Phillips replied with confidence. "Was that your reason?"

"Good lord, no," Mr. Summers lied, and became voluble. "It was Mr. Grant sent me in the first place. I shan't ever know what for, some more of his fun and games I suppose. Well, we had a bit of a misunderstanding right off, she and I. I don't understand now what she thought. But it struck me there couldn't be any harm in taking you along. Hope you didn't mind?"

"Of course not. Then when I turned it over in my head afterwards I wondered if you hadn't mistaken something."

Charley was alarmed, but he kept pretty calm. He was now ashamed of what he had felt for Rose.

"What d'you mean?" he asked.

"It's only that there's nothing to the shape of a face."

"What are you getting at?" Charley wanted to know, on the defensive because that phrase had particularly made him think of her son.

"Yet when a man marries again, he chooses the same type, or so the women say. While you and Rose were old pals, knew each other long before we ever met." There was a pause. He did not explain further. "You know, now she's gone, you're my link with her, old man," Jim Phillips said.

They'd had double whiskies for the road before they left the pub. Charley began to wonder if James wasn't a trifle sozzled. But he kept quiet.

"Look," Mr. Phillips went on, "perhaps you may consider I'm going a bit beyond it, even for between friends, but I've had no one I could talk to, all this long while. Anybody would think Ridley must remind me of her, but he doesn't, and if ever you're in my position, as I hope you never will, I dare say you'll find the same. No, when you took me up to that flat in London, I did wonder at the time if you wanted to see whether I got it too. I mean, if she should remind me, as well as you."

"I don't know what you're driving at?" Charley asked, still on the defensive.

"I'm not getting at anything, or anybody," Mr. Phillips said handsomely. "Forget it. No, I'm speaking for your own good. When she died I took it very bad, living on in the same house as I had to. I've given your friend her old room by the way. There wasn't anywhere else. And I shouldn't wonder if you didn't feel it very hard as well, situated like you were when you heard, out there. But what I'm trying to say is, it's you reminds me of her when I'm with you, there you are. Much more than your other lady friend, or even the boy now. There's nothing in faces."

"Then you did think they were like when I took you?"

"Just when I first set eyes on her I might have done, and with that contemptible remark she made after. I was a bit wild with you as a matter of fact, just for the moment. Then when I got back I read the old story I sent on."

"Which story?" he asked, glad to get off the subject.

"Didn't you try it? Oh, in one of those magazines my sister used to take when she kept house here, before I married, and I kept 'em up, I don't know why."

"I believe I did, now you come to mention this."

"Which didn't ring the bell, eh Charley? Well there's no accounting."

"I don't see much in books," Mr. Summers said.

"No more do I," Phillips agreed. "Marriage is a funny thing. And nothing at all to do with the tripe these screwy authors serve us up with."

"Did Rose ever know Arthur Middlewitch?" Charley interrupted.

"Arthur who?"

"Middlewitch."

"Never heard of him," Mr. Phillips said. "You knew her earlier than me," he pointed out.

"It's nothing. Just an idea," Charley replied.

"But to carry on with what I was in the middle of," Mr. Phillips began again, "you know, before Ridley was born, Rose got it into her head we were going to have a daughter." This gave Charley a shock because he remembered very well how, at the time, she had insisted to him that they would have a son. "They get crazes for things," Mr. Phillips was saying, "in her case it was olives, and, of course, that's a female name, anyway she was quite settled she'd have a girl." "You liar" Charley said to himself under his breath, although Rose was gone and he'd got rid of her, didn't mind any more, or so he'd been thinking. "Well, she made me promise, if anything should happen to her at the birth, that I'd never let those Grants have the kid."

"She knew about 'em, then?" Charley got out, with difficulty. What had Rose been doing to talk of a daughter, when with him she had been so full of a son?

"Of course I promised," Mr. Phillips said. "What man wouldn't. It came easy, too, this particular promise. After all having children is what we're here for," he said with assurance. "All there is to life, or that's how it strikes me. But it proves one point, she must have known something was up, at Redham, between her mother and the old man, eh? Stands out a mile she must have. Not a happy home, you know."

"Certainly is," Charley agreed, confused, several sentences behind once more.

"Which brings me to what I've been getting to," Mr. Phillips said. "Why don't you marry and settle down?"

This was a bit of a facer.

"Why don't you marry again, for that matter?" Charley asked, with the air of a man getting himself out of a tight spot.

"Who me?" Mr. Phillips demanded. "Once bitten twice shy, old chap. No, that's got a disobliging sound to it. What I meant was that, with Ridley, I've perpetuated myself, d'you get me? So you've nothing of the sort in mind?"

"Never," Charley said, and made it sound final.

"Not even with our friend upstairs you brought along?"

"I told you I work with her in the office."

"Well it's been known before, after all? It wouldn't be the first time. All right, you're not." Then he lied. "I only asked because with Rose's room being the only other one, mine's right next door, so I thought you might have imagined I was trying some funny business or something."

"That's O.K.," Charley said. "There's nothing in her direction for me or you, you can bet your life on that." He was also lying, but in his case with only half a mind to it, he was so taken up with sudden doubts of Rose, doubts which almost redisposed him to love her.

"You ought to marry. A man like you should," Mr. Phillips repeated, well content.

"Why?"

"Because you're alone, old man."

"Aren't you, as well?" Charley asked, still defensive.

"I've got Ridley."

"Of course," Charley muttered, but saying to himself "You old mutt, if you only knew."

"No, it's a duty," Mr. Phillips went on. "Because you're moping. That's what's got you, moping."

Charley stayed silent. His day to day sense of being injured by everyone, by life itself, rose up and gagged him.

"I say I hope you don't mind my speaking like this? But I've noticed things. You've been different, old chap, since you got back."

"Wouldn't you be?"

"Very likely," Mr. Phillips admitted, as though granting a favour.

"Still, we have to take the world the way we find it. There's life to live after all. You'll overlook my saying so, I'm sure, but you're mal-adjusted."

There was a silence.

"Nowadays no man's got a right to lead his own life," James went on, speaking with a fat man's conviction. "It's selfish, that's what it is, not to marry and not to have the little old comforts marriage brings. With the responsibilities."

"I'm not fit," Charley brought out with difficulty, and with a great look of pain. His self pity had at last got the better of him.

"My dear old chap, if you'd rather not discuss it, why of course. In any case, what say we wander upstairs and get a bit of sleep?"

But Charley did not move.

"After those prisoner of war camps," he began, then stopped.

"Well what about 'em? Pretty rough, what?"

"I can't," Charley said, shifting about in his chair.

"Well," Mr. Phillips said with a change of tone, "we have chewed the old rag over, haven't we? Will you just look at the time? It's beddy byes now for us, I say." As he got up to go, the younger man thought, "Why you bloody civilian."

In his bed he had a short spell of Rose before he began to feel he was back in Germany again.

The next day, the first morning of her visit, it was James called her with a cup of tea and the usual questions about whether she had been all right, slept well, and so on. But the following day, after James had been for hours in bed with her, it was Charley who brought the cup, and who sat down on the edge, looking as usual as if he was sleepwalking.

"Well Dot," he'd said, with no more than a glance in her direc-tion. But of course, on account of what she had just done with the other man, she'd absolutely shrunk away from him, couldn't help herself. It made her feel a fool even to think of it after, for he couldn't have been up to anything, not him, poor fish. So he'd drifted out, almost at once. You could never tell if he noticed.

But the first morning they had an egg for breakfast each, which made up for a good deal.

Then, when Charley was helping to clear away, he'd come on the Phillips daily help in the scullery, Rose's precious Mrs. Gubbins. James left them alone. Later on he asked Charley what had passed.

"'Imagine seeing you again,' was what she said," Charley lied, for the woman, who hardly ever spoke, had come out with, "Imagine seeing you here again."

"Now you know what you fought for, Charley boy," Mr. Phillips exclaimed. "What a welcome back, eh?" Then he told Dot this woman had been his wife's treasure, and how lucky he was to keep her.

"It's for Ridley," he went on. "Kids need a woman's eye. She'll see a sign in a kid's face that a mere man would never even notice. It's nature. So I feel safe with her looking in every day."

"He's a wonderful little chap," Miss Pitter returned. "I'm sure he's a credit to you."

"I was just wondering if you'd think it was wrong to look after him as I do. Trust my own judgement, I mean. But it's she gives me the confidence."

"Well, things won't last that way for ever, I don't suppose."

A roar of traffic kept him from hearing this.

"What's that?" he asked.

She blushed. But she did not give in. She said it again.

"Well, things won't last that way for ever, will they?"

"How d'you reckon?" James asked.

Miss Pitter actually began to shift from one foot to the other.

"I don't know what I mean really," she explained.

"No, go on," he urged.

"Well a man like you will marry a second time one of these fine days," she brought out, with some embarrassment.

"And very nicely put," Mr. Phillips rejoined. "But if ever I did, believe me, it would be for the boy's sake."

"Here's your chance, Dot," Mr. Summers interrupted. They had forgotten all about him. He was feeling extraordinarily lighthearted this first morning. "Better than the office," he added.

She was not in the least put out. She could handle him. And what was to happen had not occurred yet.

"Careful," she said. "We're not on the old advice notes now, you know," she said.

It was still the first morning, and it continued wet outside. Charley slumped back into a chair, went to sleep all over again with the paper. She'd made another general offer to help in any way, only to be refused. Then, after James had put on their lunch, he came back into the sitting room. He said to her,

"Come over here a moment."

They stood side by side once more, looking out through other leaded window panes onto the untidy back garden which was two apple trees, a dump of rubbish, and a tumble down shelter, on top of which sandbags had burst to grow ragwort. With the two hedges, it was all green and black and red, particularly a small crop of red apples half hidden, like sins, by the wet leaves, the black branches, and, on the ground, a lush rank grass.

"Rose," he said, "that's my wife, who's dead and gone now, rest her soul, she particularly wanted to have a pergola built just where the air raid shelter is now. Of course the war put paid to that idea. But when I have a minute I'm going to, after we've licked those Germans. What's your opinion? Of course there's not a great deal of space, but what I've got in mind is one of those ones with a triangular sort of roof on brick piers, with seats back to back underneath. What d'you think?"

"Why that would be lovely," she said.

"What was that? Because you see I'm beginning to realize I value your opinion."

"I said, why that would be lovely."

"Yes, and I'd have roses trained up for old times' sake. You mustn't judge of it now," he explained, referring to the desolation. "She was always on at me to clear this mess up. Then, once she was taken, there never seemed to be time."

"With roses growing all over that would be beautiful as a memorial," she said.

"She was the best little wife a man ever had," he replied, completely honest. "But I must go and see to our joint. I notice our friend's well away," he said of Charley. "He's had a bad war, you know."

"It's terrible what those poor boys must have been through," she said.

"What?" he asked, again unable to hear on account of the traffic. She repeated it.

"I'm sure he's very lucky to have you to watch over his interests at his work," he rejoined.

"Oh he's a dear," she countered, half-heartedly, thinking Mr. Phillips was a bit of a dear himself, though of course she had no earthly notion of what was to happen, or that it was to be so soon.

They never saw Ridley except at meals, for which he was most often very late, and through which he sat in a gobbling silence. It seemed he spent all his time with the Gubbins children.

At tea that first day five buzz bombs came over one after the other. They took little notice of the first three, but James and Dot were discussing whether or not they should take cover while the last two roared and rattled past. How different the second morning, bed plus one day, when the same phenomenon occurred at about the same time. Dot squealed the moment she heard the first distant clatter. James immediately hurried her into the wet dark of his broken down shelter outside. There they passionately kissed. On neither of these occasions did Charley move. In fact he was so busy thinking of himself he hardly noticed. Ridley, of course, was away, somewhere on his own.

Charley was more preoccupied that same second afternoon because he had unexpectedly run into Arthur Middlewitch in the village street, where he had gone to buy cigarettes.

"Well bless me, it's Summers isn't it?" Mr. Middlewitch had exclaimed as they ran across one another, and in exactly the tone he employed when, as civilians, they had first met some months back. "What on earth are you doing here old chap?"

"With Jim Phillips."

"Down for the August, eh?"

"Aren't you?" Charley was feeling particularly fit.

"Me? Oh me. I'm staying with old Ernie Mandrew," Mr. Middle-witch replied in a most superior tone, falling into step beside Summers. "You know, when I come to think, it was a pity you never went across with me to meet him, that time I took you to our little luncheon club." Naturally Summers had not refused to meet the man. Hearing this made him confused. "Because, if you had gone over, I might have been able to bring you back with me this evening for a cocktail," Middlewitch continued. "Marvellous place he's got, old man, simply marvellous. Crawling with domestic servants. I don't know how he does it."

"We could make merry over a cup of tea to get on with," Charley suggested, in what was, for him, a burst of sarcasm.

"Well I don't mind if I do. I'm not one for tea as a rule, but they don't open for another couple of hours yet, anyway."

So they went into a bun shop.

"You're looking a lot fitter than when I saw you last, old man," Mr. Middlewitch began, once they had found seats. "I don't mind saying I was a bit worried about you. I must have been, because I did you a good turn."

"How's that?"

"I played the Boy Scout over you, with Nance."

Mr. Summers' stomach turned inside him. He was surprised. He'd had no idea he could be so excited at the mention of her name.

"Well, a man who's fair can't allow two people he respects not to hit it off together, can he?" Mr. Middlewitch proceeded, then paused, it may have been from surprise at his using the word respect in regard to Charley.

"Ah," Mr. Summers said, to encourage him.

"You mark what I say, you're all right there, old chap. Gosh, this tea isn't going down so bad after all. Did you hear those buzz bombs yesterday? The natives weren't too happy. Laughable, really, the way they flopped down."

"What comment did she make?" Charley asked, still on about Nance.

"Don't give it another thought, Charley boy. She's all for you. Any little misunderstanding there may have been is over and done with now. Why, didn't she write?"

"Oh yes."

"Well I'm glad to have been of assistance," Mr. Middlewitch vaguely replied, already looking round the crowded tea room in case there was a pretty face. A silence fell.

"Who's in your party?" Mr. Middlewitch enquired, as it seemed with impatience.

"No one really."

"You alone then?"

"No, there's Jim Phillips we're staying with."

"Who's we, anyway?"

"Just a girl. Dorothy Pitter and me."

"You're a bit of a dark horse, Summers. Did you bring her down or what?"

"Of course," Mr. Summers replied, almost lively.

"Well then what's the form, how's the old romance proceeding, boy? Because you're not going to tell me you've got yourself engaged, or something, have you?"

"Me?" Charley asked.

"No, of course not," Mr. Middlewitch replied. He had adopted an almost bullying attitude, out of boredom perhaps. "It's not for the likes of you and me to set up a little home, not yet awhile, believe me. That's the only trouble about where I'm staying. Lots of everything except fluff. Which is why I took myself down here this afternoon, if you want to know. Come on now, what's she like?"

"There's nothing doing," Charley said, flat.

"Come off it," Mr. Middlewitch demanded. "Tell that to the Japs. What, after the greatest war in history, with everyone still at it, and all we've been through? Not to speak of these secret weapons."

Charley laughed.

"You let the grass grow under your feet," Mr. Middlewitch

exclaimed. "That's your trouble, Charley boy. God bless me," he went on, "Will you just look at the time. I must be off. Well, it's been jolly running across you like this." And he hurried out, after a blonde who was on her own. She was extremely small.

But it now seemed to Charley that he had known Dot too long to try and start anything. Also he knew he was right, for he had only to consider how she had edged away when he'd brought her tea that very morning. Though of course you never could tell, you could never tell with a woman.

He'd never once thought to visit Rose's grave.

Then, about five o'clock, back at the house, as has already been described, there was the second lot of flying bombs. When James and Dot came back from the shelter Charley noticed nothing. He had at once begun a long complaint about his coupons, and how impossible it was to choose with the few he had.

They were to go back on the morrow, bed plus two days. Phillips and Miss Pitter seemed rather to hurry the evening. They all left the pub earlier than ever, although they'd been having a very pleasant little time. But when Charley got lonely between the sheets he found, as so often, that he could not sleep. He lay there nervously wondering if he should go in to Dot. He told himself that it would mean nothing, after everything was said and done; that is, if it came to nothing, then he was just paying a call, and if it did come to something, well, it would be as much her choice as his own. Because, either way, he wouldn't be committed. Still, when it came to getting out of bed, he did not seem able to make up his mind.

At last, after a long time, he actually did go. Her door was open, the place empty. Moonlight, coming through a fake Tudor window, lay over her bed with the clothes pushed back like a breaking wave. There were no pillows, for she had taken these with her. And then he heard noises next door in James' room. They were in the act.

Of course he felt cheated, but he slept well for once.

The next morning, no one brought Miss Pitter tea.

Then, with not a word said, they'd travelled back to London in a very crowded carriage.

WHEN HE arrived that afternoon at Mrs. Frazier's, he found a letter from the handwriting expert. It said there was definitely no resemblance between the two scripts, that Miss Whitmore's note inviting him round and the letter from Rose, which he had cut out of all the love letters she had ever sent him, were written by two different people. Somehow this did not seem important now. It was out of date. Also Dot's treachery with Phillips was beginning to rankle, unsettling him. So he put Nancy's invitation in a pocket, and started off to walk in her direction. He had not decided if he would go up, before he surprised himself knocking on the pink door.

She had been in tears.

"It's Panzer," she greeted him, making way so he could enter.

Perhaps it was because of Dot, but he was very taken by how she looked.

"That's my precious puss," she explained, when he stayed silent. "I'm afraid she's been getting into bad company, the naughty girl."

"Oh," he said vaguely. He fed his eyes on her.

"I get so upset," she explained. "Of course I should have taken her round to the cats' hospital to have a little operation, but I never seemed to spare the time. Now it's too late."

"What's the matter?"

"She's to have kittens, the wicked girl, her first." As Miss Whitmore told him, two huge tears rolled down from her eyes, while her face remained expressionless. He actually laughed. Then she giggled.

"Oh, I know, I'm making a fool of myself, you don't have to tell me," she said, very friendly.

"Made more of an idiot of myself, for that matter, when I was round here," he muttered, shamefaced at once.

"I don't know. Did you?" She was sitting opposite, with the cat on her lap. "Oh, Panzer, how you could? But I'd rather you didn't give it another thought," she said to him. "It takes two to get into an argument, as my mother always will insist."

He suddenly found he was thinking of Nancy's mother as of someone quite separate from Mrs. Grant. But he did not stop to consider this.

"It's no trouble to them, is it?" he asked.

"What d'you mean?"

"They have their kittens without any fuss, don't they?"

"But I might be out at work."

"Where d'you work, then?"

"I'm on nights at the G.P.O."

He was beginning to feel easy and comfortable.

"There's this about kittens, they don't have to bother with clothing coupons," he remarked.

"You've said a whole lot there," she agreed. "I don't suppose it can be easy for you people back from Germany."

He could talk coupons as freely as he could technicalities in the office. He at once plunged into a long description of what few clothes he had, including the pink tweed he was wearing and which was useless in London. She listened with more than good grace. She joined in. And couldn't help reminding herself how she had not meant to be so friendly. It turned out his main trouble was, that he hadn't yet received the coupons to which he was entitled on discharge from the Army.

"The others said I should apply to C.A.B.," he told her. "Which is that?"

"Citizens' Advice Bureau," she explained. "But who are these people you're mentioning?"

"Why the ones I was staying with."

"Over the holiday?" she asked. "Well come on, be a friend. Who were they, then?"

"As a matter of fact one was the man I brought here."

"Oh that fat man again." That was how she dismissed Phillips. "And the other?"

"She was a girl I work with in the office."

"I thought so," she said. "It's you quiet ones all over. You're not satisfied with the life we others must lead, you have to have romance."

He was embarrassed and delighted. He laughed.

"There wasn't much of that for me, believe us," he said.

"Which is what you say," she countered. "And how am I to credit anything you tell me? After what's occurred before my eyes, and in this very room?"

"Well, it's true enough," he said. "Jim snitched her from under my nose."

"I'm not sure this is quite nice," she remarked, gravely.

"You're dead right," he said.

"I wouldn't want you to think you could tell tales, here. After all, this is my place we're sitting in."

He made no reply. Again this did the trick.

"You were too slow, I'll bet, now weren't you?" she asked.

He laughed. Then she laughed.

"It takes all sorts to make a world," she said.

"Certainly does," he agreed. He was astounded that he could be so easy, sitting opposite. Perhaps she thought that, in the circumstances, it was too comfortable for him, because she next said, with obvious malice,

"If you're short of clothing coupons, why don't you ask my precious dad for some of his?"

"How on earth?" he asked, taken aback.

"Well you seemed very thick together. I only wondered. After all, at the age he is, he can't have much need."

"I couldn't," he objected cautiously.

"That's you all over," she said. "The few times you've been here I've watched you. What harm could there be to have a go?"

He did not reply.

"Because I'll bet he's asked you for things."

"Certainly has," Mr. Summers agreed.

"What sort of things?" she demanded.

"Asked me to come here," Mr. Summers reluctantly told her.

"What else?"

Charley gave way.

"As a matter of fact he was keen that I should tell you about Arthur Middlewitch," he said.

"I knew it," she cried, indignant. "Was there ever any girl as pestered? He can't leave me alone. Why there's nothing to Art. He's all talk and no do, that lad is."

Charley kept quiet.

"A woman can tell in a moment," she said, in a most superior way.

"Hope you didn't mind me passing it on?" he asked.

"Why no, you're sweet," she answered. He was surprised. She may have seen this, because she went on to explain.

"I've a lot to answer for, the way I made your acquaintance. But you will admit you came through the door in a peculiar sort of manner, the first time. Still, as I've said, I've a responsibility, it's not everyone who's in my position, the double of a dead woman with a child. Then, when we started off on the wrong foot, like we did, we never seemed to get straight, did we?"

"There it is," he said, still cautious.

"Well I must say I appreciate your seeing it my way," she told him. "Things haven't been easy for me. You know I lost my husband. Then mum came back to keep me company. And I was just about getting straight when these beastly buzz bombs started, and she had to go away again, of course. So now perhaps you realize," she ended.

"Tough luck," he said.

He was allowing himself a long examination of her appearance, as he had never dared to when they met previously. She was very well aware of this. But what she could not know was that it was directly due to Dot. This girl's treachery with Phillips had awakened him to possibilities, and now his eyes guardedly took her in while, at the same time, as never before, he got no impression of his Rose. He was comparing Nance with Miss Pitter. So that he ignored the girl he had loved, who was gone.

Nance was not big, but she was thick and solid where Dot came spindly. She had deep blue eyes, not pale like Dot's. He could not remember the colour of Rose's eyes, he found, then at once forgot Rose again. Her hair was black and strong. Her legs were thick. Her breasts were not afraid, like Dot's. And it seemed to him that Nance was stroking the cat in a way of her own. "Quite a girl," he thought.

"Well, that's enough of my troubles," she said. "Now then, over your coupons. If you haven't had what was your due when you were discharged, why don't you take it up with your Old Comrades Association?"

"My O.C.A.," he echoed. "I hadn't thought."

"Some people are making use of you, you know."

"How d'you mean?" he asked, delighted at the attention he was getting.

"My old dad, for one."

"He's not in the O.C.A., is he?"

"Of course not. Whatever's on your mind? No, he sent you here, didn't he? And it wasn't for you he did it, you can be sure of that. He wanted to keep track, now I'm alone once more, that's all. The next thing was, he got into a spin about poor Arthur Middlewitch. So he turned to you, didn't he? It's as plain as the nose on my face." Charley immediately fixed his eyes on her nose, which she wrinkled at him. "And what's even more obvious is, that you must consider yourself for a while. I mean, if you won't, there's no one else will, is there? Look, you want to ring the people up."

"Which people?"

"Your old Association of course. Stick out for your rights. Tell them you didn't make all those sacrifices to be treated like you're being now, when you're back. Make out it's their fault."

He laughed in admiration, more particularly of her looks.

"I don't know how you poor souls get on at your work, I really don't," she said. "I'll bet you're under her thumb all right."

"Whose thumb?" He was smiling.

"Oh, you can laugh, but I'm serious. What's the girl's name?"

"Pitter," he said. "Pitter is it?" She continued, "Because it's not funny what she served on you over the August. It's serious, that is."

He was embarrassed once more. "Well it's not...we didn't," he murmured, and could not finish.

"I know," she said, laughing. "But she played you up, now didn't she?"

"All right, she did." He was smiling again.

"And are you going to lie down under it?"

"I don't know," he said.

"I'd know if I was a man and in your shoes," she brought out. She was looking straight into his eyes.

He had a brain wave. He wanted to bring the conversation back to themselves.

"Might I ask a question?" he enquired.

"Why, go ahead," she said.

"What was the reason you changed your name back to your mother's?"

She turned her eyes away at this. Yet, when she replied, it was in exactly the same tone of voice that she had been using all along.

"Because when Phil was killed I was finished," she said.

If he was surprised that he had asked, he was almost struck dumb at the reply. "I know," he feebly murmured.

"I bet you don't," she countered in a loud voice.

"With me, it was Rose Grant," he explained, and yet it was as though he could do this painlessly, as of a rib that had been removed.

"I shouldn't wonder," she said, calmer. "But speaking about them," she went on, almost at random, so as to change the conversation, "Have you been down to Redham lately?"

"No."

"I wonder what's become of my dad?"

"Why?"

"Because I haven't heard from him."

"How's that?" he asked. "I haven't called on his behalf, you understand."

"I know that," she said. "No, it's only that he hasn't sent the usual these last two weeks, as a matter of fact."

"Look, if you're short . . ." he began, like a fool.

She took him up in her old manner, in just the way she had on his previous visits.

"Who d'you think you are?" she demanded, indignant. "Why I've never heard such a thing. I should imagine not, indeed."

Then he did cleverly for himself. He made excuses and left. It was to avoid trouble, as he considered. Actually it made her feel she was in the wrong. It set him up with her once more.

DIRECTLY after the August holiday there was another, and a worse, explosion in the office. Charley was seated in Corker's room, who was saying to him,

"It won't do Summers, won't do at all. I haven't said my last word yet about this card index of yours, but, man alive, you've got to understand me. There's no visible or invisible system, or whatever it may be, it doesn't exist, which can take the place of ordinary office routine. Now d'you comprehend that?"

"Yes sir."

"Because I'm telling you for the last time, for your own good, you can't just put one system over another, and then be satisfied to sit back and use the top one without any sort of a check. Let's get down to bed rock. Everything that's ordered out is ordered by the drawing office, isn't it?"

"Yes sir."

"And everything that's been delivered has an advice note, or should have. Right?"

"Yes sir."

"These advice notes are checked off for the quantities, and all that, against the copy orders in the drawing office? Well then, there's the system, the routine we've run on all these years. When Mr. Pike, or Mr. Benfield, or even I want to look into the position with regard to any contract, we turn up the copy order and find marked there what has been delivered and when, don't we?"

Charley stayed silent. He was very upset, and this choked him.

"Whereas, with these card indexes I let you install against my business instincts," Mr. Mead continued, red in the face, his neck congested, "you've superimposed them on the drawing office, there's two checks being kept, your own and Mr. Pike's. So you rely on your own, and it's let you down. Why has it? For the reason it's not accurately kept. It's untrue to the facts."

Charley could not answer.

"And what's the outcome? The stuff's coming along all anyhow. I've been into this, Summers. Take the fifth plant now. We've got the oven bodies in, we've enough of those for the next three consignments, but there's no trays when we're gasping for 'em. And why aren't there any? I'll tell you. It's easy. Because on your cards it's shown that five more sets of trays have been delivered than have actually been received. Yet, on the copy order, there's the right number given. You've fallen down. You're squint-eyed with your own system, while we get invoiced for goods like those extra oven bodies that we don't yet require, and shan't do for another six months. Think of the financial side, man."

"Yes sir," Charley said.

"Not to mention the question of storage space. Besides that's the very job we entrusted you with. To bring the stuff along, as and when it was required."

There was a long pause.

"What's that girl of yours like?" Mr. Mead asked.

Charley saw again an empty bed, Eton blue in the moonlight.

"Hard to say," he answered, at last. He was thinking of Dot.

"Is she accurate?"

Charley did not reply.

"Well she can't be, can she?" Mr. Mead answered himself. "No, I'm not altogether blaming you, my boy," he went on. "These days there's nobody can get any assistance. And when you came with this idea of yours about a card index, Mr. Pike, he did say to me, quite rightly, that his view was you couldn't always be running into his office to look up the details in the order book. Not while he's using it making out fresh orders."

This argument seemed more promising to Charley.

"There it is, sir," he agreed.

"But dammit, that's no excuse when all's said. Two wrongs don't make a right, do they? We've got to take steps. There's nothing for it but you'll have to stay late and check through every blessed one of them cards, till you know there's not an error left. Either that, or we shall be in queer street."

"I was going to, anyhow, Mr. Mead, starting tonight," Charley said.

"I know you were," the man replied in a kinder voice. "Knowing you as I do I wouldn't have supposed any different. But what's that girl of yours like?" he repeated.

Charley tried to be loyal. He did not reply.

"There's nothing between the two of you, is there?" Mr. Mead enquired.

"How d'you mean, sir?" Charley said, although he knew only too well.

"You mustn't misunderstand me," Corker began. "I remember when I was in the Directorate in the last war, we had an instance of that very same kind. The Controller's personal assistant and his typist. She was an Irish redhead. And the end was, that by 1919 this country had one million more of what we were buying in that office than it needed. Very tricky the situation became for a week or two, after the Treasury jumped on it. They'd been looking into one another's eyes, those two had, Summers, instead of at the work piled up on their desks."

"Not me. I . . ." Charley started, then was interrupted.

"That's all right, my boy," Mr. Mead was saying, while Charley asked himself if Corker could have got hold of a buzz about their August holiday together. Because this man would never credit the truth, how Phillips had cut him out. "But it's a bit difficult for you young fellows, I shouldn't wonder, after what you've been through, prisoner of war camps, and all that," Mr. Mead was going on.

"She's not used to the work," Charley broke in, hoping to draw a red herring across the trail.

"But is she willing?" Mr. Mead asked.

Then, only because she had not gone to bed with him, Charley came right out with it,

"She's not," he said.

"I don't like that, Summers," Mr. Mead announced. "It's not fair, that isn't. We're on important government work here and if she won't pull her weight, get down to things, then she's doing her country a grave disservice, Summers. I shall have to get on to the National Service Officer about her, that's all. I shan't like doing so, but there it is."

"Let me have one more try with her, sir."

Mr. Mead ignored this.

"You mean you can't rely on what she puts down on those cards of yours? What you're saying is, she plays fast and loose with you, isn't it? Because that's not right, that isn't, not right at all."

Charley could find nothing to add.

"Why, you'd think a woman who was a woman, coming in to help a boy with your record, over a stile which is a mite too high for him," Charley winced, "you'd think any decent natured girl would get down to it, and see she did her work honestly. You know what's in my mind? That it wouldn't do her any hurt if she got herself put in uniform, scrub floors for a change with the A.T.S."

Charley felt everything was getting beyond him.

"You send her to me," Corker demanded.

"Could I have just one more shot at her, sir?"

"Can't a man handle his own staff in his own office, Summers? You'll very much oblige me by doing as I tell you. Send her straight in when you get back to your desk and let me handle this. Thank you."

Charley dared say no more. He did as he was told.

Half an hour later Miss Pitter returned. She was not in tears, as he had expected, but her face was very white, and she was obviously beside herself. She stood just within the door, looking through him as if he was moonlight.

"Well, I'm off," she said.

He got up, pale as a bed, from behind his kitchen table desk.

"How's that?" he asked.

"I've had plenty, that's how," she announced. "I told him so. 'Very good Mr. Mead, if you'll release me I'll make my application to the National Service Officer,' I said. 'Tale telling, that's all there is in this blue hole of a firm,'" I said.

He stood silent.

"And no one to speak up for me," she began again.

He still said nothing. He gaped like those bed clothes.

"D'you know what they call you here?" she went on. "'Shoot me' that's the name they have for you." It was a pure invention, which in no way upset him.

"Shoot me?" he mildly repeated.

"Because of your martyr ways, with what you've had in the war, and your Rose," she said.

It was water off a duck's back, nevertheless he remained wary. She could not now hurt him through the war, or through Rose. Then he denied his love for the third, and last, time.

"Rose?" he said. "Her? Oh, she was just a tale."

"I'll be bound," she replied. "Well I shan't be seeing you again, thank God," and rushed out, slamming the door after. He sat down once more, considerably astonished on the whole. Then she put her head in a last time. She was crying so much it made her face look like a pane of glass in the rain.

"I didn't mean what I said about you with the war," she said, and was gone. That's that, he thought, coming alive once more. He turned his mind to the effort he would have to make to go through each one of his precious cards. He dreaded it.

But he did feel somehow ashamed.

So CHARLEY came in for a period of hard work, in which he stayed late at his place of business, kept it up weekends, and quite forgot about life outside the office in an attempt to get straight with his job. Then one afternoon, about the time he was beginning to feel confident he had got the hang of those deliveries again, Miss Whitmore rang him.

"It's Nance," she said.

"Trant's?" he answered. "To do with these valves?"

"No, Nance," she said. "Is it convenient to speak?"

"I say, I'm sorry. Go ahead."

"I know you're very busy," she began, "but I'm so worried. The fact is, I've had bad news from Redham."

"Redham?" he enquired.

"Don't tell me you've put us all away out of mind. My dad of course. Mr. Grant. Art, you remember Arthur Middlewitch, now, don't you, he's heard somewhere my dad is very ill."

"Sorry to learn that," he said.

"Then it's news to you, is it? But you see I can't very well go down there myself as things are between dad and me. I was wondering if you'd mind dropping in on them some time. Just to set my nerves at rest."

"Why sure," he said. "What's happened?"

"I'm not certain. From all I can make out conditions are properly topsy turvy with them at the moment. I'd be so grateful, Charley. And they'd appreciate a visit from you."

"Glad to go," he replied. "How are you keeping?"

"I thought you'd forgotten about me."

"I have not. Tell you what. I'll call in there, then I'll come round and give you a report."

"That's very sweet," she gravely said. "Drop in for a cup of tea." She rang off. He lingered over the last phrase, whether she wasn't having him on perhaps. But she sounded really worried. So next Sunday he took a train out to Redham.

When he rang the door bell Mrs. Grant answered.

"Why Charley," she said. She kissed him. She looked just the same.

"Come into the front garden a minute," she went on. "You'll excuse the fallen leaves, but now father's laid up of course he can't see to them."

Charley was dumbfounded. So he kept silent. Mrs. Grant at once began to cry, softly.

"So you're back safe," she said between her tears. "It makes me think of my darling Rose." At this Charley's eyes immediately smarted, mostly from self pity. For this was the first time he'd had a real welcome back.

"My darling Rose," she repeated, quite naturally. "You mustn't mind. It brings the old days home to me," she said.

He did not know if he should mention his more recent visits. He thought better not, and once more took refuge in silence. But he kept hold of her hand, as though it was they who had been lovers.

"I thought I'd never get over it," Mrs. Grant began again. "Oh, and it must have hurt you, too," she said. "It's made me selfish."

"I couldn't go to the funeral," she went on, "no, I wasn't well enough. I haven't been well since it happened. Now father's very bad. Oh dear. Yes, I'll tell you about that in a minute. But I haven't asked after you yet, have I? I don't know what you'll think of me. Well, you're back now aren't you, Charley Barley?"

This calling him by his old name was almost too much for the man. He had a lump in his throat and had to swallow several times, so that he could not answer.

She gave his hand a squeeze. "Was it very bad?" she asked in just the voice his mother had used, dead these many years, and whom he never thought of, after the doctor put those stitches in his cut. This was much worse. He had to turn away. Yet he kept control of himself. Perhaps she noticed, for she continued,

"Don't you pay attention. But it is kind to come and visit us old folks. The dreadful part is that father's so ill just now. He's had a stroke. He's paralysed all down his right side, I'm afraid. He's quite conscious, which is the terrible thing, because he's lost the power of speech."

"That's bad," Charley said, recovering.

"I'm afraid he's done," Mrs. Grant said, and silently cried some more. "Sometimes I thank providence Rose is not here to see him."

"She never liked illness," Mr. Summers tried to comfort her.

"Oh this would have been different," Mrs. Grant softly objected. "She would be sitting up all night with her father if she was anywhere she could get to him. She'd never allow to have it mentioned about strangers, could she? But you were different. You remember when you had mumps so bad just before she married. Why, we had to have the doctor in to tell her it wasn't as serious as all that."

"I never knew," Charley muttered, examining in himself what he still felt for Rose, and finding nothing much.

"I often wish she had married you after all," she said, squeezing his hand again.

"There it is," Charley said. He had to be careful not to show he no longer cared about Rose. There was a silence.

"And how have you been?" he asked, because it frightened him that she should not remember his previous visit.

"Oh I've not been at all well," she replied. "But now this has happened to father, of course I've no time for my small bothers, have I? Charley, could I ask you something?"

"Why, go ahead."

"I've a little matter nagging me. There's a person should learn about Gerald. It's very awkward but I can't get in touch with them direct. They're a sort of relative. They should come down really."

"Who's that?" Charley asked, knowing full well, but anxious, for

Rose's sake, to hear it from the old lady herself. Dreadfully anxious, he realized he was.

"A Mrs. Phil. White," she replied. "Now, mind, father doesn't know I know about her, as a matter of fact," Mrs. Grant went on. "But I've been in touch on and off with her mother all these years. It's one of those little misunderstandings that occur in family life," she explained, while Charley felt surge all over him an exquisite relief. He felt this was the final confirmation that Rose was truly dead, that Nance was a real person.

"She isn't Rose," he brought out in a low voice, forgetting himself.

"Then you've known all along," Mrs. Grant said gently, missing what he had said.

"Only just recently," he answered, still quite vague, still at cross purposes.

"There's nothing to it," she said, to soften his embarrassment, as she thought. "It was just one of those things. I'll tell you. I wasn't at all in good health soon after we married, and he met this Mrs. Whitmore with someone I hope you'll never come across, for she's a wicked woman, Mrs. Frazier the name is. Then they had this girl. Oh now I see." As, at last, she had done. "You noticed the resemblance?"

He could find nothing to say. He just looked at her, and blushed.

"Oh Charley," she gently said.

He stood there.

"Why, they were not at all alike, really," she went on. From her voice he could tell that she was not blaming him.

"But how terrible for you to come back to that," she wondered aloud. "Whoever put you on to her?"

"It was Mr. Grant," he blurted, to excuse himself.

"That was cruel," she agreed. "Yet you mustn't lay blame, Charley. You know, poor dear, she lost her husband? Father was ever so worried. Oh, he thought I was in ignorance, but you can't live all those years with a man without you learn. And I didn't say anything to let on. Now he's so ill, the doctor thinks he can never get better, and there's the question of the little allowance he used to give. Then she should say goodbye, as well." Her tears began to come faster.

"She'd never take money from me," he objected, hardly knowing what he was saying.

"Whoever asked her to?" she explained. "Her coming down here is what should be arranged. She should. That's the only right thing, before it's too late. It's settled then. I knew I could rely on you, Charley. Now perhaps you'd like to see him." She began to dab a handkerchief at her round face. "Remember, he'll be able to hear every bit we speak," she warned, as she led the way into the house, and up the stairs.

Mr. Grant rested like a log in bed. All that was alive was his eyes. Charley stammered a good evening, adding a word about how well he was looking.

"Oh, he's not," Mrs. Grant broke in, "he'll never be better the doctor says," she announced loudly. "This is John,—I mean Charley Summers, dear," she went on in the same tone of voice. "Isn't it kind to pay you a visit?" Mr. Grant did not even blink. His shining blue eyes expressed nothing, although there was a sort of look of astonishment upon the whole frozen face.

It was some time before Charley could make his escape. In spite of the warning she had given, Mrs. Grant carried on in front of her helpless spouse as if he were deaf, and the man could give no sign that he heard. Charley supposed this was a judgement on Mr. Grant, but found it painful to watch, it was so innocently carried out; although Mrs. Grant's remarks on his hopeless state must come, it was plain, from an excess of feeling for her Gerald. And, when he did leave, he was not to get away at once, because he had hardly reached the bottom of the front garden before a car, with "Doctor" on the windshield, drew up at the gate.

"Good afternoon, young fellow," the elderly man inside said to Charley as he got out. Summers halted in his tracks, as though challenged. "You've been visiting here, I take it? I wonder if I might have a word. About Mrs. Grant," he said.

Charley waited.

"Quite impossible to get help these days," the doctor explained. "And it's too much for her. She has to do everything, you know."

"Can he hear?" Charley asked.

"What d'you mean, can he hear? Of course he can. I trust you haven't been saying one damn thing after another in front of my patient."

"I have not," Charley assured him, but with a great look of guilt.

"That's right," the doctor said, suspiciously. "I should hope not, indeed. No, what I wanted to impress upon you is, that we can't go on like this, with Mrs. Grant carrying everything on her own shoulders. I take it you're a relative? Because the burden's too much for her."

"When I was down, before he fell ill, she didn't recognize me," Charley said.

"Perfectly natural in her condition at the time," the doctor replied. "I've a number of cases like that, now. Comes from the bombing. After you've reached a certain age, as you'll find when you get there, nature provides her own defence, she's merciful, she draws a black-out over what she doesn't want remembered. Or rather the nervous system rejects what is surplus to its immediate requirements. But in a crisis everything is thrown overboard, of course. She recognized you today because of the shock Mr. Grant's health has been to her system. But we've got to get assistance to her, or she may slip back."

Charley had not understood. "Yes," he said.

"Very well, that's settled then, I'll rely on you," the doctor called to Charley, who was already moving away. "Excuse me," he added, "but what's the matter with your right foot?"

"It's off," Charley meekly explained. "Artificial leg."

"Really?" the doctor said. "I thought I noticed something."

HE RANG Nance to fix a date, then went to tea. He found quite a spread, fried fish warmed up, and an imitation chocolate cake she had wangled somewhere.

"You shouldn't have bothered," he said.

"It's no trouble. I couldn't let you travel all that distance to Redham for nothing," she replied. The truth was, her free time lay lonely on her. She was glad, now, to have him round.

"It's not so good," he began, and gave a description of how he had found Mr. Grant. She listened, seeming to be unmoved. "And there she was, after pretty nearly telling me not to speak a word in front of him which he wouldn't wish to hear, there she was on about he could never get well." His indignation made Charley speak out. "What d'you make of that? I felt such a twirp in front of the doctor."

"She couldn't help herself, poor thing," Miss Whitmore explained. "It was too much, you see. Don't distress yourself. You needn't suppose he would listen. Anyway we shall never know now, will we? But that's bad about his health then, Charley, isn't it?"

"Certainly is," Mr. Summers replied.

"I reckon I ought to drop in on them one day, don't you?" she said. "I could lend a hand."

"He wouldn't care for that," Charley objected. "From what he told me the other time, he was aiming to keep you dark."

"But he sent you to see me, Charley?"

"That's as may be," Mr. Summers took her up, "yet he'd never have let it out to Mrs. Grant."

"Won't you have the other piece of fish?" she asked. "Go on. I couldn't. We have a lovely canteen, really, where I work. Well, you can't tell how much he's let on to her, can you? There's not a great deal wives don't get to know, believe me."

"Yes," he said, his mouth full, "you've had experience."

If he had been looking he would have seen her eyes fill with tears at this, but he wasn't.

"Anyway," she said, "we'll never learn now about my dad, if he doesn't get better."

"Pretty rotten, though, to upset him, the shape he's in at the moment."

"Why, how d'you mean?" she asked.

"By you going down," he explained.

"Yes, but I can't just leave her to herself, can I?" she said. "With dad like that? The only bother is Panzer."

"The cat?"

"My darling puss."

"But you wouldn't be there all that amount of time."

"Oh well, you know how it is," she said, "either you do a thing properly or not at all. I was thinking I ought to go each day, after what you've told me. Why, your cup's empty. Why didn't you ask? If you don't speak up for yourself there's no one will do it for you, you know. Sitting with an empty cup, indeed."

"You are certainly looking after me," he said.

"And how do you manage at your lodgings?" she enquired. "D'you get your rations? I know those old landladies all right."

"Oh there's nothing of that sort about Mrs. Frazier," he told her. "Which reminds me. Mrs. Grant said Mrs. Frazier used to know your mother."

"It's news to me," she replied, uninterested. "Well I hope I know where my responsibility lies. I'll go down to Redham to find that poor woman, and see if I can't lend a hand round the house."

"What about your job?"

"Who, me? I'm on nights, as I told you. I've got the daylight hours to myself."

He felt absolutely comfortable. He could be free, or so he was beginning to imagine, when in her company.

"You're not like some, then," he said.

"What d'you mean? Of course I'm not. There's not everyone who's on night work."

"I didn't mean that, I meant who'll take their coats off. I had a girl in my office who wasn't fit even to copy a thing down."

"You explained about her."

"I did? Excuse us, I don't think so?"

"Wasn't she the girl you took away with you over the August?" She was laughing at him as she asked this. He ruefully laughed back.

"There you are," he said.

"I'm not," she said, "but you are," and pleasantly laughed some more.

He could not get over how easy all this was.

"No, about Redham now, you can't tell what effect you might have on his health when he sees you," he said.

"You're a man, so you think of him. I'm a woman, and I consider her. You don't want 'em both to fall into neglect, surely? I've a responsibility to those two."

"She knows about you," he carelessly announced. She cannot have liked this for she said,

"Let's have less about me and more regard to the old people. Why, I'd have no respect for myself if I didn't go down. The work here's nothing. I could look in on them every afternoon."

"Well that's grand," he said, letting it go at last. "I'm sure they'd be very grateful. I see you're using my cup."

"There wasn't anything else for it," she replied, tart. "I only had the two when you broke yours. They're a terrific price these days."

"I can't imagine what you can have thought."

"I know right enough," she said, laughing gaily.

"What did you?" he asked, very shy.

"You want to learn too much too soon," she replied. "Anyway, it took a bit of forgetting, but I've forgotten now all right."

"All's well that ends well, then."

"Least said, soonest mended," she agreed.

"She wants to keep up the allowance he made," Charley told her, greatly daring, for he did not know how she would take this.

"Why, that's generous. But you seem to be pretty well acquainted with my personal affairs now, don't you?"

He looked at her. It was all right. She was keeping quite pleasant.

"Excuse us will you, please? None of my business, naturally."

"O.K.," she said. "Only it was queer the way we met, and now here you are knowing so much I've no idea what you haven't learned."

"It's luck," he explained. "Chance, that's all."

"Have another cup," she offered. "Look," she said, "when you were down at Redham, did you ask about those spare coupons like I advised?"

"How could I?"

"Well, there's something in that. I'll tell you what. I will, when I go. It'll come easier from me."

He thanked her confusedly. He was amazed that she should be so kind.

"Have you heard anything about Art lately?" she asked.

"Art?"

"Arthur Middlewitch?"

"No, why?"

"There's a change come over him. He's not the same man at all."

"I couldn't say," he announced.

"Oh I'm not sending you after him as I did after my old dad," she laughed. "Don't you fret. No I only asked. I thought you might have come across him in the ordinary run of business."

"Not me," Charley said. "He's out of my street altogether in the C.E.G.S. Got a big job there, Arthur has."

"I wonder."

"How's that?"

"I fancy Art's in some sort of trouble. There's no other way of explaining his manner these past few weeks. And I don't know about his position with them. I shouldn't be surprised if you don't hold down just as important a position at Meads."

"Me? I'm only the office boy."

"Then why, when I rang you up, did the telephone lady call you their production manager?"

"Oh, that was just Miss Whindle."

"What are you, then?"

"That is my job as a matter of fact," he said.

"There you are. You've got to get wise to yourself. Why, if Art came to your firm he'd be glad to take a place under you."

"If he didn't sit in my own chair at my own desk."

"No, you're not being fair to the man, or to yourself," she said. Soon after this, he thought it would never do to outstay his welcome. So he made his departure. She noticed he didn't say a word about when they might meet again. Of course, it was not for her to suggest.

IN THE next three weeks he called thrice at Miss Whitmore's, but had no answer when he manhandled the dolphin on her door. She could only have been out. Finally he realized she must be going to Redham each afternoon. The following Sunday he went down there.

When he rang the bell, she answered as though it was her own house.

"Hullo dear," she said. He was touched at this.

"Come in. There's not much change in dad," she went on. Back in the hall, she dropped her voice. "Art's here," she told him.

"Oh," Mr. Summers said, suspicious.

"He's come out with it," she continued, almost in a whisper, "he's lost his job, or rather his firm have written to the M.O.L. to say they want him withdrawn. Poor old Art, it is a shame. And he's dropped in to find if dad could put a word for him. He hadn't heard, you see. Mother's with him this minute."

"You've got your mother back from Huddersfield?"

"No, Mrs. Grant, of course," she answered.

"I see."

"Oh, I'm glad I came," she said. "It was too much for her, by far. And he's so good lying in his bed, with never a murmur of any kind."

"Can he speak a bit, then?" he asked.

"Of course not. You can tell by his expression," she explained in a loud voice. "I wondered when I'd see you again," she added, more quietly.

"Called round on you twice as a matter of fact, and you were out," he told her.

"That's nice," she said. "Now you'd like a word with dad, I expect," and led him upstairs.

He found Mr. Grant lying shuteyed, but otherwise in the same position as previously, motionless, speechless, hopeless as he must have been. After Charley had muttered a greeting, Miss Whitmore rattled on to the sick man exactly as though he was a child. Even if he had so wished, Charley could not have got a word in edgeways. He looked at the lowered lids. He wondered what they covered. Then he saw Nance nod to him. He stammered a phrase, and got out of the room.

"You are mean," she said, the other side of the door. "I meant for you to talk to him a few moments."

"I couldn't," he explained, as he came down the stairs.

"I know. It is awkward at first," she agreed. "But you soon get so you don't notice."

"Will this go on for long?"

"The doctor says he may be carried off any day. Mother's being wonderful, simply wonderful."

At this moment Middlewitch and Mrs. Grant came out into the small hall, in that order. The four of them hardly had room to move. His manner with Summers was very different.

"Why, hullo, Charley my dear old man," he cried, at his most effusive. "Well, this is a bit of a surprise, running across you here," he said, as though he owned the place. "We must have a chat one of these days," he was continuing, while Charley leant across to shake Mrs. Grant by the hand.

"Why, Charley Barley," she greeted him, quite composed. "It's good of you to travel all this way to visit us old folks."

"How is he?" Charley asked.

"You've just come from him, haven't you? I heard you mount the stairs. You noticed the change there is, didn't you? He's ever so much easier."

"That's fine," Charley said.

"But the doctor says it might happen any moment," she went on calmly. Summers turned for the first time to Arthur Middlewitch. But this man's mind was plainly miles away. He was preoccupied.

"Oh, don't speak like that," Charley protested to Mrs. Grant.

"It's got to come to one and all of us, Charley," she told him, quite composed. "He doesn't suffer, I know. I know," she repeated, insistent. There was a pause.

"That's right," Charley said.

"Well I must be getting along now," Mr. Middlewitch broke in. "I'll give you a tinkle one of these days," he added to Charley. "And it certainly has been grand of you, Mrs. Grant, to listen as you've just done. I'm sure when I dropped in I never..." and he stopped. Then he hurriedly made his goodbyes, and left.

"I don't much cotton onto that young gentleman," Mrs. Grant mentioned.

"Now there's no harm in Art, mother," Nance said. "He's worried, that's all."

"I must get back to my grand old man," Mrs. Grant announced waving them into the living room. "And I know you two young people must have a deal to say to one another," she added, arch. Charley looked at her unseeing. He was shy. He could find nothing to come out with. But when Mrs. Grant was gone, and Nance was settled down opposite, it was she did all the talking.

"That's what I'll never forgive this war," she began, unexpectedly, "never so long as I live, that at the end I couldn't be with...with Phil," she brought out, and turned her face away so he couldn't see it. Charley stayed miserably silent.

"After all, that's the least you can ask of life," she went on, "to have your loved ones round you when you go. But in this war it's not what anyone can expect with these beastly bombs."

"Was he killed by a bomb, then?" was all Charley could think to ask.

"No, of course not," she replied, still speaking in the same quiet voice. "He was brought down in his airplane over Egypt. That's what's cruel, my not being there, not being able to hold his darling head. Because dad, now, has got us round him. And he's very fond of you as well, Charley. Mother told me. But when I had to let Phil go, there was none by him, no one at all. He was alone."

There followed a silence. At last Charley brought out, "You mustn't distress yourself," although she had been speaking quite collectedly. He could not look at her.

"You don't understand," she said, soft. "He died for us," she explained. She had told him this before but it was very different now, it was as if she were making him a gift. "He went out alone without me, that's what's so hard for me to bear," she ended. Then she added,

"That's why I changed my name."

There was a long silence.

"Well it certainly is good of you to come down. It's not as though you didn't have a job of your own," he managed to say.

"She's asked me to live here the next few weeks. They have a splendid train service still. I'd use her room. She takes what rest she can in an easy chair by his bed. She has to do everything for him, you know. But of course she'd rather have it that way. The only thing is Panzer."

"Panzer?" he echoed, at a loss.

"Why yes, I couldn't leave my puss the very moment she's likely to need me, could I? So this is just what I wanted to ask. Would it be all right, d'you think, if I brought her down?"

"I'm sure Mrs. Grant wouldn't . . ." he began.

"It's not that. No, what's exercising me is, will Panzer stay here?" she demanded. "Because if she started off on a long trek back home, I should go right out of my mind. I'm scatter brained enough already, though you mightn't think."

"I certainly wouldn't . . ." he began again.

"Oh but I am," she insisted at once. "Why only the other day," she went on, plunging into a long description of some minor detail she had forgotten while she was doing for Mr. Grant. When she finished he casually asked, having, as he thought, got over the awkwardness,

"Does he recognize you?"

She answered, "Would you believe, I'm sure he thinks I'm Rose, you remember that's my half sister," she explained, forgetting all about him.

Then the bell rang.

She went to answer the door. His mind was in a turmoil while he heard her say, "Yes?"

But he listened intently when he heard Mrs. Frazier explaining to Nance that she was an old friend of the family, and that she had dropped in on the chance of visiting Mr. Grant, if he was not too ill.

"I'll see," Nance replied. She then called loudly up the staircase to Mrs. Grant, "Here's a Mrs. Frazier come to call on dad."

The response was immediate. Mrs. Grant came to the head of the stairs. From where he was sitting Charley could see her face, which was hidden from the others. It was a terrible dark purple, altogether unlike her natural rosy cheeks. She at once began shouting, "I won't have that woman inside my house, I won't have her, not her I won't," and much else that was too vague, or allusive, for Charley to follow, though he could not mistake the sightless rage. At this Mrs. Frazier started off in her turn.

"This is a strange thing," she cried from below. "There's something wrong going on here, it's not right, this isn't," but she did not make too much fuss, and, when Nancy shut the door in her face, she made off down the front garden quite quietly. Miss Whitmore ran upstairs to comfort the old lady, who was loudly sobbing by the open door to Mr. Grant's room, led her back into it, and shut the door on them both.

While Charley wondered how much had come through to the old man, the sound of Mrs. Grant's crying died away, then ceased altogether.

Summers began to fidget about his coupons. And it was almost as though she were a thought reader that Nancy said, when presently she came back into the living room, "I don't forget all the time, you know," as she handed over a whole unused book of them.

"I say, you shouldn't," he began, when she cut in with,

"Don't worry your head." She spoke simply and without affectation. "He won't need very many more of those, I'm afraid," she said.

WHEN HE went down to Redham the next Saturday evening, Nancy opened the door, as she had done the last time.

"He's much better," she said in a low voice. "He's resting."

Then, as she took over Charley's hat, she added,

"See who's here." He looked down to see the bloated cat, which raised its tail and terribly glared at him.

"Yes, my own sweet puss," she went on, "who's as good as gold, that doesn't go out after nasty toms, never even tries to get back to London, does she?"

Mrs. Grant came into the hall.

"Why Charley," she said, "this is so thoughtful of you." Then she, in her turn, turned it off onto the cat. "You know I've never properly cared about them," she went on, "but this beauty is altogether different."

"Had her kittens yet?" Charley enquired.

Both women laughed.

"How could you ask such a thing?" Miss Whitmore exclaimed. "Isn't that just like a man, mother? Why you've only to glance at the poor sweet to tell, haven't you, my great, big, Panzer darling? She's going to have quads, we've settled on that, haven't we, dear?" she announced to Mrs. Grant, although there had been no word between them on it. "Two tabbies and two gingers. Wouldn't that be wonderful?" Then she realized what she had done, risked a glance at Charley, and at the old lady. But it was plain they were not making this a red herring.

"Come along," Mrs. Grant waved him into the living room, "sit down, do, and make yourself at home."

"I wouldn't wish to interrupt..." he brought out.

"Why, he's resting," the older woman explained. "He's got a bell right by his hand, on the good side, that he can thump away at when he needs. He's getting ever so expert, isn't he, Nancy?"

"Half the time he bangs the thing just to see us run," Miss Whitmore said.

"Oh he's very good, so patient really," Mrs. Grant protested, and smiled.

"Of course he is. He's a marvel," Miss Whitmore agreed. At that instant the bell did feebly jangle and Nance rushed out of the room, up the stairs.

"She's been wonderful, Charley, I shan't ever be able to forget to my dying day," Mrs. Grant told him. "More like the darling I lost than I could imagine."

"There it is," Summers said.

To his surprise she took this up.

"I could never have dreamed," she elaborated. "It's as if Rose had come back."

"There is a resemblance," Charley commented, without conviction.

"I'll never allow that," she said, in a wondering sort of voice. "But, well, the picture a mother carries is very different, I dare say. No, it's the loving kindness. Why that child's so good she hides a real heart of gold. And she's had her own dark times, too."

"Yes," Charley agreed, happy and free.

"There's something she wanted me to mention, now she's not here for the moment," Mrs. Grant said.

"Yes?" he prompted, beginning to feel excited.

"It's about Mr. Middlewitch," the older woman went on. Charley felt let down. "I don't say I think the world of that man myself, but after all we're all here to help one another, aren't we? And now I've come to realize what Nancy's nature is, I can't believe she'd be mistaken in anyone. She's so sensitive that she simply learns father's wants before he has time to realize what they may be. I know. I've seen it," she insisted.

He sat quiet, waiting, and drank in this praise.

"No, it's only that Mr. Middlewitch has lost his job. Some little disagreement at the office, nothing unpleasant I'm sure. He's told her. Now, if you could put a word in for him, where you work, I'm certain it would make all the difference. You see the control's speaking of sending him up north. Because he explained to me there's a young lady he's interested in. Just now it would break his heart to be moved out of London, with things as they are between the two of them."

"Who's the girl?" Charley asked, beginning to dread.

"Well, dear, as father always would say, a confidence is a confidence, it's sacred, and it's not for us to break it. Why, I do declare," she then cried out, delighted, "I believe I can see what's troubling you. He's nothing to her. You needn't think of that again. He even mentioned the name, as a matter of fact. She's a young lady out in South London. Now, Charley Barley, whatever made you such a goose?"

"Me?" he said. "I didn't say a word." He was horrified at what he seemed to have let out.

"You young people," she commented, peaceably. "So you will, won't you? That's settled then."

He could not be sure what she meant, did not dare ask. She saw the look on his face, and giggled.

"Don't mind me," she begged. "I might be your own mother, when all's said and done. Why not put a word in for him, which is all I'm suggesting? Every day I open the papers I see how short-handed everyone is, and I don't imagine where you work can be any different. He's a boy father helped when he first came to London, son of an old business associate I believe. I'm sure Gerald would be ever so grateful if you could. It was for father's sake Nance asked me to mention him."

"Can't rush things. I'll have to look about me," Charley promised, intending to do no such thing.

"I can set my mind at rest on that, then," Mrs. Grant announced. "But I won't breathe a word if you'd rather I didn't."

"And how have you been keeping, mother?"

"There, that's like the old days once more, your calling me mother again," she said. "Dear, dear, it does bring it all back. You two children sitting in here as bold as brass, just like you were grown up, seeming to dare father and me to come in and disturb you. Many's the laugh he and I had over it, bless him. But Rose was so wilful, wasn't she? Of course, it's true she was an only child. No one could say a thing to her, could they?"

He no longer wanted to hear about Rose. To change the subject he tried to bring things back to health.

"You're looking very fit," he said.

She misunderstood his drift.

"You don't like talking about her, do you?" she gently asked. "Yes, it does come hard at first. You know for a long time after that happened I couldn't bear it, I had to put the whole thing behind me or lose my reason. Then the doctors gave father some wrong counsel, and he used to keep on to make me remember. Oh, things weren't easy for me, I'm sure."

"I came down, d'you recollect?" he said, to get her off Rose.

"I don't know whether I do or I don't," she replied, and he was horrified to find a sudden look of sly cunning begin to spread over her placid face.

"When's the cat expecting her kittens?" he hastily enquired, proud that he'd thought of it.

She would not meet his eyes. She began looking sideways. Then he was shocked to see that she was covering her mouth with a hand.

"Asking me a lot of questions," she mumbled.

At that moment Nance came back. She took all this in, at a glance. "He only wanted his bed made more comfortable," she announced, in a cheerful tone of voice. "Now he's dozed off into such a nice sleep. And mother, I really do believe you should lie down for a moment, if you're to sit up with him later."

"Yes dear," the older woman agreed. She went out on Nancy's arm, without saying goodbye to Charley.

"Don't you go," Nancy said over her shoulder, in what he took to be a menacing voice, "I'll have something to say to you, later."

He sat on, feeling guilty.

When she came back she asked, "Now what have you been saying to her?" but, from the tone she used, she did not seem to be put out. Indeed she appeared to take everything about this house in her stride, and, at the same time, to pump life into it.

"Me? Nothing," he said.

"You've been on about your Rose, I'll be bound," she told him, and seemed disinterested. "That's always liable to bring back one of mother's turns. And Rose can still do the same with you, you know she can."

"She can't," he protested.

"Tell that to the Japs," she replied.

"Which is an Arthur Middlewitch expression," he said, with resentment.

"And why not?" she asked.

"Only that Mrs. Grant says, now, you want to find him a job."

"Don't let's argue," she answered, still quite calm and friendly. "Art's all right. He's no more than another lame dog the wrong side of a stile. No, I wasn't questioning your turning the conversation onto the daughter. It was people's hearts I blamed, which lead them to do hurt to themselves. I know. I've had some."

"You mean your husband?" he brought out, daring, and as though he had made a wicked discovery. There was a pause. He was careful not to look at her.

"Well, what did your Rose mean to you?" she began, rather wild. "Was she a part of you? Did you wake with her in the morning? Did you know what was in her mind when she was a thousand miles overseas. Oh Phil," she said, and could not go on.

He felt an absolute criminal.

"Now what's this?" he weakly protested.

"I'm sorry," she replied, pulling herself together. "It wasn't your fault. I started it," she said. "Tell you what, let's get out of here for a few minutes. Everyone's been on edge in this house, lately."

"What about your work?"

"I'm off on Saturday nights, didn't you know?"

"But can she manage? I mean, will it be all right?"

"Yes, you needn't fuss," she said. "The moment mother hears that bell he has, she's round his bed, day or night. There's not much she lets me do, really. It's everything for her, his being like he is."

"Are you certain?"

"Oh well, if you don't want to come. I was only thinking I couldn't stand this another moment, if I didn't get a breath of air."

"If you say it's O.K.," he said. It seemed heartless that Mrs. Grant should be left alone with the sick man, just when she had been taken up to rest. But he humbly realized he knew very little. And this is just what she proceeded to tell him.

"Don't look at me with that expression on your face," she said, very friendly. "You can't understand about her, never will I expect. Now, don't go and forget we're off for a stroll in less than five minutes. It would be like you," she called back to him, as she went to put on her shoes.

"Where shall we go?" she asked, when they got outside.

"Wherever you like," he offered.

"I don't know this part," she pointed out. "Lord, aren't there any Lovers' Lanes round here, or anything?"

He laughed. "I wouldn't know," he said.

"Oh yes you would, dear. Take me where you used to take her, then."

He laughed again. "You'd have to dye your hair," he said.

She wasn't going to have that.

"Here, who d'you take me for?" she demanded. "It's disgusting, that is."

"I'm sure I didn't . . ."

"Oh yes you did, or you wouldn't have said. Now where? Left or right?"

"This way," he answered, and she put her arm through his as they set off.

"You aren't leading me to one of those kid's places, six trees and a bit of railing, where they lie up of an evening?"

He risked a lot. "Wait and see," he told her. It was all right, because she laughed.

Rain had been pouring down all summer, with the result that this October was the hottest in years. It was a red sunset for them, but, even so, too cold to sit out. There was no wind, everything was quite still. They walked at a smart pace, in silence, and in five minutes were leaving the cheaper estate, on which Mr. Grant had bought his own residence, for a road which ran through wide gardens with expensive houses, one or two of which were blitzed.

Autumn was the season, most roses were dead. Petals that had dropped some months back and rotted, traces of a summer now gone, were covered by the brown leaves which even in this still air rocked down to lie deep on the ground as they walked, so that their feet rustled. Where a flying bomb had dropped recently, the drift of leaves was still green underfoot, the trees bare as deep winter. Then, just as they were passing this spot, the syrens set up a broken wailing.

"Come on," he said, turning off the road into the garden of a house in ruins.

"Why, surely you never took her here?" she asked, for the place could only have been blitzed a few days.

He laughed.

"Or are you nervous?" she wanted to know.

"Not of them," he answered.

"Why not?" she demanded, as they skirted what was still standing, against the untouched chimney a lone staircase which descended from nothing to the leaf-covered drive, the steps blotched with a dust of plaster, and all of it turned a great red by the setting sun, her face as red as his own. "Why not?" she repeated.

"Don't know," he answered, hurrying her along.

"Where are we going?" she asked, and seemed content. He knew no more than she. But when they got round the red garage, which was intact, and a privet hedge, which, in this light, and because it was shaded, burned a dark glowing violet, they found what had been the rose garden, enclosed with a low brick wall, and then they had before them, the outlines edged in red, stunted, seemingly withered, rose trees which had survived the blast as though it had never happened, and, for a screen at the back, a single line of dwarf cypresses, five feet high with brown trailing leafless briars looped from one to the other, from one black green foliage to its twin as green and black, briars that had borne gay rose, after rose, after wild rose, to sway under summer rain, to spatter the held drops, to touch a forehead, perhaps to wet the brown eyes of someone idly searching these cypresses for an abandoned nest whence fledglings, for they go before the coming of a rose, had long been gone, long ago now had flown.

Both instinctively looked back to find whether they were being followed, but all they saw was the red mound of light rubble, with the staircase and chimney lit a rosier red, and, as they turned again to themselves in the garden, the briars wreathed from one black cypress to another were aflame, as alive as live filaments in an electric light bulb, against this night's quick agony of the sun.

Then, before he knew what she was about, she had put her arms round his neck, and kissed him.

"There," she said into an ear. "That's for coming down."

But he put his hands behind her head, pressed her kissing mouth harder on his own. The night, on its way fast, was chill, and now he had again that undreamed of sharp warmth moving and living on his own, her breath an attar of roses on his deep sun-red cheek, her hair an animal over his eyes and alive, for he could see each rose glowing separate strand, then her dark body thrusting heavy at him, and her blood dark eel fingers that fumbled at his neck.

She cruelly spoiled it. She took her sweet lips off his.

"Was it like that?" she asked, as though nothing had happened.

He made to grab her up to him once more. But she twisted away.

"Was it?" she repeated. He did not realize that she was aiming at Rose.

Then, in the position she held, half in, half out of his arms, and so close that the one eye in his line of vision was in the outer corner of its socket to watch him, he saw it catch the dying sunset light around, and glow, as if she had opened the eye hole to a furnace.

He made another clutch at her, but she broke away completely. He was left, so that his arms hung at his sides, and he could not speak, paralysed, for an instant, as Mr. Grant.

"I'm sorry, dear," she said, annoyed with herself. He did not move, or speak.

"It's too cold to sit. We'd best go back," she said.

So they walked home in silence. In the dark she took his arm once more, pressed close. But he said and did nothing at all. He couldn't even feel.

WHEN THEY got home in the dark, Nance found she had left her key behind. They were obliged to ring the bell. They heard pattering footsteps. Then Mrs. Grant flung the door open.

"Oh so it's you," she said, in an accusing voice. A lock of grey hair lay unexpectedly over her forehead. "He's had a bad turn," she went on, almost wailing suddenly, "he's ever so ill, my darling is, come quick," this to Nancy, for she chose to ignore Charles. "Where could you have got to? I don't know how you could."

As the two women hurried upstairs, Miss Whitmore called out to Summers, "Wait there. Don't go," she said.

He was still absolutely dazed by the scene he had had with this girl, and it was not until Charley got into the living room, and was faced by a chair overturned, that he knew there was disaster in the wind, because the whole house had always been completely neat.

So that, on top of everything else, he began to dread what was due.

Then just as he was putting the chair to rights, a car drove up.

It was the doctor.

As Charley opened the door the doctor said, "What's this?"

"Don't know quite," he replied, ashamed.

"How's that?" the man asked, obviously despising him, as, in his turn, he hurriedly climbed out of sight into an upstairs deathly silence. Charley re-entered the living room, sat down, put his hands on his face.

The worst part was he could hear nothing, nothing at all. The eyelids burned over his eyes, and were as red as that sunset. Now that he could begin to think, he wondered if this whole affair wasn't another Dot Pitter. Then he saw he was useless on account of his being so slow. That time, in the office, when he put his face against hers because she was crying, had led to his call on Nance, which had caused him to take Dot down to Jim Phillips, which, in its turn, had pushed him on here to Nance. "Oh Rose, Rose," he cried out in himself, not noticing that he did this without having real regret, "Oh, why did you?" He began to cry, in his self pity seeing himself again with his hands, like a monkey's, hung up on the barbed wire which had confined him within the camp.

He felt a touch on his shoulder. It was Nance. She'd come back so quietly he hadn't heard. He sprang away, went to stand by the black-out.

"You shouldn't distress yourself," she gently said. "It's all my fault."

His mind came back to her kissing him. He thought she was referring to this. He said not a word.

"It was me decided we should go off out," she went on, thus disclosing that she missed the point. "You warned me, and I didn't listen," she added.

She could not think how she was to tell him what Mrs. Grant wanted. Because, while the doctor was starting his examination, the old lady had requested her to get Charley to stay over, to have a man in the house. And, after the manner he took her innocent kiss, Nance feared that Charley might accept this invitation as being from herself, for a certain purpose. Then she thought she saw this was the one way she could make him spend the night.

"I want to ask you something," she said, shyly, a bit of a martyr. He did not reply, or turn round.

"Don't go back to London this night," she asked, in a wheedling sort of voice. "You'll hardly catch the last train now," she explained. "You lie up on the sofa in this room. Maybe it won't be too bad," she said, to go as far as she dared.

She saw his back stiffen, as she imagined in refusal.

"Be a sport, Charley dear," she pleaded. "You don't have to be at work tomorrow."

He thought this must be it. He could not believe she'd ask this if she didn't mean to visit him later.

"Oh all right," he answered, and blew his nose.

"Why, that's sweet of you," she said, with a great feeling she was laying up trouble for herself, and how the one point was, that it would be in a good cause. "I've got to go back to them," she excused herself. "And when we're a bit quieter, I'll see if I can't knock you together a bite of supper. Now don't forget, you're to stay on, you know. Don't you go wandering."

When he turned about to thank Nance, to discover he did not dare hope what in the expression on her face, he found she was gone. So he sat down again. He could not tell quite what to make of it. But he knew what he wished.

Then he found the cat at his feet. It glared so directly into his eyes that he had to look away. The moment he did this, it jumped on his lap, lay heavy, and began to purr carrying its cargo of kittens. He stroked the animal, much, if only he had known, as the girl had kissed him an hour or so ago, though without the jealousy she had felt.

He noticed his fingers were brushing hairs off the cat's back, and raised the hand to sniff his nails. Then he wanted a good wash, but didn't like to move because of the creature on his knees. Oh, he felt, she could never have kissed me if it wasn't to lead somewhere, human beings don't play games like that with one another, Dot hadn't been up to anything even, it was only he'd been too slow, as Nancy said. Then what had she rushed away for, just now, he asked himself, when she twisted out of his arms? And, because she'd asked him to stay over, he had no idea at all, he could not imagine.

But what a night to choose. Wasn't it just like his luck the old man should have another bad turn, exactly when his own affairs promised better? Then, with surprising intuition, he supposed that one crisis in this life inevitably brings on another, that she wouldn't have kissed him if Mr. Grant had not been having a relapse (even if they neither of them knew), nor, and here he fell unwittingly on the truth, would she have asked him if it hadn't been for the now doubly serious illness. All the same, so to speak in spite of himself, he began to have hopes.

Yet, even if she wanted, he felt, there was nothing she could do about it. Mrs. Grant would come and go all the time, they'd never be able to avoid the old lady. But then Nance would not have invited him without she had some plan. And she'd find a way. Trust a woman, he concluded, as he heard the doctor come downstairs.

"Very sad," the doctor announced.

"It is," Charley agreed, at which he recollected himself.

"You don't mean he's..." he asked, and could not finish. After his war experiences he had a sort of holy regard for death in bed, whereas dying out of doors meant damn all to him.

"It may be any time," the doctor said. "Tell me, you aren't a relative?"

"I'm not," Charley replied. He could not think what was coming.

"You're staying here, though?"

"You bet I am."

"See they get all the rest possible, both of them, will you? Good night," the doctor ended.

Good night? Rest? Charley felt, that rather put the lid on it. Then he remembered the old man was passing on between his sheets, and felt ashamed.

He decided he must absolutely do something. So he went into the kitchen, found some dirty dishes, and got on with those.

Upstairs, in the sickroom, where Mr. Grant lay still as an alligator, and Mrs. Grant waited on a chair, up by his pillow, to hear him breathe, Nancy whispered,

"He's to stay mother. I'll make a nice bed for him, on the sofa." When Mrs. Grant did not reply, Nance got out a pair of blankets which, if she had only known, were those used by Rose before marriage, and went down to the living room.

Nance was shocked to find him absent. For a moment she wondered if the bird was flown. She discovered she could not blame him if he had gone. Then, hearing a noise in the kitchen, and thinking it might be burglars, poor old dad what a night to choose, she crept up to the door and looked through the crack. It did something to her to see him making himself useful.

But she did not yet make her presence known. She noiselessly arranged a bed on the furniture. And even that, she found, gave her a warm feeling again, his being so good, out there, with the dirty dishes. She told herself, "My girl, you're going all sentimental."

Nevertheless it was not until she was done that she went out, softly, to the sink. And, once more, he did not hear her coming, in this sickroom hush they now affected throughout the house, before she had kissed him from behind, on the neck. He jumped. She chose to ignore this.

"You're not so bad, after all," she said.

He put his arms round her and, luckily, was very gentle. He softly kissed the corners of her mouth, first one then the other.

"Oh Charley, isn't this terrible?" she asked, through it. His being so quiet, so good, melted her, and curiously urged her thoughts back to Mr. Grant. As for Charley, now that she seemed to be appealing, he felt somehow at peace. Again, more by luck than good judgement, he kept silence. He was beyond speech. He just mumbled with his lips at the corners of her mouth. This began to tickle her, and his mouth felt her smile. He kissed harder for it, only noticing those curled lips, at which she immediately drew back. And he did not press after her. He had his old feeling, that he must not be caught a second time.

She meant to tell about where he was to sleep, but she had an idea this was not quite the moment. So she held him at arm's length, with rather a martyred expression on her face.

"You're really sweet," she said.

"I'm sorry," he announced, in a low voice. He was apologising. He always would.

"What for?" she asked.

He said nothing.

"Don't you worry. You're all right," she said. "Look, I've made up your bed." She took his arm to show him. "You'll drop off in a tick of the clock."

"It doesn't matter," he assured her, as if mesmerised. "I never do much anyway."

"Why, how's that?" she demanded. "And after I've been to this trouble, all to make you comfy?"

"It's ever since I got back," he began.

"Heavens, we can't have another sick man, not just now, you know," she said.

He felt he was losing ground once more.

"I'll tell you what," she offered, as though giving a child the first refusal of a jujube. "I expect I'll be up and down all night, so I'll look to see if you want tucking in," she said.

His feelings were one tall question mark. She laughed.

"Well, you needn't look as if I'd given you a pain in the neck. Perhaps I'd better not, then."

He laughed awkwardly.

"If I were you I'd get your head down now, as my Phil used to say. I don't suppose we'll any of us get much repose this night." Then she was gone.

Now what could that mean, he asked himself, as he began to un-button his clothes?

When he had got underneath the blankets, he did not notice whether he was comfortable, or otherwise, but started to listen intently for her coming. He was struck, at once, by the absolute silence, the waiting quiet, as though something dirty was at work which might at any time come out in this darkness, and be green. Then he switched on a light, got off the sofa, and opened the door so, when she did come, that she could get in as quietly. He listened again in the doorway. What was before him of the house was in pitch darkness. He could hear no sound at all. He went back to bed. He switched out the lamp once more. Immediately he shut his eyes and rubbed them, green and red balls slowly revolved, turned pink, then were gone.

But how could she come, he asked himself, with all that dying in bed going on above? When the least movement could be heard throughout the house? He tried the sofa to find if it sounded. He bounced once, then twice, yes thrice, as he lay there. Each time it loudly groaned. There you are, he told himself, what a bloody row. She couldn't possibly manage, not here. What was that? A creak on the stairs? No, nothing. Besides, it wouldn't be decent, plumb under old Grant's bed. But who could tell about a woman? And if she did, would he be all right? He lit the lamp a second time, got himself a cigarette.

The house remained entirely still. Then he caught a sort of mutter in the springs he lay on, next, it was in the air itself, only very distant. Then, much too quick and to his great dread, it had become the vast interrupted hum of planes. They sailed by, as if revving up in hundreds up above him, roar after roar of engine, drone after drone, bound no doubt for the country where he had been imprisoned. It was as though, at a secret signal, every bomber in England, at the call of the queen, had taken off to go hugely hornet swarming, and on barbed wire. He had a horror of hornets. He felt sick. He went to the window, remembered, and rushed back to turn off the light. Shaking then, he watched the cloudless new moon sky, through glass. Each plane had one green and one red light, and that was all he knew while they rumbled over. He felt worse. The moonlit world was Cambridge and Eton blue, as he saw again in his mind the filthy moonlight on Dot's bed. He smoked a third cigarette. He got cold.

Then, almost as soon as he had slipped back under the blankets, in complete silence because the planes had passed, he fell uneasily asleep, and without another thought of Nance.

It was some time later that he was wakened by something, he did not know what, except that it was dreadful. A shout. Someone ran along to Mr. Grant's room. Nance? And slammed the door. Silence once again. Then it began in earnest. Another shout "Gerald." It was Mrs. Grant calling, so loudly that he could only just recognize her voice. "Gerald." "Gerald." And much more urgent, "D'you hear me?" "Oh d'you hear me, do speak." She was yelling now. "Gerald." After which the most frightful sobbing. "Gerald darling, Father, where are you?"; then, in a sort of torn bellow, "Father," then, finally, "Come back," and the culmination of all this was about to remind Summers of something in France which he knew, as he valued his reason, that he must always shut out. He clapped hands down tight over his ears. He concentrated on not ever remembering. On keeping himself dead empty.

He made himself study the living room. He forced himself to stay clear. And he saw the cat curled up asleep. It didn't even raise its ears. Then, at the idea that this animal could ignore crude animal cries above, which he had shut out with his wet palms, he nearly let the horror get him, for the feelings he must never have again were summoned once more when he realized the cat, they came rumbling back, as though at a signal, from a moment at night in France. But he won free. He mastered it. And, when he took his streaming hands away, everything was dead quiet.

Finally he heard her coming, at last. There could be no doubt. Instinct made him switch out the lamp. He waited in darkness.

When she got to the door, she turned every light on in this room. He sat up. "He's gone," she said, in a great voice. "It's over." She stood there proud, grave, and lovely.

"I've given her something to make her sleep," she explained, as she came over in her red dressing-gown. He could not speak. "Here, drink this," she said, "it's a drop of whisky." She did not mention that she had added a sleeping draught, to make him sleep also. In the wide sleeves her arms were like the flesh of peaches.

He took the glass. It was when he saw her as she was looking at that moment, when, finally, she brought him peace, that he knew he really loved her. But he could not tell a word of this.

She left in a few minutes, and did not come back that night. He slept like the dead. Indeed, he snored so loud he shook the springs.

A DAY OR so later, he was hauled up before Corker, who took him through those deliveries of the ten parabolam plants, in great detail. The man seemed to be satisfied because at the end he said, "Yes that's quite good," but then he added, "Now, Charley, I want to speak about yourself."

"Yes sir?"

"I've been observing you."

"Yes sir."

"What I've to say isn't easy for me, Summers." To revert thus to Charley's surname was a sign of trouble. "I think I told you before that in this war the civilians have had some. Why only the other afternoon I was obliged to send one of our typists away, out of the estimating department, for a week's rest. I can't remember her name at the moment. Yes I do. Miss Pease, of course. It's not often I can't recall a name." He paused, as if waiting for Charley to confirm this, but the young man, who lacked the self-confidence, missed his opportunity. "But I've been observing you," Mr. Mead continued. "It's not altogether your case taken on its own merits, I'm thinking of the rest of the staff who joined up, and who'll be coming back to us some day," he said, leaning backwards in the chair with a judicial expression. Once more he paused, once more Charley did not find it in him to reply.

"With your case," Mr. Mead began again, "I've a feeling I'm not getting your best at your work, not all your attention, not all of you, Summers. When everything's said and done, this is a grand opportunity for you, you know. You're the first we've had returned to the old firm, and I put you in a big position for a man of your experience, which hasn't been all that large. And what do I find after I've watched carefully, for I've kept an eye on you, mind? Of course I know there was a bit of bad luck with that girl the Ministry sent. She was no more help to you than a sick headache. In fact, I'll go this far. She was a disadvantage, Charley, and I give you credit for putting up with her like you did. No, it's not that is worrying me. It's yourself, and all the young fellows like you. Have women gotten hold of you, Summers? Is that it?"

"Me sir?" he asked.

"Yes you," Mr. Mead insisted. "You're the only other person in this room, aren't you? But I'll tell you why. I've known Rob Jordan all my life, and a year or two back, when we were talking, he got me interested in the Reform of Prisons League. I've been to several of their meetings since. It may not be a very pleasant thing to say in mixed company, Summers, but we're speaking as man to man now. It's sex is the whole trouble. There you are. Sex."

"Sex sir?" Charley echoed.

"See here, Summers, I've a right to expect a bit of co-operation from your quarter, now, haven't I? It's no good your telling me you never came across that problem, not in the four years you had behind barbed wire. Dammit man, there's things we all feel. It's nature."

"You mean girls," Charles said blankly.

"What else?" Mr. Mead enquired, in a savage voice.

"My girl died the week I got taken prisoner," Charley announced. It was a measure of how far he had forgotten Rose that he was able to say this, calm as calm, and, of his old need to cover up, that he did not now mention Nance.

"Did she?" Mr. Mead muttered. He had been flung off balance. "I see. That's different, then. I'm sorry to hear that, Charley."

"Her dad joined her just the other day. I was down there when it happened." Charley spoke with an extraordinary tone of innocence.

"What did he die of?"

"He had a second stroke."

Mr. Mead was always able to talk medical details for hours. He drew out every little thing Charley knew about Mr. Grant's illness. When he could get no more, and he had said, "It's got to come to all of us, some day," a silence fell.

"Now, my lad, to return to yourself," he said. "I may have been mistaken where you were concerned. I'll be perfectly frank and open with you. No one said a word to me, mind, but somehow I got the impression, right or wrong, that there was a little matter of account between that typist of yours we had to get rid of, between the two of you. I realize now I may have been mistaken. But in this life, Charley, and I've had a lot of experience, it's either the one thing, or the other. To put it in a nutshell, after the bad time you've had, you want to marry and settle down. Children of one's own, that's the thing. And I'll tell you this. It's not a promise, because there's others besides me to consider, but, when you do put up the banns, you just come along, and we'll see what we can arrange about giving you a rise."

Then a ludicrous accident occurred. Charley gulped, quite in the usual fashion, but swallowed the wrong way, so that he choked. He coughed once or twice, and after that held his breath, going red in the face as he did so. It crossed his mind that Mr. Mead might believe he was laughing at him, which was precisely what Corker had begun to suspect. Charley's eyes filled with tears. Mr. Mead cleared his own throat. Charley's eyes began to start out of his head, and, for every millimetre they protruded, Corker's mounting anger pushed his out an equal distance. At last the younger man grew desperate for lack of air, half rose out of his seat, made as if to bang himself on the back. Upon which Mr. Mead tumbled to it, and heartily thumped him.

When Charley had recovered, Mr. Mead said gravely,

"It can be very serious, that can."

He waited for encouragement, but the young man was still gasping.

"People have died of that," Mr. Mead was beginning, when his telephone rang. He picked up the receiver. He listened. He said "Yes

Muriel?" from which Charley was fairly certain that Corker's goi-
tred wife was on the other end. Again, a savage expression spread
over Mr. Mead's face.

"You tell that kid of mine I'll tear the heart right out of him
when I get home," he shouted, almost at once. "What's that, Muriel?
I don't care if he is seventeen. What? I can't correct my own son,
can't I? Look, I don't care if he is going into the army directly, it's
discipline he wants now, or it'll be the worse for him later on when
he's enlisted. Muriel. Now Muriel..." and there was a click over the
phone, Mrs. Mead had rung off. He put the receiver back. He
mopped his brow. "Women," he muttered, "women."

"Ought to be getting back," Charley said, out of a straight face.

"Don't mind me," Mr. Mead mumbled at random, floundering in
the chair.

When Charley got to his own room, he rang Nance.

He often did, these days. Now he no longer had a girl working in
his room, he would ask the telephone operator for a free line, and
speak to her where she was still staying on at Mrs. Grant's.

"That you?" he said, "it's me."

"Why Charley," she answered, "wait just a moment, will you,
while I light a cigarette." He gave her time to get settled. When she
said "Now," he announced,

"You'd have laughed the other minute."

"How's that?"

"Corker had me on the mat. Told me I should get married, wife
and children, and all the rest." He paused, his voice had gone anxious.

"Well?" she encouraged, not taking this up as he would have
liked.

"It was nothing really," he continued, disappointed, although he
had no hopes, "just that his wife happened to ring him, and before I
could get out of the room they were at it, hammer and tongs, over
young Arthur you know, their eldest."

"What's strange about that, then?" she enquired. "You can't bring
up a family with nothing but good wishes, can you?"

This made him wonder if he had sufficient to marry on. Then he wanted to tell her how Corker had offered a rise if he took a wife, but he did not dare. He fell silent. Upon which she gently went over yet again their little bits of news at home, that the cat had had its kittens, that Mrs. Grant was wonderful, and so on.

"Well," she said finally, "I've got to see to mother's dinner. We'll be expecting you Sunday. Thanks for ringing, dear."

He went back comforted to his work.

When he travelled down next Sunday he noticed a great change in the cat. She was thin as a board, her eyes oily with anxiousness, as she went squawking after the kittens to try to keep her family together, and everlastingly to wash them. All this was going on in the living room, where Nance took him.

"Aren't they sweet?" she explained. Indeed, for the rest of the day, he hardly raised his eyes from off them.

"She's upstairs resting," she said of Mrs. Grant.

Again he made no comment.

"Well, how have you been?" she asked. "Worrying along as usual? Why d'you worry like you do?"

He stayed silent.

"Puss never does, do you, darling?" she went on. "And if a mouse was to run right in front of your very whiskers you'd be too busy to pay attention, poor dear, wouldn't you? You know, I can't think how she manages. They're so clean you could have them on your bed, the little loves." She was fondly smiling.

He also smiled as he watched.

"Why do you worry so, Charley?" she demanded. "She doesn't, do you my sweet puss?" He rather wondered at this statement. "Is it over your work again?" she insisted.

"I'm O.K.," he assured her. He found, as he had done recently, that he was quietened by having her there, and then the kittens were domestic, like taking your slippers off to a fire. As though she could read his thoughts, she asked,

"Are you warm enough? The days are turning sharp. Shall we light it?"

"I'm O.K., honestly," he said.

"Are you certain? I never am able to tell where you're concerned, or perhaps I can, more than you imagine. Because you're good, you know. Why don't you think of yourself more often? Come on now. Let's talk about you for a change. What's worrying you? Is it to do with your work?"

"Me?" he asked. "No, everything's all right."

"But you said you'd been up on the carpet before Mr. Mead, when you called me over the phone. And I know things weren't easy a short time back, with that girl they wished on you, and you had to wet nurse. What is it, Charley? Then is it to do with your having been a prisoner, dear?"

He did glance at her, but she got no idea of what was in his mind.

"I'm back, aren't I?" he said.

"Oh dear, pity us poor women," she sighed. "Aren't some men dense?"

"Why, what d'you mean?" He had a vague impression there might be more in this than immediately appeared. He began to feel upset in his stomach.

"No more than I'm asking, slow coach," she replied. "I want you to open up."

"How's that?"

"You'll find it ever so much better after," she gently assured him. "There's something on your mind from way back, I know, and it's none of that silly old Rose business, I'm certain. So what was it like out there?"

"Oh, just ordinary, I suppose," he said with reluctance.

"I'll wager it was."

"Can't talk about that, Nance," he brought out at last, obviously distressed.

"No more you need if you don't want," she said, and his eyes went back to the kittens. "Why, here's mother," she cried.

He did not get up as Mrs. Grant came into the room. He watched the cat, which was dragging one of her kittens back by the scruff of its neck. She was crouching down as though anguished, while the kitten let out high, thin shrieks.

"Why Charley," Mrs. Grant said to him, and he looked to find the old lady dressed in black, but at her best. She seemed just the same.

"I did want to thank you," she went on, sitting between them on the sofa. "It was really wonderful, your staying with us all through that terrible night. It made the whole difference, dear, didn't it," she appealed to Nancy, "having a man in the house," she explained. Charley began to calm down again. What appeared to him to be the usualness of this conversation, settled his stomach. "Though Father didn't suffer. I was there. I know," she said. "No, he never knew what it was that struck him down at the last, but at the same time he had the comfort of his loved ones round him at the end."

She paused, and Nancy took one of her hands in her own.

"And what I should have done without you, my dear, I can't even begin to picture," Mrs. Grant said to the girl. "Why, she was no more to me than my own daughter could have been," she told Charles who, heart at rest, was, in simplicity, smiling at the kittens. "Nothing could ever be too much for her," Mrs. Grant continued, "day or night, never too much trouble, oh dear, I've been very lucky in my loved ones," the old lady came to an end, the tears rimming her eyes.

Nance murmured something. But Mrs. Grant was started.

"She'll make a splendid wife to a man one of these days," she said. "But Father was wonderful," she came back to it, in exactly the same tone of voice. "Never the least word of complaint, although he lay in a kind of terrible living grave, the poor darling. Not once a look in his eyes, even. Oh I've been fortunate in my life," Mrs. Grant announced, with utter sincerity. "I lost my only child it's true, but now I've found another. And then I was blessed with a good husband. He was a wonderful man to me. Forty-seven years we lived together, and he never gave me a moment's unease."

Charley glanced at her. He saw she was at peace, looking straight in front, the tears now running down her red cheeks. Then his eyes fell back to the cat again.

"It was all you did for him," Nance told the older woman.

"I was what Gerald made me," Mrs. Grant proudly answered.

"When I married I didn't know the littlest thing, but he took me along at his side. You can smile, dear," she said to Nancy, who was doing no such thing, "then one of these days you'll learn for yourself, you'll remember who it was told you. Oh yes, when I was young, I thought I understood all there was to know, but I soon found my mistake." She spoke quietly. Charley felt even more at peace. "And so thoughtful," she went on. "D'you know what I came upon, the morning after he died? Why a policy I'd no notion he'd been keeping up, so that I shan't want for my little comforts till I go to join him. Oh, he was a good man."

They sat tranquilly by.

"And it's something you don't discover till you've had your experience, dear," she continued to Nancy. "Life is like that. Oh, I don't mean not to have your good times when you're a girl, but, to a woman, the truth and the meaning come after she's married. So you'll find a right husband, won't you, if only to please your old mother here."

"She will," Charley echoed.

"What d'you mean, I will?" Miss Whitmore took him up, boisterously. "What do you know about it?"

"Me?" he asked, brought back to earth.

"Oh, you young people," Mrs. Grant smiled. "Now I think I'll go sit with Father again. It's my last afternoon with him." She left quite naturally.

"She's been wonderful," Nancy said.

"I expect you're a help yourself."

"Don't be stupid, silly. I only did what anyone would, who was here," she protested.

"Don't those kittens play the old cat up," he remarked.

"Yes, they are cute, aren't they?" she said.

"Well, it's a grand thing Mrs. Grant has come through the way she has," he announced. Miss Whitmore noticed he seemed much freer. "Thanks to you," he added. But she saw he was still watching the kittens.

"You're coming to the funeral tomorrow, aren't you?" she asked.

He had not intended to do this. He sat listening now, not knowing what to say.

"You could pass the night," she explained. "I'd make your bed up on the sofa, once more." He hadn't considered this.

He stayed quite still.

"I'd not let it be like the last time," she said, referring to the death of Mr. Grant, but of course he was not to know this, not at once.

He began, again, to feel the old upset in his stomach. Only, because he really loved her now, he was much shyer.

"I couldn't," he said, pushing happiness off.

"Why, whatever's to stop you? Not that old Mrs. Frazier, surely?"

"You don't understand," he said, careful not to look.

"Mother'll be terribly put out if you don't," Nancy explained. "You could be back at your office after the lunch hour."

He seized onto this.

"It's my work," he said.

"You mean, you never asked leave? You are forgetful, Charley, aren't you? And when I took the trouble to let you know, soon as ever we fixed it. Well, if you didn't get permission, it's too late now, naturally."

While she was there he was all right, and while he was busy at the office he forgot. But he was sleeping badly once more, what with his doubts and fears, this time about Nance. He knew she wouldn't come to him in this room, though sometimes she said things to make it so that he couldn't be certain. But he felt that he might have a good night's rest, at last, if he could remain on here this evening after all. He wondered how to put it.

"I might stay," he said.

"And not go to the funeral?" He looked at her. There was a half smile of complicity on her face. "Oh no, you can't do that," she went on. "It wouldn't be right. Mother wouldn't understand."

He saw he was not going to have his way. He began to feel miserable.

"Come up with you," she said. "It's not all that, sleeping on the old sofa, surely?" She kept herself from wondering what he wished to

"What in heaven's name are you getting at now?"

He spoke with a casual manner, as of a great truth.

"Comfortably," he said.

"Well they do say it should be with your boots on," she said, greatly wondering. "I mean while you're about your work. Seeing to the grandchildren, or whatever."

"That's bunk," he said.

"Oh, so it's bunk, is it?" she repeated, at a loss. Really, Charley had more a way of getting away from you than she had ever even suspected.

"Like what they tell you in the Army," he explained.

"Well, my Phil was in the R.A.F., wasn't he?" she demanded, beginning to show irritation.

"He's got hold of her tail," he said of the kitten.

"No you can't slide away from me as simply as all that," she protested. "What's up with you, Charley?"

"Me? Nothing." He was at ease, his mind a blank.

"You're not saying anything against Phil, are you?"

At that he seemed to be disturbed.

"Never even mentioned him," he said.

"That's all right then. For you know, no matter what others suffered, it was his life he gave." This was the third time she had said it, and it had been different each time. "And he died in action," she added.

"Why Nance..." he began, turning to her, distressed, "I never..."

"Very good," she said, "forget what I said. I'm funny where Phil's concerned."

"Didn't enter my head..." he protested.

"Oh, all right, don't go on," she cried out. "You needn't pay attention." Then she took pity on him, he looked so puzzled. So she raised his nearest hand, and kissed it. "There," she said.

He knew less than ever what to think, as the upset began once more in his stomach. Her mouth on his palm had been like a bird in the hand. He looked stupidly at where she had kissed him.

"They are sweet, aren't they?" she remarked.

express. All she wanted was that he should speak out, whatever might be.

"You've always something, bothering you, that you can't seem to rid yourself of," she went on, sadly, when he did not say it. "You mightn't be sitting here with me. I might be an old ghost," she said.

"Now Nance." Greatly daring he turned to her, and made as if to put an arm round her waist.

"Steady," she warned him. "We shan't want much of that, shall we, or not until after the funeral, at all events?" Then she changed the conversation. "What was it passed between Mr. Mead and his wife on the telephone, the time you rang me up about?"

"Oh you don't have to notice them," he protested. She saw with excitement that his eyes were anguished. He rapidly went on, quoting what she had commented, and without realizing it. "You won't bring up a family on no more than good wishes will you?" he said.

"But can't they get along together, then?"

"Corker's all right," he dully replied, in the dumps once more, his attention wandering back to the cat.

"Isn't that like a man all over?" she asked, boisterous again. "With not a word to spare for Mrs. Mead," she elaborated.

"She's got a goitre."

"Has she," Miss Whitmore said. "Yes, that might make a difference."

He actually laughed. She was astounded.

"What is there funny in what I've just said?" she demanded.

"Wouldn't be room on the pillow, would there?" he asked, watching the tabby kitten, free again.

"Why, Charley, that's rude," she joyfully protested.

They fell silent. When she spoke next the mood had passed, she was dead serious.

"No, it's the end of life that matters, how it finishes," she said. "Look at mother, now. Why, she was like a saint. I was proud to be here, there you are," she ended, almost in defiance, as though daring him.

"You're right," he said. "To die in bed."

He did not catch the first word, and glanced at her. But she was watching the kittens.

"Aren't they now?" she insisted. Once more he put happiness off. Then he did tell her something. It had suddenly come on the tip of his tongue.

"I had a mouse out there," he said.

She had a quick inkling of this. "And the guards took it away from you?" she asked, as if to a child. But he did not notice.

"No, I had it in a cage I made," he said.

"You don't hold it against my puss?" she enquired. She was anxious.

"Never even crossed my mind," he answered.

Mrs. Grant came down, soon after. And for the rest of the time, before he went to catch his train, he sat in a peaceable daze, while the two women lovingly talked of Mr. Grant.

NANCY stayed on at Mrs. Grant's after the funeral, and he went down there every Sunday. He loved her, although he did not say so, or even show it, while she, for her part, had made up her mind that she would marry him.

He lived quietly and hopelessly on, convinced that no girl would ever look at him, because he was too slow. He did nothing about her. He was content to bide his time, and so was she.

Mrs. Grant, who remained steadfast and kindly, often prodded Nance about Charley. It was the one point on which they disagreed, that she would not declare herself to the old lady about him. Nance turned it off by asking what Mrs. Grant would do if left alone. The answer made, was that "mother" could go live with a niece in the Midlands, a schoolteacher. To which Nance would object that, surely, she did not wish to give up her lovely home. Indeed, with what Nance, who had gone back to work, contributed each week, and with the insurance money, it was easy for Mrs. Grant to keep things going.

Nancy's real mother wrote, from where she was evacuated, to hint that she had in mind to marry again.

When Charley was down, the two younger people would go out in the evening if it was fine, and, before they came back, they would kiss a bit. This made him more miserable the rest of the week, when he had the leisure to remember. But she never kissed him indoors, after Mrs. Grant had begun to press her.

They called each other dear. And, once he had begun really to love Nancy, he did not sit with Mrs. Frazier in her room any more, which turned this lady against him.

Nancy could not forget her dead husband Phil, but she gradually came to feel about him less often, and to wonder about Charley more. Where the airman had always been gay, and on his own until his last leave, when they had been married, Charley was so helpless that she wondered how he held his job down. In a way she was waiting for him to lose it. She did not express this to herself, even, but she might have been seeing whether he could support himself, also whether he had really and truly got over Rose, which had been such a business when Father first put them in the way of each other, and it had all been so dreadful.

But what she liked about Charley was how he did not ask for anything, however small, although his need was desperate, a child could tell it. He was so trusting, she felt, that she came to trust him.

After a time she believed he was very reserved, and respected him for this. Yet she realized the war had injured him. Really what intrigued her was, that she did not know if he didn't, or just couldn't, tell about himself, tell even something of all that went on behind those marvellous brown eyes, which had so humbly implored her when she came to announce that Mr. Grant was gone, which had so often begged her since, which told her she was needed as she could never be by almost anyone, that more than anyone in the world, now they had killed Phil, it was Charley Summers who must have her.

Accordingly, some time in November, she made up her mind she'd do it. But she said nothing. She waited. Then old Ernie Mandrew sent another sad sort of note about Phil, and asked her to stay over for Christmas, to bring a boy if she liked. She saw this was her chance. She put it to Charley.

She asked what he had planned to do over the holiday. Suspecting nothing, Charley said he did not know. Then she suggested that he should come along, in almost exactly the same words he had used to Dot Pitter, on a previous occasion. The two times seemed so alike he was terrified, so much so, that she saw almost how terrified he could be, and her heart fell. But she had made up her mind, and she had to go through with it.

He produced a perfectly genuine reason against the visit. He objected that Ernie Mandrew, with all his domestics, was too much, altogether, and that the man must be in big business. She said, why didn't anyone ever inform you, he's a bookie. But Charley was very suspicious. He wanted to be told how she had got to know Mr. Mandrew. She was patient. She explained that her Phil had worked for him, in peacetime. It still looked to Charley like a trap, he did not dare think what for. Next he asked if Middlewitch was to be present. She replied that she thought she must have explained how Arthur was out, that poor Arthur had been betting, and couldn't pay up. Betting with a firm that size, Charley asked. She told him the truth. With someone else's money, she said.

"So you will, Charley Barley, won't you?" she ended.

"I might," he said, feeling sick.

THIS AFTERNOON of Christmas day, down at old Ernie Mandrew's, she took Charley out, determined by hook or by crook to bring him to the point at last, for, however little she knew about his intentions, her own mind was still made up.

"Would you ever want to have children?" she asked, as they set off together over the snow, on the way to the village. This made him think of Ridley, whom he had not considered in a long while.

"Why?" he said.

"Oh, why does a person ever put a question?" she gently enquired. "To get their answer, of course, you old silly."

"I don't know." He still did not realize that they might come on the boy when they reached the first houses, and he was not to know this until it was too late.

"Come on," she insisted. "Having children's one of the few things anyone can do for herself in this old world, that is if she can rake up a boy to do it with," she laughed.

"Would you?" he asked.

"We're not talking of me, this instant minute, thanks," she replied. "Why won't you ever tell me anything?"

"I might have one already."

"Go on," she said, laughing still. "Why, you've never been wide awake enough for that."

"I might," he insisted.

"Charley, I really do believe ... No, look here, you haven't, have you, now?"

He did not answer, or even glance at her.

"You said it in such a way that you might at that . . ." she went on, when he said nothing. "But, Charley, it would be living a lie."

"How d'you mean?"

"Well, wouldn't it?"

"I still don't get you," he cautiously explained.

"Why, being like me," she elaborated. "Not having a real father all my life. That's been my trouble. Oh it mightn't matter for a boy, but it's very different where girls are concerned."

"Rotten luck," he said.

"No, Charley, you never did, did you?"

"What would you give for me to tell?"

"But this is serious," she entreated. "You can't play about with this. It's all there is that people the same as us can do with their own lives."

"A man never knows if the kid is his own, or not."

"Now there's no need for you to be sarcastic," she protested. "I haven't brought you all this long way for that," she said, with more truth behind the remark than she proposed to reveal. "Can't you be serious, once in a while," she begged, although he was the most serious of men.

The snow, and the sun above, lit her face so that each eyelash stood out on its own, and the grain of her skin, until, with those blue eyes, and the way she had of addressing him, on which he had come to rely for peace of mind, and with her walking by his side, she grew upon him, became an embodiment of everything comforting, and true, and good. So much so, that he lost the drift of this argument. She had to press to get him to say he did not really know if he had a child.

"But who with?" she demanded. She was getting upset.

"That would be telling."

"Oh, I believe it was only your old Rose," she brought out at last, very much relieved. "And there was me, supposing all that over and done with, ages ago. Did you love her very much then, Charley?"

"It was a long time back."

"That's not much help to a girl," she replied. "Did you or did you not? That's what I want to know."

"I suppose so," he said, unmistakably with no trace of feeling.

"Oh, pity us poor women," she cried out loud, delighted, thinking this would have taught Rose, if the woman could have been here to learn it. "D'you mean you can't be certain?"

"I thought I knew, dear. Then she went and married someone else," he explained.

"Yes, but you carried on seeing her, surely? You told me."

"I did."

"Well then?" she demanded.

There was a pause.

"She properly played you up, didn't she," Miss Whitmore made comment. But Charley was several sentences behind once more.

"I didn't trust her quite the same," he brought out, with difficulty.

"When was that?" she gleefully demanded.

"After she married Jim."

"Trusting is different," she announced.

"I wouldn't know," he said. "But I seemed to need her more."

"You know a great deal more than I sometimes credit you with," she admitted, soberly, sadly.

"Was it the same with your husband?" he asked, greatly daring.

"With Phil? Oh that's all over, done now. And we didn't have a kid. I shan't forget him till the day I die, but he wouldn't want me to go on to be an old maid."

"But you never would, would you? I mean you were married once?"

"Well, of course," she said with a happy laugh. "But if you live on long enough without a man, you go back to be a virgin."

This remark enormously excited him somehow.

"You don't," he cried out.

"Then what's an old maid, then?" she wanted to know.

He could not think what to say, so stayed silent.

"Oh yes, you know all right," she insisted. "And it's not for me. No thank you. Besides, I want kids."

"Why do you?" He spoke loud.

"Because they're good for your health, if you're a woman. But that's not the real reason. I want to have them so as to love."

He was very nervous about where all this was leading. But he considered he had been let down so often, in his time, that he was not going to give himself away again just yet.

"You could love the man you married?" he asked.

"I don't see it that way," she replied. "You can't get more out of anything than you put in. And kids are your own flesh and blood. A woman risks her life having them. There's nothing more a girl can put into it than having her own children, doing everything for them, till they're of an age to look after themselves, it's her most."

"Not much of a look out for the husband, then," he had the courage to say.

"What d'you mean?" she asked. "What is there that's wrong for him, in all I've just said? I don't see life as sitting in another person's lap, as you and your Rose seem to have done together, from what Mother tells me. It's starting a home and working for it, that's what I call it," she said.

"Did your Phil see things that way?"

"You leave him out, Charley. He's nothing to do with what we're discussing."

They fell silent. They were getting near the village.

He was becoming really agitated. She could talk about Rose playing him up, yet she'd had a shot at the same game once or twice herself, or so it seemed. But then, of course, it was all his own fault, he felt. A wife and kids were not for Charley Summers. He knew that. He was too slow. He'd never find a woman to put up with him.

"Then there's Panzer," she said suddenly, and, so it appeared, at a tangent, but, in actual practice, with a great deal of purpose. "I couldn't leave her," she pointed out.

"You don't have to," he objected.

"If I married," she explained, and spoke as if talking to a child. "No," she went on, "whoever took me to be his wedded wife, would have to take my cat on with me."

"Well, why not?" he asked, wondering.

He became aware that she was watching him.

"That's all very fine, but Panzer's one of those things I'd have to get straight right off," she insisted. "Her future kittens as well, oh yes. I could never leave them behind."

He did not know what he was supposed to say. He was floundering.

"Why sure," he said. "But you'd leave Mrs. Grant?" he asked.

"No," she said. "There's not room for two in my digs, and houses aren't easy to come by these days. I'd stay on where I am now. She'd be glad to welcome my husband in her home."

"I thought she had a niece in Leicester," he brought out.

"And so she has, Charley, but she's not sure of her welcome there. Oh we've had this out. She'd be quite agreeable."

"Well that makes it easier, certainly, with the cat and her kittens."

She accepted this. "There you are," she said.

They had almost come to the single village street, in which he had met Arthur Middlewitch during the August holiday, and through which he had so often strolled with Rose, after her marriage to Phillips. It was also where Ridley used to play with the Gubbins children. He did wonder for a moment whether they would run across the boy, but the little street was quite deserted. He supposed the locals were sleeping off their Christmas dinner. He was glad, because he did not want James to know that he was down. He was not going to have him getting in first with this girl, as Jim had done the last time. Then, absolutely without warning, stepping out of a surface shelter in the roadway, and not three paces from them, was Ridley, his eyes fixed on Nance. Afterwards, when Charley went over it in his mind, he thought he had never seen such pain on any face. For the boy had blushed, blushed a deep scarlet in this snow clear light. He must have thought he was seeing his mother step, in her true colours, out of his father's microfilms. And Nance, who did not know him, passed him by.

Charley managed to turn round, without attracting her attention, in order to make the child a sign. All he could think of, and he did not know why, was to put a finger to his lips. At that, Ridley turned, and ran off fast.

Charley was so upset that he did not take in the sense of the words with which Nance then broke the silence that had fallen between them.

"We could make a go of it between us, you know, if we tried," she said.

"What's that?"

"You wouldn't have heard, would you dear?" she said gently. "I was making a proposal."

He still did not trust his ears.

"I didn't quite catch," he lied.

She stopped in her tracks. She put her hands up to the lapels of his coat.

"I was proposing, dear," she said.

He felt his heart beating so hard that he was afraid he would suffocate.

"You really mean it?" he asked, and for the rest of his life, for the life of him, he could not remember anything of what passed during the remainder of that afternoon. It was bliss.

So she had asked him to marry her, and had been accepted. She had made only one condition, which was that they should have a trial trip. So it was the same night, under Mr. Mandrew's roof, that he went to her room, for the first time in what was to be a happy married life.

She was lying stark naked on the bed, a lamp with a pink shade at her side. She had not drawn the black-out, and the electric light made the dark outside a marvellous deep blue. In an attempt to seem natural, he said something about showing a light.

"Come here, silly," was what she replied.

Then he knelt by the bed, having under his eyes the great, the overwhelming sight of the woman he loved, for the first time without her clothes. And because the lamp was lit, the pink shade seemed to spill a light of roses over her in all their summer colours, her hands that lay along her legs were red, her stomach gold, her breasts the colour of cream roses, and her neck white roses for the bride. She had shut her eyes to let him have his fill, but it was too much, for he burst into tears again, he buried his face in her side just below the ribs, and bawled like a child. "Rose," he called out, not knowing he did so, "Rose."

"There," Nancy said, "there," pressed his head with her hands. His tears wetted her. The salt water ran down between her legs. And she knew what she had taken on. It was no more or less, really, than she had expected.

TITLES IN SERIES

For a complete list of titles, visit www.nyrb.com or write to:
Catalog Requests, NYRB, 435 Hudson Street, New York, NY 10014

J.R. ACKERLEY Hindoo Holiday*
J.R. ACKERLEY My Dog Tulip*
J.R. ACKERLEY My Father and Myself*
J.R. ACKERLEY We Think the World of You*
HENRY ADAMS The Jeffersonian Transformation
RENATA ADLER Pitch Dark*
RENATA ADLER Speedboat*
AESCHYLUS Prometheus Bound; translated by Joel Agee*
LEOPOLDO ALAS His Only Son *with* Doña Berta*
CÉLESTE ALBARET Monsieur Proust
DANTE ALIGHIERI The Inferno
DANTE ALIGHIERI The New Life
KINGSLEY AMIS The Alteration*
KINGSLEY AMIS Dear Illusion: Collected Stories*
KINGSLEY AMIS Ending Up*
KINGSLEY AMIS Girl, 20*
KINGSLEY AMIS The Green Man*
KINGSLEY AMIS Lucky Jim*
KINGSLEY AMIS The Old Devils*
KINGSLEY AMIS One Fat Englishman*
KINGSLEY AMIS Take a Girl Like You*
ROBERTO ARLT The Seven Madmen*
WILLIAM ATTAWAY Blood on the Forge
W.H. AUDEN (EDITOR) The Living Thoughts of Kierkegaard
W.H. AUDEN W.H. Auden's Book of Light Verse
ERICH AUERBACH Dante: Poet of the Secular World
DOROTHY BAKER Cassandra at the Wedding*
DOROTHY BAKER Young Man with a Horn*
J.A. BAKER The Peregrine
S. JOSEPHINE BAKER Fighting for Life*
HONORÉ DE BALZAC The Human Comedy: Selected Stories*
HONORÉ DE BALZAC The Unknown Masterpiece *and* Gambara*
VICKI BAUM Grand Hotel*
SYBILLE BEDFORD A Legacy*
SYBILLE BEDFORD A Visit to Don Otavio: A Mexican Journey*
MAX BEERBOHM The Prince of Minor Writers: The Selected Essays of Max Beerbohm*
MAX BEERBOHM Seven Men
STEPHEN BENATAR Wish Her Safe at Home*
FRANS G. BENGTSSON The Long Ships*
ALEXANDER BERKMAN Prison Memoirs of an Anarchist
GEORGES BERNANOS Mouchette
MIRON BIAŁOSZEWSKI A Memoir of the Warsaw Uprising*
ADOLFO BIOY CASARES Asleep in the Sun
ADOLFO BIOY CASARES The Invention of Morel
EVE BABITZ Eve's Hollywood*
EVE BABITZ Slow Days, Fast Company: The World, the Flesh, and L.A.*
CAROLINE BLACKWOOD Corrigan*

* *Also available as an electronic book.*

CAROLINE BLACKWOOD Great Granny Webster*
RONALD BLYTHE Akenfield: Portrait of an English Village*
NICOLAS BOUVIER The Way of the World
EMMANUEL BOVE Henri Duchemin and His Shadows*
MALCOLM BRALY On the Yard*
MILLEN BRAND The Outward Room*
SIR THOMAS BROWNE Religio Medici and Urne-Buriall*
JOHN HORNE BURNS The Gallery
ROBERT BURTON The Anatomy of Melancholy
CAMARA LAYE The Radiance of the King
GIROLAMO CARDANO The Book of My Life
DON CARPENTER Hard Rain Falling*
J.L. CARR A Month in the Country*
BLAISE CENDRARS Moravagine
EILEEN CHANG Love in a Fallen City
EILEEN CHANG Naked Earth*
JOAN CHASE During the Reign of the Queen of Persia*
ELLIOTT CHAZE Black Wings Has My Angel*
UPAMANYU CHATTERJEE English, August: An Indian Story
NIRAD C. CHAUDHURI The Autobiography of an Unknown Indian
ANTON CHEKHOV Peasants and Other Stories
ANTON CHEKHOV The Prank: The Best of Young Chekhov*
GABRIEL CHEVALLIER Fear: A Novel of World War I*
JEAN-PAUL CLÉBERT Paris Vagabond*
RICHARD COBB Paris and Elsewhere
COLETTE The Pure and the Impure
JOHN COLLIER Fancies and Goodnights
CARLO COLLODI The Adventures of Pinocchio*
D.G. COMPTON The Continuous Katherine Mortenhoe
IVY COMPTON-BURNETT A House and Its Head
IVY COMPTON-BURNETT Manservant and Maidservant
BARBARA COMYNS The Vet's Daughter
BARBARA COMYNS Our Spoons Came from Woolworths*
ALBERT COSSERY The Jokers*
ALBERT COSSERY Proud Beggars*
HAROLD CRUSE The Crisis of the Negro Intellectual
ASTOLPHE DE CUSTINE Letters from Russia*
LORENZO DA PONTE Memoirs
ELIZABETH DAVID A Book of Mediterranean Food
ELIZABETH DAVID Summer Cooking
L.J. DAVIS A Meaningful Life*
AGNES DE MILLE Dance to the Piper*
VIVANT DENON No Tomorrow/Point de lendemain
MARIA DERMOÛT The Ten Thousand Things
DER NISTER The Family Mashber
TIBOR DÉRY Niki: The Story of a Dog
ANTONIO DI BENEDETTO Zama
JEAN D'ORMESSON The Glory of the Empire: A Novel, A History*
ARTHUR CONAN DOYLE The Exploits and Adventures of Brigadier Gerard
CHARLES DUFF A Handbook on Hanging
BRUCE DUFFY The World As I Found It*
DAPHNE DU MAURIER Don't Look Now: Stories
ELAINE DUNDY The Dud Avocado*

ELAINE DUNDY The Old Man and Me*

G.B. EDWARDS The Book of Ebenezer Le Page*

JOHN EHLE The Land Breakers*

MARCELLUS EMANTS A Posthumous Confession

EURIPIDES Grief Lessons: Four Plays; translated by Anne Carson

J.G. FARRELL Troubles*

J.G. FARRELL The Siege of Krishnapur*

J.G. FARRELL The Singapore Grip*

ELIZA FAY Original Letters from India

KENNETH FEARING The Big Clock

KENNETH FEARING Clark Gifford's Body

FÉLIX FÉNÉON Novels in Three Lines*

M.I. FINLEY The World of Odysseus

THOMAS FLANAGAN The Year of the French*

BENJAMIN FONDANE Existential Monday: Philosophical Essays*

SANFORD FRIEDMAN Conversations with Beethoven*

SANFORD FRIEDMAN Totempole*

MASANOBU FUKUOKA The One-Straw Revolution*

MARC FUMAROLI When the World Spoke French

CARLO EMILIO GADDA That Awful Mess on the Via Merulana

BENITO PÉREZ GÁLDOS Tristana*

MAVIS GALLANT The Cost of Living: Early and Uncollected Stories*

MAVIS GALLANT Paris Stories*

MAVIS GALLANT A Fairly Good Time *with* Green Water, Green Sky*

MAVIS GALLANT Varieties of Exile*

GABRIEL GARCÍA MÁRQUEZ Clandestine in Chile: The Adventures of Miguel Littín

LEONARD GARDNER Fat City*

ALAN GARNER Red Shift*

WILLIAM H. GASS In the Heart of the Heart of the Country: And Other Stories*

WILLIAM H. GASS On Being Blue: A Philosophical Inquiry*

THÉOPHILE GAUTIER My Fantoms

GE FEI The Invisibility Cloak

JEAN GENET Prisoner of Love

ÉLISABETH GILLE The Mirador: Dreamed Memories of Irène Némirovsky by Her Daughter*

JEAN GIONO Hill*

JOHN GLASSCO Memoirs of Montparnasse*

P.V. GLOB The Bog People: Iron-Age Man Preserved

NIKOLAI GOGOL Dead Souls*

EDMOND AND JULES DE GONCOURT Pages from the Goncourt Journals

PAUL GOODMAN Growing Up Absurd: Problems of Youth in the Organized Society*

EDWARD GOREY (EDITOR) The Haunted Looking Glass

JEREMIAS GOTTHELF The Black Spider*

A.C. GRAHAM Poems of the Late T'ang

HENRY GREEN Back*

HENRY GREEN Caught*

HENRY GREEN Loving*

WILLIAM LINDSAY GRESHAM Nightmare Alley*

HANS HERBERT GRIMM Schlump*

EMMETT GROGAN Ringolevio: A Life Played for Keeps

VASILY GROSSMAN An Armenian Sketchbook*

VASILY GROSSMAN Everything Flows*

VASILY GROSSMAN Life and Fate*

VASILY GROSSMAN The Road*

OAKLEY HALL Warlock

PATRICK HAMILTON The Slaves of Solitude*

PATRICK HAMILTON Twenty Thousand Streets Under the Sky*

PETER HANDKE Short Letter, Long Farewell

PETER HANDKE Slow Homecoming

ELIZABETH HARDWICK The New York Stories of Elizabeth Hardwick*

ELIZABETH HARDWICK Seduction and Betrayal*

ELIZABETH HARDWICK Sleepless Nights*

L.P. HARTLEY Eustace and Hilda: A Trilogy*

L.P. HARTLEY The Go-Between*

NATHANIEL HAWTHORNE Twenty Days with Julian & Little Bunny by Papa

ALFRED HAYES In Love*

ALFRED HAYES My Face for the World to See*

PAUL HAZARD The Crisis of the European Mind: 1680–1715*

GILBERT HIGHET Poets in a Landscape

RUSSELL HOBAN Turtle Diary*

JANET HOBHOUSE The Furies

HUGO VON HOFMANNSTHAL The Lord Chandos Letter*

JAMES HOGG The Private Memoirs and Confessions of a Justified Sinner

RICHARD HOLMES Shelley: The Pursuit*

ALISTAIR HORNE A Savage War of Peace: Algeria 1954–1962*

GEOFFREY HOUSEHOLD Rogue Male*

WILLIAM DEAN HOWELLS Indian Summer

BOHUMIL HRABAL Dancing Lessons for the Advanced in Age*

BOHUMIL HRABAL The Little Town Where Time Stood Still*

DOROTHY B. HUGHES The Expendable Man*

RICHARD HUGHES A High Wind in Jamaica*

RICHARD HUGHES In Hazard*

RICHARD HUGHES The Fox in the Attic (The Human Predicament, Vol. 1)*

RICHARD HUGHES The Wooden Shepherdess (The Human Predicament, Vol. 2)*

INTIZAR HUSAIN Basti*

MAUDE HUTCHINS Victorine

YASUSHI INOUE Tun-huang*

HENRY JAMES The Ivory Tower

HENRY JAMES The New York Stories of Henry James*

HENRY JAMES The Other House

HENRY JAMES The Outcry

TOVE JANSSON Fair Play *

TOVE JANSSON The Summer Book*

TOVE JANSSON The True Deceiver*

TOVE JANSSON The Woman Who Borrowed Memories: Selected Stories*

RANDALL JARRELL (EDITOR) Randall Jarrell's Book of Stories

DAVID JONES In Parenthesis

JOSEPH JOUBERT The Notebooks of Joseph Joubert; translated by Paul Auster

KABIR Songs of Kabir; translated by Arvind Krishna Mehrotra*

FRIGYES KARINTHY A Journey Round My Skull

ERICH KÄSTNER Going to the Dogs: The Story of a Moralist*

HELEN KELLER The World I Live In

YASHAR KEMAL Memed, My Hawk

YASHAR KEMAL They Burn the Thistles

MURRAY KEMPTON Part of Our Time: Some Ruins and Monuments of the Thirties*

RAYMOND KENNEDY Ride a Cockhorse*

DAVID KIDD Peking Story*

ROBERT KIRK The Secret Commonwealth of Elves, Fauns, and Fairies

ARUN KOLATKAR Jejuri

ALBERTO MORAVIA Contempt*   A.

JAN MORRIS Conundrum*

JAN MORRIS Hav*

PENELOPE MORTIMER The Pumpkin Eater*

ÁLVARO MUTIS The Adventures and Misadventures of Maqroll

L.H. MYERS The Root and the Flower*

NESCIO Amsterdam Stories*

DARCY O'BRIEN A Way of Life, Like Any Other

SILVINA OCAMPO Thus Were Their Faces*

YURI OLESHA Envy*

IONA AND PETER OPIE The Lore and Language of Schoolchildren

IRIS OWENS After Claude*

RUSSELL PAGE The Education of a Gardener

ALEXANDROS PAPADIAMANTIS The Murderess

BORIS PASTERNAK, MARINA TSVETAYEVA, AND RAINER MARIA RILKE Letters, Summer 1926

CESARE PAVESE The Moon and the Bonfires

CESARE PAVESE The Selected Works of Cesare Pavese

BORISLAV PEKIĆ Houses*

ELEANOR PERÉNYI More Was Lost: A Memoir*

LUIGI PIRANDELLO The Late Mattia Pascal

JOSEP PLA The Gray Notebook

ANDREY PLATONOV The Foundation Pit

ANDREY PLATONOV Happy Moscow

ANDREY PLATONOV Soul and Other Stories

J.F. POWERS Morte d'Urban*

J.F. POWERS The Stories of J.F. Powers*

J.F. POWERS Wheat That Springeth Green*

CHRISTOPHER PRIEST Inverted World*

BOLESŁAW PRUS The Doll*

GEORGE PSYCHOUNDAKIS The Cretan Runner: His Story of the German Occupation*

ALEXANDER PUSHKIN The Captain's Daughter*

QIU MIAOJIN Last Words from Montmartre*

RAYMOND QUENEAU We Always Treat Women Too Well

RAYMOND QUENEAU Witch Grass

RAYMOND RADIGUET Count d'Orgel's Ball

FRIEDRICH RECK Diary of a Man in Despair*

JULES RENARD Nature Stories*

JEAN RENOIR Renoir, My Father

GREGOR VON REZZORI An Ermine in Czernopol*

GREGOR VON REZZORI Memoirs of an Anti-Semite*

GREGOR VON REZZORI The Snows of Yesteryear: Portraits for an Autobiography*

TIM ROBINSON Stones of Aran: Labyrinth

TIM ROBINSON Stones of Aran: Pilgrimage

MILTON ROKEACH The Three Christs of Ypsilanti*

FR. ROLFE Hadrian the Seventh

GILLIAN ROSE Love's Work

LINDA ROSENKRANTZ Talk*

WILLIAM ROUGHEAD Classic Crimes

CONSTANCE ROURKE American Humor: A Study of the National Character

SAKI The Unrest-Cure and Other Stories; illustrated by Edward Gorey

TAYEB SALIH Season of Migration to the North

TAYEB SALIH The Wedding of Zein*

JEAN-PAUL SARTRE We Have Only This Life to Live: Selected Essays. 1939–1975

GERSHOM SCHOLEM Walter Benjamin: The Story of a Friendship*

DANIEL PAUL SCHREBER Memoirs of My Nervous Illness